THE AGENCY

THE AGENCY

The Body at the Tower

Y. S. Lee

CANDLEWICK PRESS

First U.S. edition 2010

Library of Congress Cataloging-in-Publication Data

Li, Rushang.
The body at the tower / Y. S. Lee. — 1st U.S. ed.
p. cm. — (The agency ; bk. 2)
"A Mary Quinn mystery."
Summary: As a nearly full-fledged member of the Agency,
the all-female detective unit based in Miss Scrimshaw's
Academy for Girls, Mary Quinn, disguised as a poor boy
apprentice builder, must brave the sinister underworld
of Victorian London in order to unmask a murderer.
ISBN 978-0-7636-4968-5
[1. Mystery and detective stories. 2. Sex role — Fiction.
3. Orphans — Fiction. 4. Murder — Fiction.
5. London (England) — History — 19th century — Fiction.
6. Great Britain — History — Victoria, 1837–1901 — Fiction.]
I. Title. II. Series.
PZ7.L591173Bod 2010
[Fic] — dc22 2010004645

10 11 12 13 14 15 BVG 10 9 8 7 6 5 4 3 2 1

Printed in Berryville, VA, U.S.A.

This book was typeset in Palatino.

Candlewick Press
99 Dover Street
Somerville, Massachusetts 02144

visit us at www.candlewick.com

To S., who arrived halfway through this novel

And to N., who was here the whole time

Prologue

Midnight, 30 June 1859

St. Stephen's Tower, Palace of Westminster

A sobbing man huddles on a narrow ledge, clawing at his eyes to shield them from the horror far below. It is dark, thus his terror is irrational; even if he wanted to, he could not make out what he's done, let alone note the gruesome details. Still, his mind's eye insists on the scene: gory, explicit, final. Imagination, not remorse, is at the core of his violent hysteria.

Within the hour he will exhaust himself and even fall asleep for a few minutes. When he wakes—with a start—reason will return and bring with it a degree of fatalism. Two paths now lie before him, and the choice is no longer his. He will pick himself up, carefully not looking over the edge. He will right his clothing, inspect his hands with care, and return home. And then he will wait to see what the future holds.

And he will vow to reveal the truth—but only at the time of his death.

One

Saturday, 2 July

St. John's Wood, London

The freedoms of being a boy, reflected Mary, were many. She could swing her arms as she walked. She could run if she wished. She looked tidy enough to avoid police suspicion but shabby enough to be invisible to all others. Then there was the odd sensation of lightness that came of having cropped hair; she hadn't realized how heavy her own hair was until it was gone. Her breasts were tightly bound, and even if they did ache a little at such treatment, she could at least scratch herself with impunity, scratching in public being one of those Boy Things she ought to enjoy while she could. It was therefore a shame that she wasn't enjoying the situation. Wearing boy's clothing was comfortable and amusing, and she'd enjoyed her escapades in breeches during her first-ever assignment. But this—today—was entirely different. It was serious, and she still had no idea why.

Her instructions were simple enough: to costume herself as a twelve-year-old boy and attend a meeting of the

Agency at three o'clock this afternoon. No further explanation had been offered, and by now, Mary knew better than to ask for more details. Anne and Felicity always gave precisely as much information as they deemed appropriate. Of course, such knowledge hadn't stopped her from fretting about the possibilities yesterday, overnight, and all this morning. Over the past year, she'd delighted in her training: tests, lessons, and brief assignments that offered a taste of the life to come. But there was little pleasure in her this morning. What did Anne and Felicity want? And what sort of assignment could be connected with her present guise?

The Agency had been created and was staffed entirely by women, and its genius lay in the exploitation of female stereotypes. Its secret agents disguised themselves as maids, governesses, clerks, lady companions, and other humble, powerless characters. In most situations, no matter how dangerous, few people would suspect a subservient woman of being intelligent and observant, let alone a professional spy. With this as the Agency's guiding philosophy, it made no sense whatsoever for Mary to be dressed as a boy.

She raked her fingers through her hair, then stopped abruptly midstroke: that was a girl's gesture. And the only thing worse than not understanding what she was doing was compounding it by doing a poor job, too. As she neared the top of Acacia Road, where the Agency was headquartered, Mary pressed her lips together and took several deep breaths. Her cowardly impulse was to turn and make one last circuit of Regent's Park, to spend just a little more time thinking matters through. As though she hadn't already been marching about St. John's Wood for the past two hours. As though physical movement might still her mind and soothe her nerves. As though she was calm enough to sort through the swirl of emotions clouding her brain.

It was time to act, not to think. A few brisk steps took her to the house with its wrought-iron gates and polished brass nameplate: MISS SCRIMSHAW'S ACADEMY FOR GIRLS. The Academy had been her home for years now. But today, looking at the nameplate, she willed herself to look at it as a stranger might—specifically, as a twelve-year-old boy might. The house was large and well kept, with a tidy garden and flagged path. But in contrast with those of the neighboring houses, the front steps were swept but not whitened—an essential task that proclaimed to the world that one kept servants and kept them busy rewhitening the steps each time a caller marred them with footprints. The Academy's irregularity here was the only sign of the most unusual institution that lay within.

Suddenly, the front door swung open and disgorged a pair of girls—or, rather, young ladies. They were neatly dressed, neither at the height of fashion nor in the depths of dowdiness. They were having an animated conversation. And they looked curiously at Mary, whose nose was still inches from the closed gate.

"Are you lost?" asked the taller of the two as they approached the gate.

Mary shook her head. "No, miss." Her voice came out higher than she wanted, and she cleared her throat hastily. "I was bid come here."

A fine wrinkle appeared on the girl's forehead. "By whom?"

"I mean, I've a letter to deliver."

The girl held out her hand. "Then you may give it to me."

Mary shook her head again. "Can't, miss. I'm charged to give it to Mrs. Frame and no one else. Is this her house?" She'd spent all morning working on her inflection, trying to get the accent right while keeping her voice gruff.

The girl looked imperious. "You may trust me; I'm the head girl at this Academy."

Mary knew exactly who Alice Fernie was. Head girl, indeed! She was only head of her year. "Can't, miss. Orders."

Head Girl's face twisted into a scolding look, but before she could speak again, her companion said, "Never mind, Alice. We'll be late if we stop to argue with him."

"I'm not *arguing*; I'm just saying . . ."

The second girl unlatched the gate and nodded kindly to Mary. "Go on, then."

Mary tugged her cap respectfully and dodged around the pair, leaving Alice scowling into the road. As she walked around to the side door—the front door wasn't for the likes of humbly dressed messenger boys—she grinned broadly. Her disguise had passed well enough before Alice and Martha Mason, which was a start.

Her small stock of confidence plummeted, though, as she walked down the familiar corridors, heavy boots shuffling against the carpet runners. It was one thing to slip past a pair of schoolgirls, and another to confront the managers of the Agency. As she neared the heavy oak door of Anne Treleaven's office, her stomach twisted and she felt a wave of dizziness. She'd been too overwrought to eat breakfast. Or, for that matter, last night's dinner.

As she raised one hand to knock, she had a sudden memory of doing precisely this, feeling exactly this way, just over a year earlier. That was when she'd learned of the existence of the Agency and embarked on her training as a secret agent. And here she was, not fourteen months later, feeling as confused and anxious as she had back then. The thought gave her courage. She was not the same girl she'd been last spring—untrained, ignorant, hotheaded. Over the past year she'd learned so much. But it wasn't the physical techniques—sleight of hand, disguise, combat—that showed how she'd matured. It was her understanding of people, of calculated risk, that showed how she'd changed—as well as what remained for her to learn. It was all thanks to these women. She trusted them. And that trust would conquer the fear that made such a hard knot in her stomach.

Somehow.

* * *

"You ought not have accepted the contract, Felicity."

Felicity Frame's confident smile did not waver. "It's an excellent contract: interesting, lucrative, and one that brings us to the attention of certain Powers That Be at Westminster. If we impress them with our work in this instance, this could be the start of a whole new era for the Agency."

Anne Treleaven was careful to keep her expression neutral. "Such grandiose claims do not change the fact that you acted inappropriately. We've never before accepted work without making a joint decision."

"I hadn't time to consult and discuss; I had to move quickly in order to secure the client." Felicity paused and studied Anne's face. "You're still cross with me."

"I'm not cross." Anne's voice vibrated with suppressed tension. "But I am concerned about both your actions and your plan for carrying out the work."

Felicity looked suddenly weary. "Don't tell me—"

A knock on the door interrupted them. Four hesitant small raps, to be precise.

Felicity shot Anne a look. "Expecting someone?"

"No." The clock on Anne's desk showed it was just before eleven o'clock. "Come in."

The door opened slowly to reveal a slight, scruffy-looking boy. He wore a clean but much-patched suit of clothes, a round-brimmed cap, and unpolished boots that made a heavy clumping sound on the wooden floor as he advanced.

Anne frowned. "Who are you?"

The boy slowly tugged off his cap and wedged it between elbow and ribs. His hair was dark and badly cut. "Mark, ma'am." He paused, and then grinned wryly. "Mark Quinn."

Anne's jaw went slack.

Felicity gave a strange, high-pitched squawk.

Mary swept them both a neat little bow.

After her initial paralysis, Anne jumped up and grasped Mary by the shoulders. "Look at you! I can't—you—how—?"

Mary grinned and twirled about in a distinctly unboyish manner. She'd never heard Anne sputter before.

Felicity, too, came over to inspect her face. "Turn toward the light."

Anne's recovery was swift. "Well, my dear," she said with artificial calm, "you make a charming boy."

"Did you cut your own hair?" demanded Felicity.

"Yes, Mrs. Frame."

A subtle look of satisfaction crept over her face. "Rather a drastic step, don't you think?"

"I didn't think you would ask me to dress as a boy except for a serious purpose."

"Precisely."

"We arranged to meet with you this afternoon," said Anne. "I suppose you came early on purpose?"

Mary nodded. "I thought it a better test of the disguise."

"A sensible initiative."

"Thank you, Miss Treleaven." Mary glowed at the restrained praise. Anne was never lavish with compliments; even such measured approval meant much from her.

"Since you're here, we may as well have our meeting," said Felicity with patent satisfaction. "Unless, Miss Treleaven, you've an objection . . . ?"

A look that Mary couldn't decipher flickered between the two managers. There was a prolonged silence, broken at last by Anne. "Do begin, Mrs. Frame."

Felicity smiled and passed Mary an illustrated newspaper printed in lurid colors. "We may as well start here."

THE EYE ON LONDON

"NEWS FOR THE PEOPLE" FRIDAY, 1 JULY 1859

CURSE OF THE CLOCK TOWER!

THE GHOST OF PARLIAMENT STRIKES AGAIN?

Late last night, tragedy struck outside the Houses of Parliament: master carpenter John Wick, 32, of Lambeth, fell to his death from the pinnacle of St. Stephen's Tower, better known as the clock tower of the Houses of Parliament. It is not known how he came to fall from the 300-foot-high tower, which is still under construction. The Metropolitan Police refuse to confirm whether or not the death was an accident, but the building site was cordoned off this morning and is likely to remain so for the entire day. It was surrounded for the better part of the morning by a circle of builders and other laborers, who narrowly observed the travails of the police and other officials as they carried out their grisly duties.

Mrs. Betty Hawden, proprietress of a small coffee shop across from the Houses of Parliament, witnessed the removal of the unfortunate corpse early this morning. "It was terrible, just dreadful," she said, still visibly shaken, although speaking several hours afterward. "His poor broken body . . . and the expression on his face!" Owing to its convenient proximity to the building site, Mrs. Hawden's coffee shop was a hive of activity earlier today, with many of the dead man's workmates and acquaintances coming in to hear "the latest." And "the latest" generally included a discussion of the subject which official sources continue to deny, and which we at the *Eye on London* vow to pursue—THE CURSE OF THE CLOCK TOWER.

There followed a series of vivid illustrations depicting scenes of struggle, blood, and horror which corresponded only loosely to the article in question.

Mary shook her head and looked up at Anne and Felicity. "I must be reading the wrong article," she said. "Did you mean the one about the ghost of parliament?"

Anne nodded.

Mary scanned the pictures swiftly and shook her head again. "I'm sorry; I don't understand what this could possibly have to do with the Agency. Or, frankly, why we're even looking at this scandal sheet." Her fingertips were already smudged with cheap ink.

Felicity tilted her head to one side. "You don't think we can learn from the gutter press?"

"Well, not *facts,*" said Mary. "I suppose it's useful for the perspective it provides: someone, somewhere in London, might believe in the ghost of the clock tower. But we know better." She searched her two employers' faces. "Don't we?"

Felicity grinned, a broad, toothy, unladylike smile. "We think we do. But this news item definitely has to do with the Agency, and specifically with you."

Had she been alone with Felicity, Mary might have risked a joke about an Agency for the Control of Supernatural Phenomena. However, Anne's presence meant that she merely said, "Please tell me more."

"Setting aside the question of ghosts," said Felicity, "a suspicious death occurred two nights ago at St. Stephen's Tower. The accident occurred despite the presence of night watchmen at the Houses of Parliament, in a highly public part of town. And the death occurred after hours, which is certainly suggestive."

Mary swallowed. She'd been too quick to assume that the entire story was a fabrication, dead man and all. "So the authorities are concerned with the cause of the carpenter's—Mr. Wick's—death?"

"Mr. Wick was a bricklayer, not a carpenter; the article is, as you might expect, riddled with errors." Amusement curved Felicity's full lips. "But his death demands an explanation. This is normally a task for the police, of course. Scotland Yard have inspected the site and found no conclusive evidence. No witnesses have come forward.

There is to be an inquest on Wednesday, but if no other evidence is uncovered, the verdict will have to be one of death by misadventure."

Misadventure. It seemed a coy, silly way of saying "ghastly accident."

"And the Agency . . . ?" asked Mary. Things were falling into place now, but after jumping to one conclusion, she was reluctant to make other assumptions.

"We've been asked by the first commissioner of the Parliamentary Committee of Works to inquire into two related matters: the first is to monitor any gossip or anxiety about Mr. Wick's death. We may pick up information that Scotland Yard is unable to uncover, simply because we'll be on site in an unofficial capacity."

Mary's skin tingled at the word *we*. She had the prospect of becoming a full-fledged member of the Agency in just over six months' time.

If she worked hard.

If she continued to improve.

If Anne and Felicity so decided.

"As for the second matter, the new commissioner of works is concerned by the high rate of accidents on the building site, coupled with the fact that the tower's construction is grossly behind schedule. This is the kernel of the hysterical mention of ghosts and a curse in that scandal sheet: apparently, some say that a man killed in the original fire of 1834, the one that burned down the Houses of Parliament, haunts the site in ghostly form. This rumor seems to have been absolutely fatal to site discipline.

"The commissioner finds this impossible to investigate formally, of course: no man he interviewed would confess to believing the story of the ghost, but it still seems to be at the heart of the matter. But he also believes that having someone on the ground, so to speak, would be useful. Perhaps a superstitious belief in ghosts has delayed the works. Or, alternatively, perhaps the men are in no condition to report to work; perhaps they are flouting safety practices, and the foremen condone it; perhaps . . ." Felicity made an eloquent gesture. "Much is possible."

"And our knowledge of building practices is limited," said Anne. "For that reason, I was extremely surprised when the commissioner approached the Agency."

Mary was startled. "He didn't know . . . ?"

Felicity shook her head. "No. The fact that we're an all-female agency is still very much a secret."

"I've always wondered, Mrs. Frame: how do you manage to keep that secret when you meet with clients?" Mary asked the question timidly. Felicity was generally more forthcoming than Anne, but perhaps this was too nosy—a look into the inner workings of the Agency.

Felicity grinned again. "In several ways. We correspond by post a great deal; in meetings, Anne or I sometimes appear in the guise of a clerk or secretary representing the head of the Agency; and, when required, I make a rather convincing man."

Mary bit back a gasp. Felicity was tall and curvy, with

a beautiful and distinctly feminine face. Picturing her in a cravat and beard required more imagination than Mary possessed. Surely Anne Treleaven, a thin, austere-looking woman in her middle thirties, would make a more plausible man?

"To return to the point," said Anne, "the job requires an agent who can pass unnoticed on a building site; however, we know very little about its practical realities." She paused. "We could, I suppose, have declined the assignment . . ." The look she shot Felicity was ripe with meaning.

"But we didn't," said Felicity firmly, "for a number of excellent reasons I shan't enumerate now. The point is, no grown man could plausibly work on a building site without a trade or any general experience. And it would be exceptionally difficult for a grown woman—me, for example—to pass as a teenage apprentice. The difference in costume between a gentleman and a working man is quite unforgiving." Felicity sounded wistful.

"The Agency has no expertise in exclusively male environments," said Anne quietly. Again, that current of tension flashed between the two managers.

Felicity leaned forward. "We've two choices: to post an agent near the building site—for example, working in a neighboring pub or shop or selling food on the street—or to find an agent who can pass as a relatively young boy beginning his first job as a builder's assistant."

Mary blinked. "I see." And she did—perhaps rather

more than she wanted. There was a strange, hollow feeling in her chest that she didn't care to analyze.

Anne leaned forward and fixed Mary with a steady gaze. "Before Mrs. Frame goes into further detail, I shall ask the usual question: Do you wish to learn more? Or will you decline the assignment?" It was disconcerting, how Anne sometimes read her thoughts so accurately. "You may take a day to consider."

Anne's gentle tone—the more remarkable because her voice was normally so clipped—made Mary bristle defensively. "There is no need. I accept the assignment." Her voice was almost angry.

Anne looked at her carefully. "You are certain? I need not remind you that it is unwise to take on an assignment unless you are fully prepared, both physically and mentally." She laid a subtle emphasis on the last word. "If you—"

"I'm fine." Mary interrupted her for the first time ever. In the past, she had always been too much in awe to be so rude. "Please—tell me what the assignment will involve. I'll perform whatever tasks you set."

There was a short silence, during which Anne and Felicity again exchanged quick looks. Mary clenched the edge of her wooden chair and willed the tight feeling in her chest to vanish.

Finally, Felicity cleared her throat. "You will disguise yourself as an eleven- or twelve-year-old boy taking on his first job at a building site. The position will be forgiving of your lack of experience. Your task is to uncover information pertinent to the death of Mr. Wick, as well as to the possible causes of injury and delay on the site. This includes an investigation into the ghost stories, which may or may not have a basis in fact.

"You will begin by questioning the men and boys, and simply keeping your ears open. The engineer in charge of the site, a Mr. Harkness, already reports directly to the commissioner and his paperwork is all copied to the Committee of Works, so any evidence you find will be unofficial. The information you collect will determine your subsequent actions, of course. As you can see, it's an open-ended task which begins in a straightforward fashion." Felicity paused, but when Mary did not immediately reply, she hurried on. "You've already demonstrated that you can pass as a boy, and I'll spend some time coaching you on the finer points. As you know, it's primarily a matter of posture and movement, rather than costuming. You're young and slim and strong, so there's already a natural resemblance, and lots of boys' voices haven't broken at that age."

Mary nodded. Her fingers were very cold now, and she felt curiously numb. Felicity was always persuasive—a trick of her voice rather than her facility with words—and Mary hated to disappoint. "Very well," she said. "When must I begin?"

Anne frowned slightly, possibly at her phrasing. "There are still a few arrangements to make concerning your false identity as a boy—such as ensuring that there's a place for you on site. Mr. Harkness is deemed reliable, but he will not be privy to your real identity. Add to that time to work on your masculine persona. . . . I should say you could begin no earlier than Wednesday or Thursday."

Felicity compressed her lips. "Too long, I think. Ideally, you'd start on Monday."

Mary nodded. "Very well."

"Report back here after luncheon tomorrow," said Felicity. She nodded at Mary briskly, and glanced at Anne. The meeting was over, and Mary was dismissed.

She stood clumsily, mechanically scrunching the *Eye* in her hand. "Thank you." For what, she had no idea.

Two

A bell was ringing.

A clear, high-pitched, arrhythmic clatter.

A G—not that she cared one way or another.

Mary clutched her pillow tighter and let the note resound through her weary brain, refusing to analyze the sound, unwilling to connect it with any sort of meaning. There were always bells ringing at the Academy. Her life, since the age of twelve, had been governed by these bells. She'd never thought to resent them until today.

The bell finally stopped its nagging and Mary rolled onto her back, crinoline collapsing beneath her weight. A lock of hair—short, jagged, unfamiliar—jabbed her left eye. The plaster ceiling was annoyingly creamy and perfect—the result of a much-needed replastering last summer. She missed the old, yellowed ceiling, with its hairline fissures and occasional nicks.

That tight sensation in her chest was still expanding, and she hugged the pillow tighter in an effort to combat it. What was wrong with her, anyway? She'd just been handed the most exciting assignment of her nascent career, and the only responses she could summon were panic and nausea. Was this sort of work—spying and covert observation—not for her, after all? Perhaps she ought to be a good little governess or a nice little nurse or a quiet little clerk. Anything but the luckiest, most ungrateful girl in London.

Was she even still a girl? She was eighteen sometime this year—that much she knew, although the exact date was lost to her precarious, unhappy childhood. She was a woman now, and if she'd hoped that wisdom, perspective, and confidence would come with that, she'd been sadly mistaken.

Three quiet raps at the door interrupted her brooding. She kept silent.

A pause, and then the three raps came again. "Mary?" The voice was female, of course, but muffled by the thick wooden door.

Three—no, six—deliberate knocks. She remained mute.

The brass doorknob turned, and Mary scowled. Naturally, she'd forgotten to lock the door. Some secret agent she was. "This is a private room," she said in her iciest voice as the door began to swing open. "Kindly shut the door."

Anne Treleaven's thin, spectacled face appeared in the

gap. "I'd like a word with you, Mary, later this evening if not now."

Mary leaped up so quickly that she felt dizzy. "Miss Treleaven! I'm so very sorry. I thought you were one of the girls—not that that's an excuse, either—but if—I mean, had I known . . ."

Anne waved her into silence. "No need for that, Mary. I just want to speak with you."

"Of course." Mary scrambled to pull out the desk chair.

They sat facing each other, Anne on the chair and Mary on the edge of the bed. It was Anne who broke the heavy silence. "It can be difficult to find privacy in a boarding school."

Mary's fierce blush ebbed a little. "I'm fortunate to have a single room; I know that."

Anne leaned forward abruptly, folding her hands together in her schoolteacher's manner. "My dear, I want to talk to you about this assignment."

Mary's gut clenched. "I thought it was all arranged, Miss Treleaven."

Anne nodded. "It is. But it's clear to me that this assignment holds special difficulties for you. We'll discuss those now."

Mary immediately opened her mouth to argue the point, but something about Anne's look stopped her voice. In the end, all she managed was a toneless "What do you mean?"

"I'd like to venture a theory, Mary. You'll do me the favor of hearing it out before pronouncing judgment?" It was a courteous command, not a question.

Mary swallowed and bowed her head.

Anne spoke slowly, quietly. "Your childhood was, by any standards, a tragic one. You lost your father and witnessed your mother's painful death. By the age of ten, you knew hunger, danger, and violence. In the years that you were homeless, you passed yourself off as a boy for reasons of safety. It was easier to move about the city and to avert rape, and it gave you a better chance of survival. It wasn't until you came to the Academy that you were free to conduct your life as a girl without fear of ill treatment or exploitation. Am I correct?"

Mary managed a single nod.

"A return to boy's costume"—Anne appeared to choose her words with great care—"must evoke a return to the same dangers and privations."

Mary forgot her promise to listen quietly. "It's not the same thing at all! I'm well aware that it's a temporary, theoretical return."

Anne nodded. "Of course; you are too intelligent to believe otherwise. However, what I am suggesting is that somehow, at the back of your mind, those fears are still with you. The suggestion that you relive those days—even strictly as an assignment, with every certainty of returning to your real life—may distress you." She made a small, frustrated gesture. "I am not phrasing this well. I mean that, even seen as playacting, the idea of passing as a boy must be an extremely unpleasant reminder of your past."

The backs of Mary's eyes prickled, and she dared not look at Anne when she spoke. "During my first case . . . at the Thorolds' house . . . I had some boys' clothing. I didn't mind running about in trousers then." She bit her lower lip. "I—I quite enjoyed it." Her voice cracked on the penultimate word.

"True. Is it not possible that you saw the act differently then? As an adventure or a game?"

"Unlike this one?"

"Possibly. Or perhaps it was different because you chose to do that, and this time it is an assignment." Anne sighed. "Mind and memory and emotion are so complex."

Mary stared at her hands, clasped tightly in her lap. Their outlines blurred, and then doubled, but it wasn't until the first hot tear splashed down that she understood why.

"My dear." Anne offered her a clean handkerchief. "Regardless of the assignment, you are our first concern here. We would not require you to do anything that made you . . ."

"Afraid?"

"Yes."

Mary sniffled and wiped her eyes. She had no idea whether Anne was correct. Her surmises seemed . . . airy. Mystical. Preposterous. Yet she couldn't reject them outright.

They sat in silence for a few minutes. The light coming through the window was a rich gold that warmed and softened everything in the room: the waning of an unusually glorious summer day. It was warm, but Mary's hands were cold and numb.

"I'll leave you to your thoughts," said Anne eventually. "And I'll have a dinner tray sent up." The dinner hour: that was what the bell had announced.

Mary nodded. "Thank you."

Anne stood and rested her hand lightly on top of Mary's head, just for a moment. "Don't stay up all night thinking," she said. "Trust your instincts."

A moment later, Mary was alone.

Three

Sunday, 3 July

The Agency's headquarters

When Mary reentered the office the following afternoon, again dressed as Mark, she had the distinct impression she was interrupting. It wasn't clear what: Anne and Felicity sat in their customary chairs and greeted her with their usual brevity. Yet there was something in the careful blankness of Anne's expression, a latent glitter in Felicity's eyes, that made her hesitate. A moment later, it was gone.

Anne motioned her to sit down. "What made you decide to accept the assignment?" Her voice was dry, almost neutral, yet tinged with concern.

Mary sat up straight. "I thought a great deal about our conversation," she began carefully. "I hadn't been able to identify my fear until you suggested it to me. I didn't want to think about it, and I certainly didn't want to believe your theory—but I think you were right." She met Anne's eyes freely and offered her a small smile. "I must learn to conquer my fears rather than try to ignore them."

Felicity shot a quick glance at Anne, then looked back at Mary.

"So you're still afraid," said Anne.

"Yes. But now I know it—and with that fear in mind, I choose to accept this assignment." She hoped she sounded more confident than she felt.

There was a long silence. Anne and Felicity both stared hard at her, as though expecting her to crack. To change her mind.

Mary held their gazes, waiting.

Finally, Felicity nodded. "Very well; you've chosen. We shall—"

"There's just one more thing."

Anne raised one fine eyebrow. "What is that?"

Mary swallowed. "I shall need to live in lodgings, if I am truly to pass as Mark Quinn. I took a room at a lodging house in Lambeth this morning."

Both women were silent with astonishment.

After several long seconds, Mary said tentatively, "I'll begin with the practical reasons: the workers I meet on the building site might ask whereabouts I live. It would be rather unusual for Mark to live in St. John's Wood, and it would be useful to have a generally known address. If anybody inquired into the address, a lodging house would give nothing away—whereas it would be extremely odd for me to live at a girls' boarding school."

"And there are reasons apart from the practical?" prompted Anne.

Mary took a deep breath. "It will be simpler if I don't alternate between being myself and being Mark. I will make a more convincing boy if I am not a girl as well. And . . ." Her voice wobbled, and she waited a moment before going on. "And when I was younger, and passing as a boy, I never left the role. I should like to re-create that situation."

Anne frowned. "Why? Why deliberately return yourself to a frightening and dangerous past?"

Mary hesitated. "I don't know quite how to explain it. I think—I believe—that it might help me to stop fearing it."

"Strong reason," murmured Anne. "Are there others?"

And, Mary thought, *if I don't return to the comforts of the Academy, I'll be less inclined to give up or give in partway.* "No," she said.

There was a pause, during which the two women looked at each other. After several moments, Anne nodded once. "I shall organize our information network so that you can communicate with us while undercover. There's a pub near Westminster where you may leave a written message, in code, by giving a password. But to collect messages, we'll use somewhere in Lambeth itself. We've a contact in a baker's shop in The Cut who might prove useful." She looked at Mary. "However, should you change your mind, at any time . . ."

Mary was already on her feet. "Thank you. I shan't."

"Wait a moment," said Felicity. "That extra coaching

I promised you: meet me before dinner this evening and we'll go for a walk. Perhaps down the pub."

Mary knew she ought to look pleased, even excited at the prospect. But the best she could manage was a nod before bolting from the room. She just managed to close the door behind her when her knees wobbled. She leaned into the wall for a moment, eyes shut. It was done. But instead of relief, she felt the wild thrill of fear grip her again. Had she taken on too much?

"Of course not." The words came from within the office, but made her start all the same. The voice was Anne's.

"And you approve of this scheme?" That was Felicity.

Hesitation, then a low reply that Mary didn't catch. Anne and Felicity must be speaking much more loudly than usual for the sound to carry through the heavy oak door. Mary stood perfectly still. Never before had she known Anne and Felicity to quarrel. They politely disagreed, on occasion, in ladylike tones. But this waspish severity was new.

Mary understood now what she'd interrupted, and the understanding was unwelcome. She had walked into the middle of a dispute—about the case, about the Agency, about her? She had no idea, and it was beneath her to stay and listen. Even if she could make out the words, she couldn't eavesdrop on her employers.

As she forced her heavy feet into motion, Mary felt her fear drain away—yet it came as no relief.

For this time, it was replaced by dread.

Four

Monday, 4 July

On the road to the Palace of Westminster

It was only a short walk across the Thames from Mary's new lodgings in Lambeth to the building site in Westminster. Nervous as she was about the first day of the assignment, she forced her attention outward, to streets she would come to know well. All about her, men, women, and children shuffled slowly workward, or perhaps home again after a night shift. The pubs did steady business as laborers drank their breakfast pints. Occasionally, a fresh scent—new bread from a bakeshop, a barrowful of lilies going to a florist's—cut through the thick, earthy, acidic smells of the city. She dodged a wagon heaped high with sides of beef and grinned at the pack of dogs trailing it hopefully.

Her destination, St. Stephen's Tower, loomed over all this. It was designed to look glorious and imperial, but the effect was spoiled from her angle by the absence of hands on two of the clock faces. To Mary the tower merely looked blind, a spindly, helpless outcast marooned by the river's edge. As she stepped onto Westminster Bridge, she realized she was breathing shallowly. How foolish to think she could mitigate the odor of the river! She inhaled a careful breath and forced herself to take measure of its stench. Yes, it was still intensely familiar, if slightly less disgusting because of the cooler weather. After last year's Great Stink, appalled Londoners had spent months arguing about the need to clean up the Thames. Campaigners crusaded, newspapers excoriated, politicians pontificated. But like most Londoners, Mary would believe it only once she saw the results. For now, she was grateful that the stink was no worse than last year.

She slowed her pace along the bridge, taking a long, deliberate look at the Palace of Westminster. Every child knew that this was the seat of government, where the House of Lords and House of Commons met. Yet she'd never paid close attention to the actual buildings, sprawling and imposing as they were. They'd been under construction since well before she was born. For most Londoners now, the palace's twenty-five-year reconstruction was merely an obvious, unfunny joke about government and the ruling classes.

Nothing moved inside Palace Yard. It was too early for the lawmakers and too late for the night watchmen. The entrance to the building site was separate and there would be no need to enter the palace itself, no dangerous mingling of peers and working men. Even so, she made a circuit around the palace proper, entranced now by its colossal mass, its relentless detail. It was a revelation: not beautiful in a restrained, classical way, but fierce and extravagantly Gothic. The intricacy of the design was hypnotic, overwhelmingly so, and the arrogance and tradition it represented made itself felt in the pit of her stomach.

She passed the length of the palace in a daze, and on looping back up toward St. Stephen's Tower, had to stop to remind herself of who she wasn't. She touched the back of her neck self-consciously. Although she looked the part of a twelve-year-old boy, she still didn't quite feel it. Last night's coaching session with Felicity—a pint and a cold meat pie eaten out of hand in a public house—had been of some use. But it had also intensified her awareness of the very different world of men. Years in an all-girls school had changed her. And now, behind the site fencing there would be swarms of men and boys, roaring and swearing and doing whatever it was builders did while preparing to work, and they would all scrutinize her and know immediately if something was amiss. Of course, it was much too late to turn back. Mary took a deep breath, wiped her damp palms on her trousers, and marched through the narrow entrance gate into the building site proper.

She was braced for a wall of noise, an audience of raucous, suspicious masculinity. Yet, if anything, the building site was quieter than the street. Small clusters of men chatted as they unpacked tools or swallowed the last bits of breakfast or inspected the incomplete work. None looked up as she passed.

There didn't appear to be much order to the site—not to an outsider, at least. A small shed to her right seemed to function as an office; at least it contained a desk covered with several inches of papers, but no person. No one appeared to challenge her presence, so she walked about the site slowly, simply looking.

She'd imagined a building site to be like a cross between a factory and an anthill: scores of people milling about, busily doing nothing, until a giant bell rang calling them to work, at which point they would all fall into line. Yet what she saw seemed more leisurely and self-directed. Already a pair of bricklayers had begun to mix up some mortar, and other tradesmen seemed to be finding their places for the day. None took any notice of her, and she suspected that it wasn't due to the excellence of her masculine costume.

On the south side of the building site, a cluster of perhaps half a dozen men and boys loitered purposefully in the shadow of the palace. As she drew nearer, Mary realized they were all hovering around one man. He was perhaps in his late forties, with the usual beard and mustache and well-fed paunch. He was also the only man on site wearing a collar and tie, which meant the chances were good that he was the site engineer, Mr. Harkness. The fact that he looked tired and harassed rather confirmed this.

"I understand," he was saying, "that you're short-handed at the moment. I shall try to find a man to assist you this week, but it is your responsibility to engage a new member for your gang."

The workman he addressed—a tall, powerfully built man in his middle thirties—glowered with frustration. "Don't I know it! But it takes time, that. We're missing an experienced bricklayer, not some useless apprentice."

A muscle jumped under Harkness's left eye. "I know," he said in a placating tone. "As I said, I shall do my best."

The foreman pushed his way out of the crowd, his face dark with anger. "'I shall do my best,'" he simpered, imitating Harkness's tones. "Bloody useless son of a—" His eyes met Mary's and flared with temper. "What the hell you staring at, boy?"

She quickly averted her eyes and edged deeper into the pack. So that man had been Wick's workmate. She wondered if they'd been friends.

It took a long time for Harkness to give each laborer his directions. When Mary finally presented herself, he stared at her for a long moment with red-rimmed eyes. "Who?"

Had she not spoken clearly enough? "Mark Quinn, sir. I'm to begin today as an errand boy, if you please."

The twitch came again, and he pressed a weary hand to his disobedient eye. "As a general errand boy?"

Mary tried to look confident. "Yes, sir." What could

have gone wrong? Had someone failed to organize the position? Did she — her stomach plunged at the idea — did she not look the part? A few men nearby had stopped and looked at her curiously as soon as she'd addressed Harkness. Perhaps they could tell, somehow. . . .

Harkness scrubbed his face abruptly with one hand. "And how old are you — what did you say your name was?"

"Quinn, sir. I'm twelve."

"Quinn. Twelve. And you want work as an errand boy."

"Yes, sir." Mary was beginning to think Harkness very slow indeed.

"Hmph." He eyed her speculatively. "Nicely spoken . . ."

Damn it all. She'd worked so hard to make her voice gruff and diffident, to get the accent just right, but she'd compromised the role from the start by using the wrong vocabulary. What sort of boy would say "begin" instead of "start" or "if you please" instead of simply "please"? Five seconds into the job and she'd already made her first blunder.

Harkness fumbled in his inner coat pocket and pulled out a battered sheaf of papers. "Read that."

Burning with shame, Mary took the bundle and read blankly, automatically, from the top. "'The recasting of the bell by the Whitechapel Foundry is merely the first—' "

The papers were snatched from her grasp. "Bless me, you can read."

Of course she could—and Harkness's realization made her feel sick. Mary Quinn read fluently, but "Mark" Quinn wouldn't read or write; he'd be fortunate to sign his own name. And she, of all people, ought to have known that. But she'd been so busy kicking herself for the first mistake that she'd compounded it with a second—perhaps even greater—error. Her pulse thudded, and her cheeks were flushed. She was furious with herself yet terrified of making a third and even greater faux pas. What was *wrong* with her? No wonder the laborers nearby stared at her.

Harkness fixed her with another shrewd look. "I ask you again: why are you here as an errand boy?"

There was nothing to do but to brazen it out. "Sir?"

"You make a bad job of playing the fool, Quinn."

He was right. But she'd try, nevertheless. Mary thrust her hands into her pockets and stared at the ground. "I can't do anything else, sir. There's no money for school fees or to buy an apprenticeship."

Harkness folded his arms and looked interested for the first time. "For a bright boy like you?"

"No, sir."

"No Christian charity willing to educate you?"

"No, sir."

"Hm."

There was a long pause, during which Mary concentrated hard on the toes of her new-but-old boots. Her responses to this personal line of questioning wouldn't stand up for long. The last thing she needed was for a kindly employer to research her story. Finally, she looked up. Her face was warm with tension, but Harkness must have seen what he was looking for.

"Never be ashamed to admit want if it is not your fault," he said quietly.

Mary nodded slightly. "Yes, sir." Where was this conversation leading?

"I have nothing better for you at the moment, Quinn."

Mary frowned. "Nothing better . . . ?"

"Than a post as general errand boy. Not right now."

"Th-th-at's all I want, sir," she stammered, trying to salvage her role. "I just need . . ."

But Harkness was shaking his head. "I don't know when something more suited to your abilities will come along. But do your best and prove yourself, and we'll see. He shall provide."

"'He,' Mr. Harkness?"

"The Lord, child."

"Of course, the Lord." She ought to have guessed.

"You'll work under the bricklayers, assisting with any tasks they set you. Their foreman's named Keenan. You'll also be in charge of making tea in time for elevenses. One of the other boys, Jenkins, will show you the routine. Mine is a teetotal building site, Quinn, so if the men send you for spirits, you're not to oblige. Hot tea is all that's required to sustain the soul, not the offerings of the public house."

Mary nodded. She wasn't sure about souls, but she now had a good idea about Harkness's popularity among the men.

"And—er—since you are better educated than the average errand boy, Quinn, you may find that the others—well, they may not take to you as quickly as they might to someone of their own class. In those instances, remember, child, to turn the other cheek, and also that from those to whom much is given . . ." Harkness paused expectantly.

"Much is expected," mumbled Mary. The look of gratification on Harkness's face was familiar. "May I go, sir?"

Twitch. "Yes, yes, run along."

She was only too relieved to flee. Three minutes and two colossal mistakes. At this rate, she'd not last the hour. After all that work—cutting her hair, Felicity's coaching—she had failed the very first challenge. Even more humiliating, the role of a poor working child was not unfamiliar to her: after her mother's death, she had indeed been poor, uneducated, and desperate. She'd been homeless at times. She'd gone hungry. She'd passed as a boy to avoid rape. But today's abysmal performance showed how deeply she'd lost touch with that part of her childhood. It came as a profound and unwelcome shock.

Five

Mary circled the building site, looking for a stack of bricks and men with trowels. It was a good opportunity to walk the site and explore its corners. It was a cramped, untidy place to work, with a great number of laborers moving awkwardly about the large tower at its center. St. Stephen's Tower was the last element of the palace to be finished. With the Houses of Parliament in daily use and densely built-up streets all around, there was little space to store building materials and equipment except in the construction zone. Wherever the workers stood, the palace loomed over them, making a pinched space feel even smaller.

All the same, Mary wondered if there might be a more efficient way of doing things. She felt her ignorance here. If she knew more about building practices, she'd be better able to assess Harkness's efficiency as an engineer in charge. Not for the first time since accepting this assignment, she thought of James Easton. She would have given much for his assessment of the site, and the job. But this was an entirely theoretical temptation: James was in India, and she'd never see him again.

Eventually, she noticed a fair-haired man, whistling as he slapped some mortar onto a mortarboard. "'Scuse me—you Mr. Keenan?" Mary kept her diction indistinct, a little reluctant. She could try to blur her accent a bit more, but the fact remained that she'd already set herself apart. It was too late to change things.

The man looked up. His good humor seemed at odds with his face, which bore the souvenirs of a fistfight: one eye puffy and discolored, lip split. "What's that?"

"Mr. Harkness sent me to help out."

"Ah. You want Keenan—dark chap over there." He pointed to a tall, thickset man a little way off. He was scowling, but even without the surly expression Mary would have recognized him as the man who'd snarled at her not half an hour before.

She sighed inwardly. Of course the bad-tempered bricklayer would be the foreman. Still, perhaps that was relevant to Wick's death, too. She approached him reluctantly, as he was clearly preoccupied.

"You're awful small," he said in response to her explanation.

"I'm stronger than I look."

"Aye? I hope so." Something happened when he spoke that made words sound like threats, even when they were simple instructions. He wasn't generous with them, either:

he simply nodded at a pole lying on the ground. "You're Reid's hod carrier today." Then he strode away.

Mary struggled to make sense of the contraption, a long stick topped by three wooden planks that together formed three sides of a box. Unfortunately, she had no idea what to do with it, or whom to ask for assistance. The cheerful young man, perhaps? But when she looked around, he'd disappeared with his trowel and mortarboard.

When Keenan came back to her a few minutes later, his face was flushed with temper. "Still mucking about? I told you to get moving."

"I'm sorry. I don't know how to use this."

His face darkened some more. "Useless brat. Never seen a hod before?"

"N-no, sir."

"Then what you doing working on a building site?"

"I want to learn, sir."

Keenan cursed. "Not with me for a bloody nursemaid, you won't. I got bleedin' work to do." He looked about for a moment, then bellowed, "Stubbs!"

Another youngish man, with curly ginger hair and an astounding number of freckles, appeared. "Mr. Keenan?"

"Show this brat what's what."

Once Keenan was at a safe distance, Stubbs looked at Mary. "What's he want you to do?"

"Be Reid's hod carrier." Mary spoke the strange words tentatively. "This is the hod?" She hefted the pole and box.

Stubbs laughed, a single brief snort. "Aye. You hold it like this." In a single deft motion, he swung the stick over one shoulder so that the three planks were behind him. "You fill it with bricks—at your size, not many, maybe three or four—and carry it to your brickie. You said Reid, did you? He's over that way, round the corner."

"That's all?" It seemed absurdly straightforward.

"You fetch whatever he tells you to. You can carry mortar and trowels in it, or anything else he needs."

He gave her the hod and she hefted it experimentally. Not bad, but . . . "Why not use a wheelbarrow?"

"Sometimes you climb with the hod—up scaffolding, like." He grinned at her expression. "Not today, though—I'm doing the tricky bits while we're shorthanded."

"Oh. You missing a hod carrier?" Mary followed him toward a large pile of bricks.

Stubbs frowned down at her. "You new?"

She nodded. "Started this morning."

"Oh. Suppose you ain't heard, then." He paused and his round face turned somber. "One of ours, a brickie, died last week. Until Keenan finds a new one, the other hod carrier, Smith, is filling in. Not that he's a proper brickie or nothing. But he can lay a simple wall while Keenan and Reid do the rest."

Mary frowned. The explanation was almost as confusing as the situation. So bricklayers and hod carriers worked in teams, and it sounded as though this was a disrupted team of five: three bricklayers, Wick, Keenan, and Reid, supported by the hod carriers Stubbs and Smith. With Wick's death, it was up to Keenan to find a new bricklayer to join his permanent team, rather than for Harkness to hire another solo bricklayer. Like the hod itself, it seemed strange but made sense once you thought about it. The men were accustomed to working with one another and would have their own efficient habits and systems. Hire a gang of brickies and, she supposed, they would work together smoothly from the start.

"Here." Stubbs stopped by the brick pile. "Hold steady, now." Mary braced her shoulders as Stubbs loaded three bricks onto the hod. "All right, there?"

"I can take another one."

He looked at her critically. "Best not. Save your strength, lad; you'll be doing this for hours."

It was good advice. The hod itself was not light, and with three bricks on it, the combined weight was as much as Mary could manage while dodging through the yard. Stubbs's directions were approximate but she soon spotted the blond man, Reid, squatting on his haunches, whistling again as he sized up his day's work. Despite his propensity for fistfights, he seemed as good-tempered as Keenan was hostile, and this made her all the more grateful not to be working directly under Keenan.

"Three bricks?" he exclaimed as she set down the hod.

Mary flushed. "Sorry, sir. I'll try to bring more next time."

"Don't hurt yourself," he said, amiably enough. "But

Lord love me if you ain't the tiniest hod carrier I ever seen."

"Still growing, sir," she mumbled.

"If you don't grow no bigger, be something else," he advised. "A glazier, maybe."

Mary nodded and fled back to the brick pile. As the morning wore on, she became more skilled at loading bricks onto the hod and carrying them efficiently. Some time later—she couldn't have said how long, but hours rather than minutes—she became aware of another boy watching her. He stood about twenty yards off, hands in pockets, staring at her openly.

Mary straightened from her task—sweeping up mortar dust and brick rubble—and stared back. After several moments, she nodded a brusque acknowledgment. But instead of responding, the boy merely continued to stare aggressively. Mary kept at her work.

After a few minutes, he finally spoke. "Suppose you's Quinn."

Mary looked up again. He was closer, but no less truculent. She nodded once and went on with her sweeping.

"You don't look so posh."

So it had come to haunt her already. "I'm not."

" 'F you's so posh, why'd you steal my job?"

"What—this job?" She was genuinely surprised. "You've still got a job, haven't you?"

"Don't be stupid—I mean the tea round."

Ah: the teetotaling tea round. "So you're Jenkins."

"Yeah, and *you stole my job*."

What was it with building sites and fistfights? First Reid looked as if he'd been brawling, and now this little fool was clearly frantic for a scrap. She turned her back and kept sweeping.

He circled around and shouted, "Think you's too good for to talk to me?"

"No."

"Well, then? What you got to say?"

"Nothing."

"Nothing except lies."

There was only one way to end this. She looked straight at him and said, "You calling me a liar?"

"A liar and a thief!"

She snorted. If he wanted a fight, he'd get one. And she would win: her years on the street had taught her this, at least. "Of all the stupid . . ."

"Don't you call me stupid!" He marched toward her, stiff with outrage. He was a small boy, no taller than she and scrawny to boot, and he looked utterly ridiculous—a bantam rooster defending his turf. He'd never won a fist-fight in his life, she'd wager. Still, he hurled himself at her, arms windmilling furiously.

Mary dodged his fist with an economical twist to the left and tapped him sharply on the chin, sending him stumbling.

He stopped short of falling, spun about, and flew at her again.

She skipped aside and he tripped himself with his own momentum.

Screaming with outrage, he picked himself up and came back for more.

It was no contest. Mary wasn't even fighting; merely defending herself and keeping him at bay, waiting for him to exhaust himself. Her restraint only inflamed Jenkins further. He fought with passion and energy and utter lack of skill, and this combination made what ought to have been comical seem tragic instead. If Mary chose, she could finish him in half a minute. As it was, their fistfight dragged on and they attracted a casual, jeering ring of laborers who shouted advice and insults in equal quantity.

Finally, a new voice sliced through the noise: "WHAT is going on here? Stop this, instantly!"

Mary looked toward its source—Harkness—and in that instant, Jenkins landed his only blow, a strange accidental swing that made her nose spurt blood. She gasped with surprise, felt a stab of anger. Street fighting had no rules, of course, but that had been damned underhanded all the same. She spun, caught his shoulder, and delivered a solid jab that made her knuckles—and presumably Jenkins's head—ring.

"Stop it, NOW!"

A couple of men finally stepped forward, half-heartedly offering to hold the fighters. But it was now unnecessary. Mary stood perfectly still, allowing the blood welling from her nose to drip onto the cobblestones unchecked. Jenkins writhed silently, cradling one side of his face.

"What the blazes is the matter here?" Harkness glared from Jenkins to Mary and back again.

Neither spoke.

"Quinn! Explain yourself!"

What could she say? "Jenkins and I were fighting, sir."

There was a rumble of amusement from their audience.

The top of Harkness's head went pink. "All of you, clear off! Back to work!" As the men receded, chuckling, Harkness returned his attention to Mary. "WHY were you fighting?"

"He called me a liar and a thief, sir. I called him stupid."

"I see. And who began this childishness?"

Mary glanced at Jenkins. He was still clutching his face and appeared to be choking back tears. Eventually, he managed to gasp, "Me, sir."

Harkness stared at them for a long minute, that muscle beneath his eye spasming repeatedly. "I am very disappointed in you both. I expected better from you, Jenkins, because you've worked on this building site for nearly two years. And I expected better from you especially, Quinn, because . . ."

As the clichés began, Mary wondered whether Harkness would inquire into the root of the dispute. What was special about the tea round? Why had Jenkins been willing to attack her for it? She was also annoyed by her inability to blend in on a building site. In her first five minutes on the job, she'd nearly blown her cover, twice. Now she had drawn the attention of nearly every man on site by getting into a fistfight.

". . . Do I make myself clear?"

She nodded. "Yes, sir."

Jenkins, still clutching his face, made a noise that could have been "Yes, sir."

"Then shake hands like men."

As Jenkins released his cheek to offer his hand, Mary saw that he was indeed crying. Yet through the tears, he mumbled, "No hard feelings."

She looked into his eyes, startled and cautious. "Same here."

"I don't want to hear of further fisticuffs—or any sort of squabbling—between the two of you."

Mary mopped her nose with her sleeve. The bleeding seemed to be slowing.

"Oh, for heaven's sake." A large linen handkerchief was thrust into her face.

She took it. "Thank you, sir." It smelled of scent: the discreet, expensive type.

"Now back to work, both of you."

As Harkness disappeared back into his office, Mary and Jenkins remained where they were, stiff and uncertain. Finally, Jenkins said, "S'pose we best start the tea round."

Mary glanced up with some surprise. One of the

working clock faces showed the time as a quarter past ten. "Now? Bit early, isn't it?"

He shot her a wary look. "Lots to do. Come on." Perhaps it was a boy thing: girls could hold grudges forever and a day, but it seemed Jenkins really had forgotten the fight. He quizzed her as they walked around the perimeter of the site. "You go to Harky's church?"

"No."

"How'd you get the job, then?"

She shrugged. "Said I needed it."

Jenkins examined her through slitted eyes. "Hmph."

"How'd you get *your* job?" And why was simply asking for one so improbable?

"Most of us boys here is the same: got in through our old men."

"How old are you?"

"How old d'you think?"

Mary looked at him carefully. He was a scrawny, freckly little thing—an eight-year-old with an old man's eyes. "Thirteen."

He looked gratified. "Thirteen next month. How old's you?"

"Twelve."

"This ain't your first job, then."

"First job on a building site," said Mary, truthfully enough. She looked about. "Where're we going?"

A sly look crossed Jenkins's swollen face. "Sure you's not churchy?"

"I've already said I'm not."

"Not a teetotaler?"

"A teetotaler?" It was a large word for a boy like Jenkins.

"One of 'em what thinks a little beer is poison."

"No, I'm not."

"Then how come you's Harky's pet?"

"How can I be his pet when I only started today?" This was exactly what she'd feared—but Jenkins's answer surprised her.

"You's on the tea round. Took me a year 'n a half to get on the tea round, and here you are on your first day taking it over."

Mary was mystified. "I don't know why that is. And what's so special about the tea round, anyway?"

Jenkins looked at her suspiciously. "If I tell you, you got to share the take."

Take? Mary had a sudden idea of what that might be: teetotaling plus tea drinking could equal a nice little profit. "I'm not sure what you mean, but I don't mind sharing. What is it?"

"We'll go halves," Jenkins persisted.

"Halves on what?"

Jenkins was becoming agitated again, and their pace accelerated. By this time, they'd done two full circuits of the building site. "You can't tell Harky."

"All right," Mary said promptly.

"Promise!"

"Promise."

"Swear on your mother's life?"

"She's dead."

"Then swear on her grave!" he insisted.

"I swear. Now, what are you talking about?"

Jenkins grinned, then winced. His cheek was already bruising. "I'll show you."

They began with the joiners, who greeted Jenkins with sharp, plaintive relief. Why was he so late that morning? They'd all but given up hope. Who's the other lad? New tea boy. Ah. They wanted how much? Why, the bleedin' little highwaymen . . . and, to a man, they dug into their pockets, came up with a couple of coins, and tossed them to Jenkins with grumpy satisfaction.

Jenkins and Mary made a full circuit of the building site, and Mary realized with excitement what an extraordinarily perfect task it was for her. In this way, she met nearly every artisan and laborer on site. They knew who she was; she would soon know their domains; and she would have a reason to visit them all on a regular basis, and have a quick chat besides. It was nothing short of miraculous—as though Harkness were aware of her true assignment.

"Does everybody give you some money?" she asked Jenkins. "Apart from Mr. Harkness?"

Jenkins looked at her as though she was daft. " 'Course they do! Who wouldn't?"

After canvassing each worker on site, Jenkins had a

heavy pocketful of coppers that clinked pleasantly as he led Mary to a nearby public house. Apart from its name, there was nothing fresh or lovely about the Blue Bell. It was dank and dark, and the fug of a thousand gin-sodden nights was visible in the air. It was also quite full, and Mary had the strong impression that most of its denizens had been there since the night before.

Jenkins swaggered up to the bar, one hand in his pocket, and leaned on it in a self-important fashion. The bar was as high as his shoulder, which spoiled the effect somewhat.

"Late today, Master Jenkins," said the barman. He was fat and sweat-stained.

Jenkins shrugged elaborately. "Got me 'n associate. You won't be seeing me no more, Mr. Lamb." His voice was still a thin treble, and it sounded doubly shrill in this cave-like pub.

Mr. Lamb looked at Mary without much interest. "The usual?"

Mary glanced at Jenkins. "What's the usual?"

"Pint o' rum," said Jenkins with authority. "Rum every day, and whiskey on Saturdays."

As Mr. Lamb filled a dirty bottle under Jenkins's supervision, Mary glanced around the pub. The unvarnished floorboards were sticky beneath her boots. Small, furtive movements in the corners of the room suggested the presence of rats. There was one small window in the far wall, so dirty that at first she thought it was a particularly sooty painting. And sprawled around the room, threatening the rotting furniture, were small heaps of men and women in the last stages of inebriation. No one was merry in this pub; that phase had passed hours before. Instead, they stared at Mary and Jenkins—and at nothing in particular—with glassy, bloodshot eyes. Only their drinking arms worked with monotonous regularity, raising mugs to mouths.

"Cheers, then," said Jenkins, nudging her in the ribs.

Two small tumblers of amber liquid sat on the bar, and Jenkins's fingers were curled around one. His keen eyes were focused on her face, and Mary understood the test: she had to prove that she wasn't, after all, Harkness's teetotaling pet.

She picked up the other tumbler. "Cheers." As the first waft of raw spirits hit the back of her throat, she realized she should never have tried to down it all in one go. Her throat contracted. Her stomach lurched. Her eyes watered. She swallowed anyway, and as the liquid burned its way down her gullet, she began a mighty coughing fit that made flashing lights appear in her otherwise dim vision.

At the Academy, the ladies drank wine with dinner, and Mary had tried punch and other well-diluted drinks a few times. But never had she encountered neat spirits. And Jenkins had carried out his task well, watching Mr. Lamb carefully so that the publican couldn't dilute the rum, as was his usual practice with inattentive customers. When Mary was able to stand upright, she received a watery impression of Jenkins and Mr. Lamb grinning at her. She wiped her eyes and mopped her damp forehead and tried not to gasp for air.

"Strongest rum in London," Jenkins announced with pride.

She cleared her throat. "Not bad." Her voice was raspy—but that was actually an advantage in her being Mark.

He smirked. "Guess you's not a teetotaler now."

Jenkins's timing was just right. By the time they had made a vast pot of real tea and decanted the rum into a separate teapot, it was nearly eleven o'clock. A few coins still jingled in Jenkins's pocket, and he fished them out with satisfaction.

"Fourpence." He counted out four ha'pennies with loving care and handed them over reluctantly. "Halves, mind. You swore."

"I know." The money clearly meant more to Jenkins than it did to her, but it would have been ridiculously out of character not to take it. His eyes followed her hand as she pocketed the coins, and she wondered if they'd still be there at day's end or whether Jenkins would try to steal them back. She thought not. The fight had resolved matters between them.

"And don't you go nowhere but the Blue Bell; other pubs is dearer." He sounded for all the world like a frugal housewife giving instructions to a servant.

She bit back a smile. "Can't Harky smell the rum? How can he not?"

"Dunno. He's never said nothing, though, and I been on the tea round for months."

No bell tolled, but precisely on the hour, the laborers downed tools and began to drift toward the "tea table"—a broad plank balanced between a pair of carpenter's horses. Harkness was first in the queue, by common consent. Mary was still feeling the effects of the rum, not only in her throat, but in a slight tipsiness that made her feel extremely conspicuous. She was quite sure that her cheeks were flushed and that she smelled of drink. Yet Harkness seemed not to notice.

As he returned to his office, the men clustered about the tea station in earnest. Oddments of food—slabs of bread-and-butter and hunks of cold boiled meat, the occasional pastry—appeared in their hands as if from nowhere, along with their own thick, glazed mugs. Despite the differences in costume and context, Mary couldn't help thinking back to the last time she'd helped pour tea at a social gathering: beside Angelica Thorold in Chelsea. This time, she made sure to hold the enormous teapot in an awkward grasp. Tea pouring was a feminine technique, so she tried not to look too practiced as she filled the mugs halfway with weak black tea. Jenkins then topped them up with rum.

With Harkness gone, the general mood should have lifted. After all, what was likelier to produce gossip and levity than food, drink, and a change of pace? Yet for the most part, the laborers remained silent and solemn. A few of them chaffed her: *Not too much of that there tea, lad; don't you know it's the devil's drink?* Then, to Jenkins: *Go on, give us a drop more rum; don't be stingy now, son.* Or, *You're a pretty pair, you with your black eye and him with that bloody nose.* But once they had their tea, the men retreated into clusters that reflected their trades: glaziers with glaziers, stonemasons with stonemasons. And they drank their illicit rum without much relish.

"Ain't no one talking," muttered Jenkins.

So she hadn't imagined the tension. "Why's that?"

"Cor, you don't know nothing, do you?"

"Tell me then, if you're so clever."

Jenkins glanced about furtively. They'd served all the builders by now and were nowhere near any of them. All the same, he spoke barely above a whisper. "One o' them brickies, chap named Wick, offed himself the other night. His body was right over there."

A jolt shot through Mary. "He *killed* himself?"

"That's what I said," hissed Jenkins. "He jumped off the tower."

"How d'you know?"

Jenkins glanced around. " 'S plain. He were up there at night, and the police ain't done nothing. If he got pushed, the Yard"—he pronounced this nickname with over-casual pride—"the Yard'd nick somebody for it."

"They might still be looking."

Jenkins made a scoffing noise. "Not Scotland Yard. If they ain't found no one, ain't nobody to find."

Mary looked at him thoughtfully. She'd initially dismissed the lad as a bit dim: why else would he pick a fight he had no chance of winning? But now she wondered. He was sharp enough to make the tea round into a profitable venture. He had a reasoned theory as to Wick's death. She'd have to watch the lad—and watch her own behavior around him. He might be totally uncritical of the police, but he was clever enough to catch any slips she might make in the role of Mark Quinn.

If Wick had in fact thrown himself from the tower, there had been no conflict and there was no killer. But there was still the question of motive. What would drive a man to kill himself? Despair? Debt? And what of his choice of method? Many suicides chose the river, from sheer familiarity, or poison, for its swift neatness. But jumping from a tower was a dramatic final gesture. Had he intended something by that? It could even have been a message to his employers. . . .

"Time to clear up." Jenkins raised the rum pot aloft and tipped the last few drops from the spout directly into his mouth.

She glanced about. There was indeed a general dispersal of the laborers. "What should I do with this cold tea?"

He jerked his thumb over his shoulder.

Mary nodded. In a well-run household, spent tea leaves were either used to clean carpets or sold to a rag-and-bone man. Here, however, the nearby Thames served as sink, sewer, bathtub, and well, all in one.

When she returned, Jenkins was sniffing cautiously at the chipped milk jug. "Go halves?"

Mary shook her head. It was probably out of character to decline free food of any sort, but there were little curds of solid milk clinging to the edges of the pitcher, and the fluid itself was a funny bluish gray. She just couldn't bring herself to drink it.

He knocked that back, too, then pulled a face. "Phew. Bit past it, that."

Mary grinned. She could remember a time when she'd have choked back the milk, too. "I'll put all this away. Then what?"

"Back to work, if you's such a goody-goody."

"And if I'm not?"

"'Up to you, isn't it?"

Six

Bit slippy out here," said the coachman as he unfolded the carriage steps. He held out his arm, much as he would to a lady.

The boots that swung out of the carriage were distinctly male, as was the hand that waved him away. "I'm perfectly able to descend three steps unassisted, Barker." To prove it, he climbed down quickly and slammed the carriage door himself. He was far from old—his hair was dark, unmixed with gray, and his face was unlined—but he didn't move like a young man. There was something stiff about his gait.

Barker was unperturbed. "Very good, sir."

The gentleman scanned the building site, a deep frown drawing his brows together. The palace, still unfinished after all these years, loomed over the workers like an ungainly child squatting over an anthill. "You may go; I'll get a cab when I'm done."

"If it's all the same to you, sir, I'll wait. It may be difficult to find a cab in these parts."

Difficult to find a taxi in front of the blasted Houses of Parliament? His head swiveled sharply toward the coachman. "George told you to wait?"

Barker didn't even have the grace to look sheepish. "Yes, sir."

He sighed. There was no point in making a scene now. But once he got hold of his infernal, domineering, bleating nanny of a brother, he would create such a stinking row that no one would doubt he was entirely recovered. "I'll be no more than half an hour."

"Very good, sir."

The gentleman stood on the pavement, taking in the scene. It was strange to be back on an English building site. In the smoggy London daylight, the workmen looked pale and drawn, their tools dull. It was a chalky light, a light that grayed everything it touched. For a moment, despite all that had happened in India, he found himself longing for the hectic tropical sunshine that polished objects to brilliance and made colors glow. He hadn't fully understood the meaning of *illumination* until he'd gone east.

He shivered automatically, then glanced over his shoulder to see if Barker had noticed. As well as being gray and sooty, London was damp. Although he would never admit it to George, he was perpetually cold these days, even in his winter suits. Never mind. He straightened, walked through the site gate with a firm, even step, and rapped twice on the door frame of the flimsy office shed.

"Young James Easton! My dear fellow!" Philip Harkness sprang from his chair and shook his hand enthusiastically. "How absolutely delightful to see you once more. How long has it been?" He was talking very loudly, in the way people often do to the elderly.

James knew he was rather altered since he'd last seen Harkness, but the man's look of pity was still disheartening. "Hello, Harkness. I believe it's been a little more than two years."

"Yes, yes—I believe you were engaged in an Oriental venture until quite recently!"

This was disingenuous; the man knew very well what had taken him abroad, and why he was back in England. It was probably why Harkness had asked him to call; everyone wanted to hear the tale firsthand. "For less than a year."

"Then you'd had enough, hey?"

He'd not oblige. "They got what they needed from me."

"I heard about the malarial fever. Bad luck, old chap—all that nasty swamp air, was it?"

"I don't know, really. But I'm quite well now—fully recovered, in fact." He paused. "You're looking, ah, prosperous." Since James had seen him last, Harkness had gone bald and grown distinctly fat. It wasn't a rosy, jolly-country-squire type of fat, but a pasty, bloated look—

a rim of extra face framed his features, and his neck overflowed his boiled collar. His complexion was as gray as the London sky. Stress, James supposed, from this cursed job. That intermittent twitch could be put down to the same cause.

Harkness laughed overheartily and pushed the sole chair toward him. "Do sit down, dear boy. You're looking rather peaky, if you don't mind my saying so."

He did mind. "I feel fine, thank you. I'll lean on this desk." Perhaps it had been a mistake to call upon his father's old friend. In years past, Philip Harkness had been a regular visitor to the Easton household. But since their father's death, James and George had rather lost touch with him. Harkness seemed awkward and blustering today, quite unlike the kind, competent man James remembered from his childhood.

"And how's your dear brother?"

Awkwardly, they navigated the basics of the missing years: James's education and apprenticeship, past projects, George's interests, the brothers' personal lives. James was eager to question Harkness about the site: How had he come to accept the job? What were its challenges? And, most tantalizingly, why the hell was it twenty-five years behind schedule? As soon as he turned the conversation, however, Harkness's tension doubled. He stammered, talked around questions, and fidgeted with his elegant new fountain-style pen until his fingers were stained with ink. The more James persisted, the more evasive

Harkness became, until pity finally curbed James's curiosity. Obviously, Harkness's nervous condition was directly related to this disaster of a building site.

He checked his watch. He'd been with Harkness only a quarter of an hour, but it felt much longer. "I had better not keep you," he murmured, taking a step toward the door.

Harkness jumped up eagerly, holding out a restraining hand. "So soon? Why, I'd expected to take you to luncheon. At my club, you know. They do a rather decent roast, and I hear the wine cellar's not bad, either."

James's face froze. Kind as the offer was, he couldn't imagine anything he'd like less. "Er—well, you must be absurdly busy. A site like this . . ."

Another forced laugh. "That's precisely what I want to talk to you about, my dear young man. A site like this, indeed!"

If the site was such a challenge, how could the man think of taking a protracted luncheon? Such negligence was unworthy of Harkness—or at least of the man his father had esteemed. Today's visit had definitely been a mistake. "Perhaps another day," he parried. "Or come to dinner sometime. George'd be delighted to see you."

Harkness leapt toward the doorway, blocking his exit. "Actually . . ."

Forced to a halt, James stared at him blankly.

"I'd like to suggest—well, not to put too fine a point on it—I've a proposition for you."

"A proposition."

Another of those dreadful chortles. "Sit down, sit down, my dear young man. No need to look so suspicious!"

James sat with great reluctance. "What on earth are you talking about?"

Harkness made a few false starts but eventually managed to say, "Well, then. You know about the dreadful accident that occurred last week. . . ."

James nodded. There had been a sentence about it in *The Times*. "A bricklayer fell from the tower, after hours. No witnesses."

Harkness flinched. "Er—yes. Tragic accident. The man was young, had a family . . . It's been ghastly." He mopped his forehead with a large, crumpled handkerchief. "Absolutely ghastly."

James waited a few moments, but Harkness didn't go on. "Is there to be a review or an inquiry of some sort?" he guessed.

Harkness grimaced. "You were always a bright young chap. The first commissioner of works wants an independent engineer's report as to the safety conditions on the site. He gave me to understand that no blame attaches to me," he added hastily, "but the Committee of Works wants the matter to be absolutely clear. If the man was there after hours, and the equipment was all safe . . . You see what I mean," he finished.

James did see. If they could prove that the man had

died of his own carelessness, it cleared Harkness and the committee of responsibility. That was the critical point, and it should have been obvious even to a child. Yet he could also understand Harkness's agony, and why he should dance around the subject. A man was dead; while one wanted desperately not to be at fault, one could hardly go about proving one's own innocence. The only useful report was that of a neutral and qualified inspector. "Whom have they appointed?"

Harkness tittered nervously. "My dear fellow, they've left the appointment in my hands!"

"But that's a conflict of interest! How could such a report ever be deemed impartial?" James realized he'd jumped up and was pacing the length of the tiny office. He was slightly out of breath, which annoyed him greatly.

Harkness looked pained, and that little muscle below his eye began jumping so vigorously that he was forced to still it with his hand. "I was an idealist at your age, too."

And now what are you? James repressed the sneer: too cheap, too obvious. Harkness clearly considered himself a realist—although, from the look of him, this exerted an unhealthy strain on his conscience.

After a minute, Harkness spoke again, choosing his words slowly. "The commissioner has made it clear that from his perspective, and that of the Committee of Works, I am not to blame for this man's unfortunate death. But the commissioner wishes to confirm that the death was, in fact, an accident. A most tragic accident, but an accident nonetheless." As he spoke, Harkness's voice gained conviction. "He is also under a great deal of pressure to begin an inquiry immediately. There simply isn't time to appoint an engineer through the committee — so many meetings, so much discussion, you understand. And time is pressing on."

"So the commissioner has left things in your hands for the sake of efficiency?" *And a sure outcome.*

"I won't pretend that it's not a deeply awkward task. It certainly goes against the grain."

James nodded. He could agree with that statement, at least.

"You are too intelligent not to see what I'm asking, James, so I'll be blunt: are you willing to conduct this review?"

His immediate instinct was to refuse. It was a curious task, and a distasteful one, too. Even setting aside the question of impartiality, his findings would damage someone wherever he found fault. He drew breath to say so — and the rasping sensation in his lungs made him pause, reminding him in one breath of both malarial fever and professional failure. He had fallen gravely ill in Calcutta, had come close to death. He'd learned an equally brutal lesson in local politics, finding his work obstructed and his projects undermined because he lacked important sponsors.

He was quick to learn. Even in England — perhaps especially in England — it would do Easton Engineering good to impress the first commissioner of works. The man was enormously influential, both in his official capacity and in his private life. If James had learned only one thing in Calcutta, it was that connections were paramount. Perhaps he, too, was becoming a realist.

And yet. And yet. He couldn't possibly accept Harkness's offer.

Could he?

Harkness smiled once more, the first natural smile he'd shown since the real conversation began. "You're thinking too hard, young James. It's a plum job, the sort of job you and your brother could use. Just think of it: a spot of work, a short report, and the heartfelt gratitude of the commissioner."

He didn't need the older man to tell him that. He looked about the office, taking in the careless heaps of papers spilling from cabinet to desk to floor; at the grubby walls and makeshift furniture. Did he really want to conduct a professional review of this old family friend? How could he find against him? Yet how could he not, if that was what conscience dictated?

But what a cowardly reason to refuse the work. If he took the job, he wouldn't be Harkness's lapdog. He'd be precisely what the commissioner had specified: an independent engineer. His own professional pride demanded that he be impartial, even if he didn't care about justice and truth.

Fine words, he taunted himself. *Justice* and *truth* might

sound very well, but who would believe him once they learned of his long-standing family connection with Harkness? That was why he must decline the work, no matter how tempting. He'd find another way to build important connections.

"You're a first-class engineer, Easton—you and your brother both—and I thought it might be useful to you in the future to have made the acquaintance of such a man as the first commissioner of works."

Why was Harkness trying to sell him the job? How many candidates had already declined, and for what reasons? James knew he wasn't the preeminent engineer of his generation—not yet, at any rate. Easton Engineering was still a small firm, his reputation not yet made. He couldn't have been anybody's first choice. "Why me?" he said slowly.

Harkness looked startled. "Well, I've just said you're a sound man, a top-class engineer . . . and of course, our long friendship and my affection for your father's memory make me glad to do you a good turn. Why, you don't doubt your ability to conduct a simple assessment of the safety precautions on site, do you?"

"I don't," said James. His brain was turning rapidly. Too rapidly, perhaps. He wasn't normally the dithering sort, but today he was both tempted and repelled in equal measure. And then a solution came to him. "I'd welcome the job if I were independently appointed by the commissioner himself."

"But my dear young man, it's the same thing: As I said earlier, the commissioner has left the matter entirely with me. My choice is his choice." Harkness's overpatient tone suggested that James was being obtuse.

"With respect, sir, it's not the same thing at all."

"You always were stubborn." Harkness showed him a smile, but it was strained. "But you're not foolish. Are you willing to risk the benefits this job will bring to you and your brother, all for a mere formality?"

James drew a deep breath. "Yes, sir. I am." The compromise was far from perfect, said his weary conscience, but it hurt less than rejecting the enticing offer outright.

Harkness looked nettled. "Very well. I shall mention your . . . scruples to the commissioner. For your sake, young James, I hope he's inclined to accommodate your whim."

On his way back to the carriage, James lingered by the entrance, observing the builders at work. It was difficult to pinpoint what was wrong on a building site simply by looking, but he had a strong impression that all was not right in Palace Yard. Many mocked the idea of instinct, but he'd learned years ago to trust his. This appointment—if he got it—would not be a straightforward one.

He shivered, then glanced over one shoulder to see if Barker had noticed. Just at that moment, a dark-haired lad ran lightly down the length of the yard. James's eye followed him automatically—and then with deliberation. He frowned. The lad was oddly familiar. Was there something distinctive about the way he moved? No. Perhaps the profile—had he encountered the child before? But he was out of sight a few seconds later, and James blinked and shook his head. Impossible to pick out a twelve-year-old boy in a city of millions.

The only reasonable explanation was that the lad had something of Alfred Quigley about him. Ever since the murder of his young assistant over a year before, James had been haunted by echoes of the scrappy, resourceful boy wherever he went. The sharp treble of a boy's voice; a thatch of mousy hair; that funny, bouncy way of walking particular to preadolescent boys. All these things followed James and weighed on his conscience. They probably always would.

He shook his head again to clear the fog—and then realized that the fog was all around him. Alfred Quigley was a memory that invariably led to another, one on which he couldn't afford to dwell. Over the past year, he'd succeeded in thinking less and less about Mary Quinn. Yet even now, if he let his imagination stray . . .

Well. There was no point.

Absolutely none.

James climbed back into the carriage, waving off Barker's helpful hand. But as he settled into the padded bench, he shivered once again.

Instinct.

Seven

Somebody was staring at her. Mary could feel it, like a warm patch of sunlight on the back of her neck. But when she turned to see who it might be, there was no one: only a tall, thin man departing the site. She frowned after him. Judging from the way he moved, he was elderly or an invalid of some sort. Apart from that, little distinguished him from the dozens of be-suited, be-hatted gentlemen outside the Houses of Parliament.

And yet.

Still frowning, she watched him climb into a carriage. There was something familiar about that, too, although she couldn't place it. The driver was just another ordinary-looking middle-aged man. But she'd seen him before. She was still trying to remember where and when as the carriage disappeared into the stream of traffic, leaving her staring after it.

"Seed a ghost or something?" piped a voice in her ear.

She started and turned to find Jenkins smirking at her. "Yeah, the ghost of the clock tower."

He snorted. "Ghost won't help you shift them bricks."

She sighed. "It's heavy work."

"Carrying bricks? It's easy-peasy. How many bricks you carry at a time?"

"Three."

"Three! Delicate little girl, ain't you?"

"You couldn't take more." She glanced about, but the brickies were nowhere in sight. Good. Another minute's banter with Jenkins and with luck she could lead him back to the subject of the dead man, Wick.

"Watch me!" He leaned the hod at a forty-five-degree angle against the nearest wall and loaded it with care, distributing the bricks so the weight fell evenly. "You ready?" he called when the hod was prepared.

"Six bricks is awfully heavy," she said.

"It's nothing, with this method," he said grandly. "Easy-peasy, like I said."

"Suit yourself."

Jenkins braced himself beneath the hod and, with an enormous effort, lifted its cradle over one shoulder. In theory, it might have worked. In practice, however, he was much too short and weak: the length of the hod's stick, intended for an adult, made the six-brick load teeter precariously above his head. Immediately, it began to waver.

Mary reached out to steady the hod.

"I can do it!" Jenkins insisted, his face already scarlet with exertion.

"Let me help you!"

"Let me alone!" He swatted away her outstretched hands and, in that moment, lost his last bit of control over the hod. Mary just had time to jump clear as the six bricks smashed to the ground.

"What the devil is going on here!" The roar came from a third party, a livid man some fifty feet behind them.

She froze guiltily.

Jenkins scrambled clear of the mess and made to scamper off, but Keenan was moving fast and almost upon them. A moment later, he seized each of them by an ear.

Jenkins yelped.

Mary sucked in a sharp breath but made no sound.

"Hold this brat," snarled Keenan, shoving Jenkins toward another man. Mary hadn't the leisure to notice whom. Then he turned his full attention to her, shaking her like a particularly wet and wrinkled piece of washing. Her head snapped back and forth on her shoulders, and her eyes began to water. "Where the hell do you think you are? Little Lord Fauntleroy's nursery school?" snarled Keenan. "This is a building site, you bleedin' lazy little scoundrel!" He didn't appear to expect a response and didn't stop shaking her long enough to permit any. "Of all the stupid, wasteful, mutton-headed things to do! Why is that Jenkins brat here to begin with? Why ain't you carrying the blasted hod? What the hell you playing at, Quinn?"

He might have kept shaking her until she fainted, but somewhere in that storm of fury and nausea, Mary dimly registered a placatory voice. "Aw, Keenan, he's only a kid. Thrash him if you want, but don't shake him to pieces."

No change for a few dreadful seconds. Then there was a reluctant slowing of the shaking action. It finally stopped altogether, but Keenan kept a firm grip on Mary's hair. Slowly, the world turned the right way up once more. The flashes of black and red in her vision subsided. She began to discern faces again, prominent among them Keenan's enraged features, only a few inches from hers.

Instead of relief or remorse, Mary was gripped with a boiling sense of outrage. She wanted to attack Keenan, to kick and punch and bite him until he knew what she was feeling. But even in the first rush of fury, a distant common sense prevailed: Keenan could smash her to a pulp. He was a large, powerful man and she was a slight woman. There would be no contest.

She stood as still as she could manage, swallowing huge gulps of air and glowering at him through her tousled fringe. They stood there for several minutes, bricklayer and assistant, staring at each other, hating each other. Keenan panted with the effort of shaking her. With visible effort, he turned his gaze to the fallen bricks: three chipped, one broken in two. It was as well that Jenkins was so short; had the bricks fallen from a greater height, they might all have been wasted. As it was . . .

"We can use these chipped ones," said Stubbs mildly,

scooping them up with the two undamaged bricks. "Turn them the other way out."

Keenan grunted, still staring at the mess. Finally, his gaze reverted to Mary. "You're a lucky bastard," he muttered. "That's only fourpence off your wages, for the broken one."

She forced herself to nod.

"But I'm still going to teach you a lesson," he continued with grim satisfaction. "You'll know better than to play about on a building site when I'm done—and that includes you." He wheeled about and stabbed a finger at Jenkins, who dangled limply from Smith's fist. "Hold this one!" snapped Keenan, shoving Mary toward Reid.

She stumbled once, then was caught in a firm, dispassionate grip. Reid's hands were heavy on her shoulders, and she was suddenly grateful he'd caught her so well. Her breasts were tightly bound, of course, but the binding itself might be noticeable were he to grip her across the chest. Her pulse, already racing, sprinted even faster at the thought. Furious as she was, she now felt a fresh stab of something else: fear.

She knew better than to offer excuses—or worse, to plead. Instead, she stared defiantly at Keenan as he unbuckled his belt. She stood very still as he doubled it in his hand, weighing the thickness of the leather and the heft of the buckle.

"Now," he said in a new, soft voice, "who's first?" He

looked from Mary to Jenkins, an unpleasant smile stretching his mouth.

Silence. Mary didn't look at Jenkins, didn't look anywhere except at Keenan's brutal, ruddy face. She hated him with everything in her and didn't bother to disguise it. All her senses were heightened in this moment: she heard the different layers of traffic, both on the river and in the streets just beyond the site walls; felt the dank heaviness of the air on her forehead and the coarse fabric of her shirt again her neck; tasted the bitterness of rage in her mouth; and amid the sticky, complicated smells of the city, she smelled something new and sharp and warm. Something ammoniac . . .

Beside her, Jenkins whimpered very quietly and she suddenly understood what had happened. A glance confirmed it: his trousers had a darker patch that clung to his leg, and a small pool of urine was collecting beside his right foot.

Keenan hadn't missed it, either. A sadistic sneer twisted his mouth and he stared at Jenkins, inspecting him carefully as he might a defective tool. "You dirty little scoundrel. Your mummy lets you do that at home, does she?"

Jenkins made a choked, rattling sound in his throat.

"What was that?"

Mary stared at Jenkins, willing him to buck up. The more fear he showed, and the less control he had over his body and his voice, the more Keenan would enjoy this and the more vicious energy he would put into it. But Jenkins was scared witless. He could no more control his bladder and his voice than Mary could the weather.

"No answer?" Keenan's voice was still ominously soft.

Jenkins was shaking now, a shivering so violent that his teeth began to chatter.

"Disgusting," said Keenan. "Give him here, Smith."

In one swift motion, Keenan seized Jenkins and yanked his wet breeches to the ground. Any pity Mary might have felt for the boy was now consumed in her own burgeoning sense of panic. This was it. In a few minutes, she would be publicly, literally, exposed. A fine trembling began in her throat, then spread to her limbs. She fought it desperately but not well enough. Her lungs squeezed tight. She couldn't get enough air.

"Easy," murmured Reid, pressing firmly on her shoulders. "Easy, lad."

He sounds as if he's talking to a horse, she thought hysterically.

The belt really did whistle faintly as it sliced through the air; that wasn't merely a cliché. As it struck Jenkins's pale, skinny rump, it made a meaty, loud *thwock* that resounded clearly across the now-still site. All had downed tools; all were watching. Apart from the rhythm of the belt—*shweeeee-THWOCK, shweeeee-THWOCK*—the only sounds were Jenkins's half-suppressed screams and Keenan's grunts of exertion.

Two strokes.

Three.

With the fourth, a bright seam of blood welled up. Mary forced herself to keep looking, to take in the details: perfect stillness all around, men practically holding their breath rather than disrupt Keenan's show. Nobody moved to step in; no one opened a mouth to object. They were *enjoying* themselves, the hateful pigs.

Five.

Small rivulets of blood dripped down the boy's legs, onto his breeches, staining the dusty ground.

Six.

Jenkins stopped shrieking and began merely to cry, a keening, childish sound that sliced through Mary's contained panic. What would a brutal beating do to such a fragile, undergrown boy? Would Keenan stop before he caused permanent damage, or did he not care?

Seven.

Was there nothing she could do? Nothing at all?

Eight.

She tasted blood. Why? Must have bitten her lower lip.

"Keenan." The voice came from just above her head.

Shweeeee-THWOCK.

Shweeeee-THWOCK.

"Keenan!" More forceful, now. "Enough, man."

A pause in the rhythm. "Shut it, Reid."

A resumption. Eleven?

Sweat trickled into her eyes, its sting a welcome distraction from her trembling limbs, her panic-squeezed lungs. The pain of the lashing didn't matter; all she wanted was for her unmasking to be over and done with.

And then a cry, shrill but authoritative: "What the blazes do you think you're doing?"

What does it look like? Fortunately, the hysterical giggle in her throat didn't climb high enough to be heard.

Keenan swung the belt one last time but rather halfheartedly, as though acknowledging that the game was over.

"Why are you all standing about? Back to work, all of you! Except you, Keenan—what is the meaning of this?" Mr. Harkness was standing before them. Slowly, the other trades melted back toward their tasks.

Keenan looked mutinous. He stared at Harkness for a long minute, his chest rising and falling rapidly. "Why, Mr. Harkness, sir," he finally said, his voice velvety and dangerous, "how kind of you to take an interest in a matter of site discipline."

Bright patches of red appeared on Harkness's cheeks and on the top of his bald head. "I said, what is the meaning of this?" His voice was shrill, the twitch going double-time.

Another silence. The only sound now was of Jenkins's sobbing. Eventually, Keenan said, "The lad's got to be punished."

"What for?"

"Playing the fool. Damaging materials."

Harkness took a deep breath and turned to Mary. "Is this true?"

From the corner of her eye, she saw Keenan's face twist with rage. "Yes, sir."

Harkness looked surprised. "You willfully damaged Keenan's property?"

"Not on purpose, sir. But between us, Jenkins and I broke a brick."

"A brick!" Harkness turned back to Keenan. "You would thrash a pair of children within an inch of their lives for *one* damaged brick?"

"I thrashed them for playing the fool. They've no business messing about with tools. The damage could have been much worse."

Harkness's face turned pale. Through clenched teeth he said, "Unless you wish your entire gang dismissed, you'll remember who's in charge of this building site, Keenan. Quinn will no longer assist any of you. You'll work shorthanded until you find another bricklayer, and I expect to see progress as usual."

Keenan flushed a shade darker but didn't reply.

"Do you hear and understand?" roared Harkness.

"Yes. Sir." He spat the words as though they tasted bitter. "And I'll remember this. Sir."

If Harkness was troubled by the threat, he gave no sign of it. "Come then, children." He beckoned to Mary and Jenkins, and she suddenly realized she'd been holding her breath. Although the other workmen made a show of returning to their tasks, they stared openly as the three of them marched past: Harkness in the lead, Jenkins hobbling as best he could, Mary bringing up the rear.

She could feel Keenan's gaze on their backs. It was nothing like warm sunlight, more like an icy drill through her skull. Her thoughts were all confusion, her legs rubbery beneath her. She was still trembling, although this time it was with relief. But even as she followed Harkness and Jenkins, she began to wonder about the significance of Harkness's rescue. He hadn't intervened in time to save Jenkins from a savage beating. But in saving her from a similar lashing, Harkness had safeguarded her identity, and thus the entire assignment. She had to ask whether he knew the truth, or any part of it. And if so, what he expected in return.

Eight

Miss Phlox's lodging house
Coral Street, Lambeth

Coral Street was lively in the evening, with children and women calling to one another across the street and over garden walls. Washing was pegged out on clotheslines; itinerant hawkers stocked their pushcarts for the evening's sales; an umbrella repairman was at work on a front step. It was a bustling domestic scene of the sort that still, occasionally, gave Mary a pang. Tonight, it made her eyes prickle. Had her father lived, that could have been her family's fate: a modest but cozy home, younger brothers and sisters, and supper around the table every night.

Tired as she was, Mary knew the scene in her mind was improbable. Her parents had been very poor, her father away at sea more often than not, her brothers stillborn. Yet she clung stubbornly to the possibility. Her father had been a brave, intelligent, principled man and his death had destroyed all their lives. That was what she knew. Automatically, her hand moved toward her throat to touch the jade pendant he had left her. In the next fraction of a moment, she remembered that it was far away: safe in her desk at the Academy, along with her identity as a young woman. For now, she was simply a boy named Mark, and if she didn't want to foul up matters entirely, she'd better remember it.

She entered Miss Phlox's lodging house by the side door. One step, and she was enveloped by the hot, dense fug of washing day: boiling water, lye soap, blueing, and hot starch. Winnie, the maid of all work, was ironing bedsheets in the kitchen and glanced up as Mary entered. "Supper's in the larder." Her voice was breathless, making her sound even younger than her twelve or thirteen years.

"Thank you." Mary was suddenly ravenous, and it took only a moment to cram down the two thin slices of bread-and-butter that constituted "supper."

Winnie put the irons back in the fire to reheat and drew Mary a mug of small beer. Her eyes were fixed on Mary's face. When Mary met her gaze, she looked away, but the next moment resumed her staring. She'd been fascinated by "Mark" Quinn from the moment they'd met.

Mary swallowed her beer and tried to look oblivious. There were plenty of good reasons for Winnie to gawk at her. She was a new lodger, and therefore a novelty; she might have dirty smears on her face; she might be . . . Mary gave up. She knew very well the reason why the maid of all work looked at her with such analytical curiosity: Winnie was Chinese, like Mary's father, and thus curious about Mary's appearance. The dark hair. The geometry of her features. The "exotic" aspect that people so often remarked upon. For Winnie, these things probably added up to something very specific.

Mary cleared out of the kitchen as quickly as possible. She had no idea how to manage Winnie's curiosity and wanted to avoid all conversation with the girl until she'd decided on a strategy. Should she deny everything? It was true that she didn't look properly mixed race. Her skin was pale and her eyes round, so that much of the time she passed quite easily as black Irish. Even persistent questioners generally wanted to know whether she was Italian or Spanish. And that was just fine with Mary. The last thing she wanted was to acknowledge her Chinese heritage and deal with the questions and hostility it would inevitably invoke. Certainly not yet. She pushed away those thoughts as she climbed the second flight of stairs to her room, steeling herself for the next challenge: a roommate who'd just moved in today.

As Mary opened the door to her room, she saw a man sitting on the bed, pulling off his boots and enriching the small room with the stink of sweaty feet. He looked up, his gaze both wary and weary.

"H'lo," she gulped. She sounded authentically nervous, in any case.

" 'Lo."

What was the etiquette in situations like this? Later tonight, she'd be sharing a bed with this stranger—an uncomfortable fact of life when lodgings were cheap and beds dear. But how much did men talk among themselves? How would they organize who slept at which end? And how on earth would she guard her secret from him? "I'm Quinn," she offered tentatively.

He nodded. "Rogers."

When it became apparent that he had nothing else to say, she hung her cap and jacket on a peg behind the door. At the small washstand, the water jug was partly filled and the scratchy towel carefully used on one half only. She washed briskly, scrubbing her face and neck and wetting her hair to rid it of grime. This was the best she'd be able to do for some time. At Miss Phlox's, baths cost extra and were available only on Wednesdays and Saturdays. But even if she had the money, there was no way to manage a bath with privacy.

It was intolerable in here, under Rogers's steady gaze. It wasn't a hostile look, she decided—more like the disappointment that came of finding that one wasn't alone. She knew precisely how he felt. She had to do something. Anything, rather than sit here in stifling silence.

The dusky walk back to Westminster felt long this time. All along the streets, yellowy light glowed behind curtained windows. The effect was cozy and exclusive, and Mary felt a sharp, bittersweet longing to be at home at the Academy. Ordinarily, the prospect of an armchair and a cup of tea was dully domestic; tonight, it could not have seemed more appealing. The streets quieted dramatically as she crossed the bridge, passing into Westminster. Few lived here, and the area bustled only during the day. Her feet ached. Her muscles felt stiff. And she was so busy yawning that she nearly walked straight into a shadowy figure skirting along the tall wooden fence that divided the building site from the street.

Her training saved her. Before her mind could fully register the man and form a plan, she'd tucked herself into the shadows and gone motionless. Even so, the man seemed to sense something: he, too, stilled, glancing over his shoulder at the streetscape. After several long seconds, he resumed movement, but it was stealthier now, and he looked about at intervals.

Mary remained frozen, her back against the fence. The man was tall and powerful-looking in silhouette, although she couldn't see his features or even make out his profile in the dim light. He wore a jacket and trousers rather than a suit, but this information was of marginal use: who ever went prowling in his Sunday suit? He could be any of a million working men in London.

He wasted no time on the padlocked gate, instead choosing a section of the wooden fence. Another rapid survey of the scene. After a pause, he removed something small from his pocket and, with a swift, low hand thrust, slammed it into the high wooden fence. It was a short, violent gesture, akin to stabbing a man in the thigh. He scanned the road one more time and, apparently satisfied, appeared to walk straight up the fence panel in one fluid movement. He paused at the top for a moment, then swung himself over and landed with a soft thud.

Mary grinned and slithered out from the shadows to the spot where he'd been. Sure enough, there was a small metal half-moon embedded in the fence. It was only two inches wide by one inch deep, but it offered the experienced user a toehold from which to clamber over the fence. She'd used one herself from time to time in her past life.

She considered the climbing grip thoughtfully. Impossible not to follow him. The difficulty was that he was almost certainly headed for Harkness's office, which lay in direct view of this entry point. She could hardly follow his route and expect to go unnoticed. Neither could she borrow the climbing grip to use on a different part of the fence; he would certainly miss it. No, she would have to find her own way in. And now that she was fully alert, the challenge was both alluring and energizing.

The first matter was to work out where the night watchmen were. There were two, she recalled, who reported to Harkness at day's end. There would be others at different posts around the palace, guarding the House of Commons and House of Lords, but she would assume for now that they remained within their separate jurisdictions. Caution struggled with impulse. Caution won—a sign of how far she'd progressed since her early days in training, she thought with a touch of pride. She made a circuit of the building site, listening carefully and looking for the telltale glint of the watchmen's lanterns.

Nothing.

Were they asleep? Gossiping comfortably in some inner sanctum? Whatever the case, they certainly weren't doing their jobs. Mary's lip curled with distaste. She disliked sloppiness, even if it might make her task easier. She stopped and listened again. To one side there were the sounds of the Thames: the sticky footsteps and excited calls of scavengers both human and animal; boatmen's voices and the splash of their oars; someone, somewhere, crying. From the other side rose the noises of the city—horseshoes and wheels on cobblestones, voices raised in taverns and houses, the constant murmur of millions of human lives intersecting. But the site itself was eerily quiet.

She chose as her entrance the site's east wall, feeling her way along the fence until she found—by touch, not sight—the point she wanted. One of the fence planks was loose, and it tilted under the pressure of her hand. She smiled. An unsupervised length of fence away from the gaze of the high street was a powerful temptation to boys. Jenkins and his mates had likely worried away at this plank until it became a convenient cat flap, giving them access to the site away from Harkness's watchful eye.

She was just small enough to squeeze through the gap. Inside, she stayed low to the ground and listened again: still nothing. It was a good opportunity to scan the site. Places always looked different by night and it was especially true of this building site, which to her was still so unfamiliar even by day. Distance and dimension were distorted. Heaps of building materials and scaffolding frames took on strange shapes, both occult and comical. And St. Stephen's Tower itself seemed higher and more splendid than ever.

A faint scraping noise recalled her to the task at hand and she began to move toward its source, somewhere near Harkness's office. Oddly, there was no sign of a light burning inside the small hut and the man hadn't been carrying a dark-lantern. The door, however, was slightly ajar and so she edged closer to the doorjamb and peeked through the gap.

The only reason she saw him in the near darkness was because he moved quickly. He took three decisive steps to Harkness's desk, dipped into the top drawer, and pocketed something without pausing to examine it. A slight shiver ran through her frame: this was no ordinary theft.

She had made no noise, but suddenly he was on the alert—as though he could sense her close scrutiny. His movements ceased. Slowly, she eased back slightly. He wouldn't be able to see her, but all the same . . .

He pivoted toward the entrance. On instinct, she glided away from the office door and around the corner—and instantly was glad she had. His head popped out a second later, scanning the dark silence. A moment's hesitation would have meant discovery. Still, his suspicions were not allayed. He moved cautiously but with impressive speed, conducting a thorough search of the area just outside the office. Mary was now on the retreat, keeping an eye on her quarry while in turn becoming his.

The strange, silent pursuit continued. He seemed increasingly certain that there was something or someone to find, while Mary moved faster toward her exit. She rounded a corner and came to a halt, blinking as she considered the solid wall before her. The wall couldn't have sprung up in a matter of minutes. Had she come the wrong way? Then her eyes adjusted and she realized the "wall" was a shadow cast by some scaffolding in the moonlight.

The moon. It had shown itself while she was outside the office, spying on the thief. While most nights she'd have welcomed it, tonight it hampered her escape. Not only did it make her easier to spot, but it also changed the appearance of nearly everything on site. Still, she moved with noiseless speed.

A small, open strip of land now stretched between her and the fence. The man was no longer absolutely silent in his pursuit. Was he less certain of his way? Or was he merely allowing her to hear him, hoping that she'd panic and make an error? Either way, he was close behind now. Had she time to cross the unsheltered patch? She glanced about, looking for hiding places: a heap of rubble, a lean-to containing lumber, the entrance to the tower. None held out any hope of concealment if he followed; all were dead ends.

She drew one last deep breath, not caring if it was audible. This was her last chance. She sprinted with all her strength across the open stretch, her boots ringing clearly against the paving stones. As she dived for the fence, wriggling and kicking through the narrow gap, the boards snagged against her clothes and scraped her hips and shins. She tumbled out into the street, laughing silently now as she heard her pursuer struggling and swearing. The wooden plank slapped down into place, possibly clipping him on its way. An adult would never fit through the gap. Not an adult male, at any rate.

She scrambled up and kept running, knowing she was in the clear but impelled by a surge of energy to keep moving, to clear out, to distance herself from that terrifying, exhilarating escapade. She was nearly back at Miss Phlox's before she slowed to a walk. It was dark night now; she had no idea what time. Her lungs tingled. The grazed skin of her hips and shins stung. When she let herself in the narrow gate, a sudden, deep exhaustion gripped her. The front step, a wide slab of stone, looked wonderfully inviting; she could have curled up right there and gone straight to sleep. Instead, she stumbled up the two flights of stairs and fell into bed, fully clothed, unheeding of Rogers's lumpy form and deep snores. Within seconds, she was asleep.

Nine

Tuesday, 5 July

Mary didn't sleep for long. Dawn came early, and with it consciousness. Her eyes popped open and she lay, tense and still, wondering just where the hell she was and who lay beside her. Then, as memory returned, her tension eased a little. The dingy yellowed wall, the scratchy mattress with a valley in the middle, the clatter of carts in the street below—all these were part of her new life in Lambeth. Or, rather, Mark Quinn's life.

Beside her, Rogers snored at full bore, rolled snugly inside the greasy blanket they were meant to share. He was welcome to it. Mary lay still, watching the weak light—one could hardly say "sunlight," it was so gray—grow stronger. She felt a knife-like pain deep in her belly. Not hunger, but the desperate need to pass water. Yet she could hardly do so now, with Rogers in the room. Instead, she forced herself to think about yesterday's events.

Foremost in her mind was the fate of Jenkins. After that beating, he wouldn't walk properly for days, and there was a good chance his lacerations would become dangerously infected. Yet Harkness had packed him off with the day's wages and the bland assurance that once recovered, he would again have a place on the building site. But even assuming that Jenkins healed properly and came back to his job, there remained the question of how he was to live in the meantime. Without a wage, without medicine. It was an outrage. The least she could do was try to help him, if teetotaling, cliché-spouting, church-going Harkness would do nothing else. She would contact the Agency today and find out Jenkins's address.

Harkness's duty to Jenkins led to the question of his relationships with the other laborers. Although Harkness's building site might officially be teetotal, in practice he couldn't possibly prevent the men from drinking beer or spirits. At the noon meal, they had the chance to nip out to a pub, or they could bring a flask onto the site. That meant he was either terribly naive or rather clever at cost cutting: most building sites provided men with beer for refreshment and nutriment, and spirits to warm them in damp weather. But if Harkness provided only tea—and cheap tea, and not enough of it—that would leave a small surplus in the budget. It was brilliant: Harkness made a small profit on the drinks supply, and Jenkins made an even smaller profit provisioning the men. It was a perfect exercise in free-market economics, and the only people losing out were the workers themselves.

Was Harkness the sort of man to attempt such a thing? Character was so difficult to read. Apart from that unfortunate twitch, he looked like many a middle-aged gentleman in England, with his neatly trimmed beard and thinning hair. His face was neither benevolent nor stern, and his well-fed cheeks served as a counterweight to the anxious creases in his forehead, the twitch beneath his left eye. He might, or he might not, in about equal measure. Besides, there was likely nothing strictly illegal about serving tea instead of beer. Probably the site budget allowed for such small variances.

Her thoughts circled back to the bricklayers—to Keenan's violence, which prompted a further question about Reid's bruises. Was he a habitual brawler? The sort who got drunk and became aggressive, and sought out fistfights as a form of recreation? Or was there more to his bruised appearance? He'd seemed otherwise peaceable, in contrast with Keenan. Reid's greeny-yellow eye might signify nothing, but it merited consideration, nonetheless.

Church bells chimed seven o'clock while Rogers snored on. Would he never wake? Mary continued to lie still, listening to the household rustle to life. Creaking floorboards. Violent coughing. Clatter of shoes on the uncarpeted stairs. Outside, somebody pumped the handle of a well, filling bucket after bucket of water. Her bladder throbbed at the taunting sound. Should she risk it? She would be late for work if he slept any longer. She might be late as it was. But what if Rogers awoke while she was on the chamber pot? She stared at the ceiling for an agonizing half minute. No. She'd have to take the chance.

As she cautiously swung her legs over the side, he erupted in a fit of snorts and sneezes. Instantly, she lay down again. Closed her eyes. Feigned sleep. Rogers yawned, sneezed, yawned again. Then, finally, she felt his bulk shift as he sat up. Grunted. Sneezed again. Then, with a sigh, he dragged the heavy basin from beneath the bed. It was a long, splashy, hissing sort of piss, one that made her own bladder scream in protest. Mary gritted her teeth. Listened to him lace up his boots and clomp about for a few minutes before the door finally slammed behind him. She waited another ten seconds—it was all she could manage—then tumbled from the bed and scrabbled for the brimming chamber pot.

Lightning wash. Bowl of porridge. Smart pace to Palace Yard. And Mary arrived, breathless and sweaty, to discover that she was among the first on site. Strangely enough, though, she didn't overhear any discussion of last night's break-in. Had it gone unnoticed? Harkness's office generally looked as though it had been ransacked, so any minor disorder was likely to go unobserved. And the man had seemed to know what he was looking for. It had taken him only a few seconds to pocket the item he sought. Mary hoped this was the explanation. The other possibility, which made her much more nervous, was that the men were reluctant to talk while she was about.

As she passed the joiners, one of them summoned her with a crooked finger.

"Sir?"

"You hammered out nails before, sonny?"

"No, sir."

"Right. Well, the thing is to take your time and not rush it. Else you'll smash your finger and spoil the nail, and then I'd have to thrash you, as well." He chuckled at his little joke as he demonstrated the technique. "Like so. Now let's see you try it."

Mary hefted the hammer he'd given her and attempted to imitate his deft actions. The result wasn't terrible—she hadn't actually bent the nail farther—but it was far from straight. She frowned. "I'll get better."

The joiner snorted. "Not holding the hammer like that, you won't. What d'you think it is—a frying pan?" He showed her how to hold it. "Try again, now."

She tried again. A little better.

"Can tell you ain't used to proper work," he said, pleasantly enough. "Got hands like a little princeling, you have. Try again."

Mary flushed. The dirt beneath her fingernails was authentic enough, but she couldn't hide her lack of calluses. She brought the hammer down firmly this time, and quite miraculously the nail unbent.

"That's it. Now, here's your lot," said the joiner, jingling a leather pouch. Something about it appeared to disturb him and he peered inside. "But this ain't the half of it. Cam! Where's the rest of them nails?"

"In the pouch!" shouted a heavyset man.

"I got the pouch!"

"Then that's all there is!"

The man frowned. " 'S funny. I could have swore there was a fortnight's worth in here." He stared once again into the canvas pouch, his forehead wrinkled. Then, with a shrug, he handed the pouch to Mary. "Give us a shout when you've finished — maybe them other nails will have turned up by then."

"Yes, sir."

It was a fascinating insight into so-called unskilled labor. Her time was worth almost nothing — certainly less than the cost of the bent nails — but she still had much to learn, even in these most menial tasks. The joiners seemed content to ignore her and let her do her best. It was a pleasant change from yesterday, and Mary was reminded, once again, of how dramatically the experience of work depended upon one's employers. It was a sensation of helplessness that she disliked intensely, and she was called upon only to play at it, to tolerate bad behavior for the sake of a larger purpose. What must it be like to be so powerless all the time?

The joiners were only a short distance away. As Mary worked, she picked up scraps of their conversation —

mainly querying one another about supplies and passing idle comments as they organized their day's work. At one point, she heard the man called Lemmon say, "Harky's in a right tizz this morning."

His friend smirked. "Ain't a mystery why."

"Shhh." A third carpenter jerked his chin in Mary's direction and raised his eyebrow significantly.

Lemmon glanced over at Mary, who was frowning at a bent nail with great concentration. "You think . . . ?"

He shrugged. "Maybe."

The three men squinted at her for a long moment, then Lemmon shook his head decisively. "Nah. Just a kid." But he was speaking in an undertone, now.

"Turned up two days ago? Harky's pet? Don't know his arse from his elbow?" The third man leaned in and delivered the final, undeniable piece of evidence: "And don't forget—Harky rescued him from Keenan, though the Jenkins kid got it bad enough."

"Aw, no kid ought to be thrashed like that."

"Yeah—Jenkins neither, for all he's a nosy little whoreson."

Lemmon snorted. "All right, then. What's Harky want a pet for?"

The suspicious carpenter sighed in exasperation. "Don't you lot notice anything? Harky's lost control of this site. First that malarkey about the ghost. Then Wick. And yesterday, one of the glaziers said some bigwig's coming to check on Harky's work. It ain't regular."

Lemmon considered that for a moment. "But what's that got to do with anything? What could a kid like that do for Harky?"

"Listen. Carry tales. Get a man sacked . . ." His voice trailed off suggestively.

The three men stared at Mary once more. She tried not to look self-conscious, to appear utterly absorbed in her task. When the joiners had begun muttering, her first worry had been about her gender. Could they possibly imagine that Mark Quinn was anything other than a twelve-year-old boy? Yet when talk switched to her being Harkness's spy, she felt no relief. They were still too close to the truth.

The carpenters weren't alone in their suspicion of her. This became clear as the morning wore on and Mary made the rounds, collecting money for the rum ration. The men paid up, of course, but with much less of the good-natured teasing she'd heard yesterday. Some trades simply found their pennies and handed them over, preserving a circumspect silence while she was within earshot. During the tea break, the men accepted refreshment from her but then retreated into their separate groups to talk. And was it her imagination, or were their voices more hushed than they had been yesterday? It wasn't just Jenkins's absence that dried them up. Of that she was increasingly certain.

Ten

James arrived at Palace Yard on foot. Barker didn't know this, of course; he'd deposited James at the site entrance half an hour earlier and driven off, secure in the delusion that his young employer was going straight inside. Instead, James had taken the opportunity to walk around the Houses of Parliament. He examined the buildings, assessed the pace of work, noted the general atmosphere on the job. This would be his last chance to poke about the place anonymously, and he intended to take full advantage.

Even from the street, it was clear to James that the site was run in a typically sloppy fashion, with little in the way of safety precautions. The whole organization, or lack thereof, bespoke a casual attitude to the value of human life. Unless he was much mistaken, Harkness would have no limit on the number of men permitted in the belfry at one time, no particular rules for working on high scaffolds, no regular inspections of equipment. Yet this was still normal practice. James had a reputation on his own sites for being rather scrupulous, and he knew that many of his colleagues—especially older ones like Harkness—thought such scruples excessive.

Yet for some reason, Harkness had asked him to perform the evaluation. The question still troubled him. Was it his youth? Did Harkness hope that would translate to inexperience, malleability? There was also the family connection. Harkness might expect a certain deference from James because of it. If either assumption was true, he'd soon receive a sharp surprise. James was confident in his own abilities—to an extent that made some call it arrogance, he knew—and quite incapable of backing down from a point if he was right.

But perhaps he was being too cynical. He had, after all, been in India for nearly a year and was thus quite ignorant of industry gossip. Coming to such a long-running and rumor-laden job without expectations would be an advantage. Or perhaps Harkness simply, as he'd said, wanted to do him a good turn and help him to build connections. James repressed his misgivings and strode through the gate. He was becoming paranoid, that was all. Nothing could be more straightforward than a safety review.

As he entered the site, a flash of movement caught his eye: the same errand boy he'd seen yesterday. Again, James felt that odd pulse of recognition. Where had he seen this child before? At second glance, it was obvious that the boy was nothing like Alfred Quigley: he was a good two or three years older and a completely different type. Perhaps this was the son of someone he knew—a laborer he'd employed. But would that account for the child's almost disturbing aura of familiarity?

He realized he was staring into space. With a shake of his head, he rapped on the office door, rather more loudly than he'd intended. "Harkness?"

"My dear boy! Or, I should say, my dear *Easton*. You're a colleague now."

The corner of James's mouth quirked up in appreciation of his sudden promotion. "You must have a good deal of pull with the commissioner, sir; I received his letter of appointment first thing this morning."

"I shouldn't say that," said Harkness with a blush. "That is, it's a rather urgent task, as I believe I explained yesterday, and the commissioner is very efficient . . ." He harrumphed and rushed on. "Now, I imagine you'll need assistance with your tasks . . ."

"I'm quite capable of doing the work on my own," said James promptly. "I wouldn't have accepted the job if I weren't completely recovered."

"No, no," said Harkness with a laugh. "I wasn't referring to your health, my dear boy. I only meant an errand boy to assist you with measurements and the like. I took the liberty of arranging—well, allow me simply to call him in." He stepped out of the office before James could respond, and a minute later reappeared with the dark-haired boy in tow. "This is Mr. Easton, of Eastman Engineering," he was saying. "Easton, this is one of the brightest boys I've had the pleasure of employing; I think you'll find him quite useful.

"His name's Quinn. Mark Quinn."

James scarcely heard the introduction; his gaze was already riveted on the "boy." The ground rolled beneath his feet, a minor earthquake that made every nerve in his body quiver. He was unable to look anywhere but into those eyes. They were nut-brown today, though he knew very well that in some lights they glinted green. They were framed by thick black lashes, arched brows, and a thatch of untidy dark hair. The face wore an expression of surprise and dismay that was instantly, unmistakably familiar.

James turned pale, felt his blood rush toward his toes. His stomach turned over violently—but not unpleasantly. For a moment, he simply stood stupidly and gaped, while the "boy" stared back at him. A chain of expressions flitted across her face. Embarrassment. Panic. And something else . . .

"You!" The word left his body on a rush of air—a boyish gasp that annoyed him immensely. It also triggered a coughing fit. He hunched over, cursing his damaged health and wondering if it were possible to appear calm and authoritative while hacking up a lung. When he looked up, his ears were ringing and dark spots swam in his vision.

"My dear boy! Are you quite all right?"

He nodded, unwilling to risk speech just yet. A surreptitious glance at his handkerchief showed no blood, thank God. The seconds ticked past. He had to say something, damn it all. It was a large effort, but he cut through Harkness's well-meaning blather with, "It's merely a slight cough—nothing at all to do with malaria." He looked straight at Mary as he spoke, but her expression was now neutral. Damn. He'd given her the advantage of time to recover.

"If you say so, of course . . ." Harkness sounded unconvinced. "As I was saying, Quinn ought to be of assistance to you. He's a bright lad who wishes to learn more about the trade. Isn't that right, sonny?"

"Yes, sir."

"Well then, that's all arranged. I suppose you'd like a tour of the site, Easton?"

He was so greatly altered that she wondered, at first, if she'd have recognized him at all. He was still tall, of course, but his shoulders now seemed too broad for his thin frame. He was sun-browned, but instead of looking healthy and relaxed, he seemed to vibrate with an underlying tension. And his features had a harsh cast that was new to her. He'd always looked serious—severe, even—but this saturnine expression was new. Then her gaze locked with his, and she felt a deep surge of warmth curl through her entire body. *Of course* she'd have recognized him; she'd know those eyes anywhere. She felt breathless. It was hard to look away now, but she managed—and then wondered if averting her gaze had seemed coy.

The tour of the site seemed to go on for hours. Harkness pattered nervously, James nodded his comprehension, and she followed the men in silence. What an absurd, improbable stroke of fate that she should meet James Easton here, when she was masked in this guise. Had he requested an assistant, or was that Harkness's doing? And—again—what did that suggest about Harkness's intentions for her? He couldn't possibly know the truth about her disguise.

Could he?

And then they were alone. Mary stood very still, nerves humming, bracing herself for his attack. Her situation was awkward and potentially scandalous: perfect fodder for the sort of cocky, blistering observation he loved to make. No doubt he'd been crafting a series of withering, faux-innocent remarks throughout the tour, to be delivered with his usual insolent drawl. Her only surprise was that he'd managed to restrain himself in Harkness's presence.

She waited.

And waited.

And waited some more.

After a full five minutes' silence, she raised her eyes to his face.

He was staring at the laborers working at the base of the tower but, as though sensing her unspoken question, turned to look at her. "I think," he said in a conversational tone, "we'll begin with the stonemasons. Er—Quinn, isn't it?"

It continued like this all afternoon. They—or rather, James—observed workers, inspected scaffolds, examined safety equipment, and took note of difficult or dangerous bits of work. He worked without haste, but covered a lot of ground nonetheless. And throughout their labors, he treated her with remote courtesy, exactly as he would any young assistant.

She hadn't seen him in over a year. Had never expected to meet him again. Even so, it seemed impossible that given her surname and confronted with her face, he had indeed forgotten all about her. She could have sworn that in those first, tingling moments, he'd recognized her immediately. That gasp—hadn't it been a gasp of surprise? He might have covered it with a coughing fit, but she hadn't mistaken that light of recognition in his eyes.

Or had she? Common sense told her that if he truly didn't remember, it would be cause for celebration. It would be, by far, the simplest, safest state of affairs. Yet if she was perfectly honest, this simplest, safest state of affairs bruised her pride. The—what was he? A bit young to be a man, but certainly not a boy—damn it all . . . he, James, had kissed her. Yes, he'd been concussed, and light-headed with smoke inhalation, and probably delirious to boot—but he'd pinned her against a wall and kissed her. Twice. She shivered with pleasure at the memory. So yes, a part of her hoped that, despite the complications it would create, James wasn't unmoved by "Mark Quinn."

Yet if he *had* made the connection, would he simply think her face vaguely, perhaps only slightly, familiar? That stung even more. How many girls had James kissed? More than a few, judging by those kisses. (*And how might you know?* taunted her inner voice. *Who else has kissed* you?) It would be even worse if he knew her face but couldn't place it.

Be rational, came the inner voice, cool and precise this time. Although he'd seen her in boy's clothing once before, his lack of recognition now was actually a compliment on the excellence of her disguise. And if her features seemed slightly familiar, he would likely assume this was merely in the way that most children seemed—their unformed faces so often all but interchangeable to adults.

It was only at day's end that he showed signs of seeing her as an individual rather than a moderately useful tool. "Quinn."

She looked up—and caught her breath. He was looking straight at her. "Y-yes, sir."

"Mr. Harkness mentioned that you're new to the trade."

She nodded slowly.

His eyes wandered over her roughly shorn hair, the grubby boy's attire. A faint smile curled the corner of his mouth. "What brought you here?"

"Sir?"

"To this site. It's unusual for a lad to find work on a

building site without previous experience or connections. You must have impressed Mr. Harkness."

"He's been very kind to me."

"I see." His gaze seemed to snag somewhere at the level of her waist—she was holding a roll of drawings—and lingered for so long that she squirmed with discomfort. "What did you do before coming here?"

She hesitated. Part of her wanted to shout, *As if you don't know!* "Bits of all sorts, sir. Errands. Nothing as you'd call a trade." That was truthful—and vague—enough.

"No. That's quite clear."

She waited, but he didn't elaborate. "Why's that, sir?" she asked eventually.

He nodded toward the scrolls of paper. "Your hands are soft and pale—not working hands." That quarter smile reappeared, and this time there was a glint in his eyes. "Some might even say lady's hands."

She froze, scarcely able to breathe. Now was the time for a clever, snappy retort, but her wits were frozen, too. The best she could manage was to gape at him with her mouth closed instead of open.

James shrugged and made a show of consulting his watch. "Ah—six o'clock. Mustn't keep you, young Quinn."

It took a moment for the words to register. When they did, she was furious. Still, there wasn't a thing she could safely do or say apart from, "Yes, sir."

The blasted man only grinned. "See you tomorrow, laddie."

Eleven

There was a bakery on The Cut, not far from Miss Phlox's house. As arranged with Anne Treleaven, Mary stopped there each evening to buy "a plain roll, the brownest they got." Once outside, she tore eagerly into the bread. She was perennially hungry these days. But tonight at the bun's squishy center she found a ball of paper the size of a green pea. On it was scribbled an address in Bermondsey, with additional terse directions. It was often difficult to find one's way about dockside areas, owing to the absence of street signs. It took only a moment to commit the directions to memory. Then she dropped the scrap into a particularly nasty puddle, where it was promptly obliterated by the wheels of a passing dray.

London was a transitional sort of place in the evenings. Thousands of people had finished their day's work and were now pouring out from the heart of town toward the suburbs: shabby-suited clerks trudging across bridges, weary-looking market traders dragging the last of their wares with them, laborers with toolbags slung across their backs. Yet there were a few bodies tacking their way against the rush. Already, new vendors were arriving to sell coffee at street stalls; to set up the late markets where the last of the day's—and yesterday's, and last week's—meat and vegetables were sold at knock-down prices; and to sweep the streets of a long day's dust and refuse.

It wasn't difficult for Mary to resist the third-rate scraps laid out on the crude stalls that sprang up just outside the Borough Market each evening. But all around her, poor people bargained for slimy vegetables, wormy fruit, and rank meat because they could afford these and nothing else. She thought of Jenkins knocking back the dregs of sour milk at yesterday's morning tea break, and of the hunger that must be even greater because he'd earned no wages today. The thought made her walk faster.

Near Tower Bridge, the stench of the tanneries struck her like a physical blow. Rotting flesh, caustic lime, animal dung—these were the constant perfumes of Bermondsey. They made the Thames itself smell acceptable. Jenkins's address turned out to be a bedraggled little terraced house not a hundred yards from one of the larger tanneries. Outside this strip of houses, a large flock of dirty children clustered near the gutter. They ought to have been playing boisterously, but this group seemed as downtrodden as their surroundings. A few bickered among themselves, but otherwise they seemed too listless to do anything much except sit in the road and watch Mary's passage with glassy, tired eyes.

She rapped on the front door and waited. Nothing. She knocked again, and this time, a voice from within snapped, "Well, what d'you want, then?"

"Please, I'm here to see Peter Jenkins."

There was a long silence. Just as Mary was about to repeat herself, the door jerked open a couple of inches and a pair of bloodshot eyes stared down at her with suspicion. "Jenkins?"

"Yes, ma'am." It was a guess; she couldn't see much through the narrow gap, but the voice was more alto than tenor.

The door opened wider, and Mary saw a wild halo of gray hair and a shapeless dress draped over a humped back. "Jenkins be down there," their owner said curtly, jerking her chin toward the interior.

Mary tried not to flinch as the smell of the house—dirty hair, mold, sweat, and decay, all compounded with the stink of rot and excrement—embraced her. She trod cautiously; if the street had been dim, the house itself was in near darkness. It took several moments for her eyes to adjust. Eventually, she made out a square wooden hatch toward the back of the house. It opened with a reluctant squeal to reveal a rotting wooden ladder disappearing down into what looked like a cellar.

She paused and looked back over her shoulder for confirmation, but the woman had already lost interest.

"Hello?" Mary called down tentatively. In sensation novels, this was the part where the intrepid hero got clubbed over the head only to awake several hours later, bound hand and foot, in the villain's lair. Mary turned her head abruptly—but of course there was nobody.

There was also no response from below, only a faint rustling that might be human. She had a rushlight in her pocket, but it wouldn't do much good here. With an inner sigh, she prepared to descend. Now that she'd come this far, there was no point in turning back.

She was slim and light, but even so she descended slowly, testing each rung before transferring her weight onto it. There were only six rungs before her foot touched earth instead of wood. She stopped again to let her eyes adjust to this new level of darkness. A small grate at the top of the wall nearest the street was the only source of light and air.

"Hello? Jenkins?"

If she hadn't been completely still, she might have missed the rustling noise from the corner.

As it was, she squinted but could see nothing clearly. "Jenkins? It's Quinn."

Silence.

If the rustling had stopped, it probably wasn't rats. "I know you can hear me."

Finally, from the same corner came a petulant sigh—and a voice. "Piss off!"

Mary grinned. Definitely Jenkins. She made her way

to the corner by instinct more than anything else.

He was there, lying belly-down on a straw pallet with a hunted but defiant look in his eyes. "I said, piss off! You got no call coming in here where you's not invited."

She ignored this. "I brought you some stuff."

"I don't want it," came the automatic response.

"Wait till you see it first." She rummaged in a pocket and brought forth a small handful of pennies and ha'pennies: all the ready money Mark Quinn had in the world. "Still don't want it?" she asked, and grinned when he scowled but remained silent. She placed the coppers in a neat heap by Jenkins's elbow and dug out a long twist of paper from a different pocket.

"What's that?" His tone was surly, but his eyes intrigued.

"Powdered willow bark." At his blank expression, she explained, "For the pain."

"Oh." His eyes followed her movements now as though she was a conjuror.

From her jacket she produced a two-pound loaf of bread—white, with a golden crust, the most luxurious type one could buy.

His eyes widened and he sniffed appreciatively.

Finally, she pulled a small flask from her pocket and sloshed it encouragingly. "Still going to tell me to piss off?"

"Aw, stuff it." But Jenkins's tone was distinctly pleased.

It was the first time she'd heard it so, she realized with some surprise. Even on site, even mucking about, he'd never sounded this happy. Or this boyish. She opened the sachet and watched him tip the bitter powder down his throat without a grimace.

He took a mouthful of rum next and gave an appreciative "Hooo-aaarh!"

Silently, she hacked several thick slices from the loaf with her pocketknife. As he munched, washing down every few bites with a swig of rum, she poked the pile of coppers with the toe of her boot. "Anything else you need? I can fetch it for you."

He looked tempted, then shook his head decisively. "Naw. I can't take your money."

"It's your share of the tea round."

"I ain't never made that much on the tea round." But his gaze was focused on the pennies as though hypnotized.

"Did today." A rotten lie, but it was the most plausible reason she had. She just hoped Jenkins needed the money enough to force himself to believe it. "I went around with Reid—he was collecting for Wick's widow—and the men all coughed up, for him and for me."

"Hunh."

"Men didn't seem too happy about it, though—Reid collecting."

"For Wick, you mean. No—he were a natural-born scoundrel, that one. Bet the glaziers didn't give nothing."

"Yeah—how'd you know?"

Jenkins grimaced. "I just know. Wick and Keenan—nobody wants to give 'em anything, 'cause they's always on the take."

Interesting. "What d'you mean?"

Jenkins merely gave her a sharp look. "I ain't got to explain everything. Just watch and you'll see." And that was all he would say on the subject.

Mary's eyes had now adjusted to the near blackness, and she could make out the general shapes of things. They were in a small, low-ceilinged, earthen-floored cellar. It held no furniture, no hearth, no place to eat, and certainly no place to wash. Only a few clues suggested that human beings attempted to live here: two small piles of matted straw and rags, representing beds; a dented pail without a handle; and a candle stub.

She tried not to look at him with pity. Jenkins's backside was obviously badly lacerated and in need of treatment, and he was wearing the same clothes she'd last seen him in. Quite likely, they were the only clothes he owned. Given the filth and poverty in which he lived, it was surprising only that he wasn't already feverish with infection.

"Who else lives here?" she asked.

A pause. Then, "Me dad and the babies."

No mother—that wasn't unusual. "Baby brothers?"

"Sisters. They ain't such babies now. Next year, maybe, Jenny'll be old enough to work."

Old enough to work was a relative concept. At the Jenkinses' level of poverty, Jenny might be five or six years old, at most. "What's your father do?"

"What's it to you?"

"Nothing. I just—you said he's a builder, right? Because that's how you got your job."

"None of your business."

"All right," she said mildly. It sounded as though she was dismissed. "I'll come back and see you in a few days, if you like."

Jenkins's gaze was riveted to the pennies once again, and he shrugged ungraciously. "Suit yourself."

She unfolded her legs, stood, and promptly banged her head on the ceiling. If she, a fairly small woman, was too tall for this cellar, how on earth could a grown man like Jenkins Senior live here? And why was his son so protective of him? "Right. See you."

Jenkins merely grunted. But as she climbed the rickety ladder out of the cellar, she heard him say, "Quinn."

She paused, her hand on the top rung, anxious now to escape that dank pit. "Yeah?"

He was poking at the small pile of pennies and ha'pennies as though testing a hallucination. It seemed difficult for him to meet her gaze. "Thanks."

She nodded once and tried to smile, but suddenly it was all too much: the cellar; the stench; the utter desperation all about her. She scrabbled her way up and tore out of the house, nearly knocking down the hunched woman who'd admitted her, not stopping to apologize. She pelted past the children, who blinked at her with their owlish, drugged eyes—sedated with a blend of starvation and opium, no doubt. And she didn't stop running until she was back in Lambeth.

Near Coral Street, she stumbled into a quiet alley and vomited. Bread, ale, that extra bun—all her meager supper accounted for. But even once her stomach was empty, the retching continued in long, violent spasms that shook her frame, making her gasp and choke. She tasted salt water on her lips, and found that she was crying. What for? Not for Peter Jenkins, entirely. And not for the others she'd seen in his street. It was absurd. Childish. Weak. But for several minutes she couldn't stop.

When she finally did, she was empty: dry of tears, her stomach hollow. She felt cold. She shook with exhaustion. And she was still in an alley in Lambeth, dressed as Mark Quinn. Swallowing the remaining bitterness in her mouth, she wondered what that meant. Mary took a few steps toward Coral Street, preparing herself for what awaited her there: Rogers, that lumpy bed, a fractured night's sleep. Versus a long walk, her own bedroom, a return to her cosseted life as Mary Quinn. It was still there. She still existed. She could go back to the Agency now, or tomorrow, or at the end of this case. And somehow, knowing that was enough—for tonight, at least.

Twelve

Wednesday, 6 July

Palace Yard, Westminster

It was the morning of the inquest. Both James and Harkness were in attendance, one as an observer, the other as a witness. And while Mary understood that a formal inquest wasn't the place for Mark Quinn, on site she felt marooned. Although the atmosphere in Palace Yard had always seemed tense to Mary, today at least there was a specific reason for such a feeling of constant strain. The main exception was a pair of laborers who slowly unloaded a cart of supplies, bickering the entire time:

"I wouldn't be Harky for all the tea in China."

"Why not?"

"What, and go to one of them inquests? Don't you know nothing?"

"It ain't nothing but a room full of people."

"Yeah, and a stiff."

"What?"

"Jesus but you's ignorant, Batesy. Some sawbones is going to slice open Wick's body in front of all the world and make them watch. That's what a inquest is, you duffer."

"Ohhhhhh . . ."

"Yeah, 'oh.' I couldn't never watch, no matter what no judge said. I'd be sick straight off, swear I would."

Despite the prevailing mood, Mary found it difficult not to smile at Batesy's sophisticated mate. She could have set him straight on the difference between inquest and autopsy, although Mark Quinn likely couldn't. But such light moments were rare and there was little else to break up her morning's work, ferrying barrowfuls of wood shavings and other rubbish to the bonfire pile.

It was a couple of hours later that she noticed a stranger poking his nose through the entrance gate. He was scruffy for a gentleman: his trousers bagged at the knees, and one coat sleeve was striped with something pale—chalk, perhaps. He peered into Harkness's office, apparently tempted by what he saw within. One silent step closer—a glance around—and he immediately spotted Mary, watching him with open curiosity from several yards away.

Instantly, he straightened and spun toward her. "Hello, laddie, Mr. Harkness about?" His voice was warm and friendly, the sort of voice that made one relax and encouraged one to trust him.

Perhaps that was why she did not. "No, sir."

"Not on site? When d'you expect him?"

"Don't know, sir. He didn't say."

He pulled a face. "Funny sort of management on

his part, eh? And what are you lot supposed to do in the meantime?" He was now standing very close—practically on her feet.

She shrugged and edged back half a step. "Carry on, I suppose." His gaze was intent upon her face, as though he were memorizing her features. It made her want to squirm. Few adults spared "Mark" a glance, unless she'd done something unusual to draw their attention. It had happened with Harkness, and then with Keenan. What had she done now?

"You're new," he announced.

"Third day, sir." Had she seen him somewhere before? The trouble was, he was utterly unremarkable: a fair-haired man with a closely trimmed beard and even, unmemorable features. He was neither young nor old, neither handsome nor ugly.

"Like it so far?"

"Well enough, sir." He was definitely up to something. No gentleman on legitimate business would waste this much time on an errand boy.

"I would have thought," he said idly, "that Mr. Harkness would have a secretary, or a clerk, to manage the site while he's gone. Where did you say he'd gone to?"

Aha! That was his aim. Her voice was a little prim as she said, "I didn't, sir."

He grinned at that, and Mary blinked. All the bland neutrality was gone, replaced by a slightly crooked, lazy charm. "You're a clever lad—too sharp for the likes of me."

Mary couldn't help grinning back. "I don't think so, sir."

"Oh, but I do. Very well: I confess. I already know that Mr. Harkness went to the inquest into the death of John Wick. But now that the inquest's been adjourned . . ." He noted Mary's big eyes and grinned. "Oh—didn't you hear? I thought boys like you knew everything the moment it happened."

She shook her head. "What did they say, sir?"

"Why should I tell you? Find out for yourself, lazy-bones!"

"I am, sir, by asking you—I'm trying, anyway."

He smirked. "Cheeky little fart." But when she continued to stand there, waiting for an answer, he looked at her more closely. "Stubborn too. Hmm . . . Well, you might as well know: there's no verdict yet. Instead, they're awaiting the result of a safety review to be conducted on the building site. First I'd heard of it, I don't mind confessing to you. First I've heard of the chappie engaged to do it, as well—fellow called Easton." He fixed her with a keen eye. "You know him, sonny?"

She looked noncommittal. "Everybody here does, sir."

"Hmph. Naturally. Er—where was I? Oh yes—I am a member of the press, seeking to interview Mr. Harkness and Mr. Easton vis-à-vis the inquest of John Wick. And," he added, holding up a warning finger, "before you summon your two largest stonemasons to turn me out on my ear, have the kindness to remember that we gentlemen of the press, though humble, help to fashion public opinion even as we serve the public desire for knowledge and advancement."

Despite her mistrust, Mary was amused. "You write for a newspaper?"

"Precisely! I knew you were clever."

"What newspaper?"

He looked at her with renewed interest. "My, my—we have a connoisseur of the daily news!"

She squirmed. Perhaps the question had been a bit out of character. . . .

"The fine and noble organ for which I write is dedicated to spreading the truth, to educating the populace, and, above all, to entertaining the masses. Can you guess its title?"

"No, sir."

"I must confess myself deeply grieved, young man. It's none other than *The Eye on London*. You know it now, don't you?"

She bit back a grin. "Yes, sir." *The Eye!* How apt. It was a newspaper that contained even less sense than the man's speech.

He was glancing about again, and though he seemed nonchalant, Mary was willing to bet he didn't miss much. "I say, is that lad Jenkins not about?"

"Jenkins is injured, sir. Off for a week, at least."

"Dearie me." But he didn't look much distressed. "And what's your name?"

She hesitated for a fraction of a second. "Quinn, sir. Mark Quinn."

"Octavius Jones, at your service." He shook hands with her solemnly. "I think we might be of use to each other, young Quinn."

"Sir?"

"Bright lad like you . . . I'm sure you see all sorts in the course of your workday."

"All sorts of what, sir?"

He grinned again and gave her a sharp look. "That's precisely what I mean. There's something not right about this site—and I don't mean just the death of that laborer. I daresay you've heard that before now."

Mary nodded slowly. Jenkins's words—"always on the take"—echoed in her mind. She had a deal of catching up to do, if she was to be of any use to the Agency.

"Well, then: I've an interest in uncovering the truth. I don't even know what that truth is right now. But if you see or hear anything that strikes you as unusual, I want to know about it. And I'll make it worth your while. What d'you say to that?" He jingled some coins in his trouser pocket.

She nodded, silently vowing to avoid Octavius Jones at all costs. He seemed entirely too much of a risk. She was wondering how to escape his presence when she heard an irritable bark from close behind her: "Quinn!"

She jumped—rather guiltily—and saw James stalking toward them, his expression stormy. "Sir!" Her voice was breathless, and she hoped he'd interpret it as surprise—nothing else.

Octavius Jones perked up and spun to face James. "Mr. Easton, of Easton Engineering, I presume?"

James's glare was fixed firmly on Mary. "Enough loitering and gossip. We've work to do." He brushed past Jones with scarcely a glance. "This is a closed building site. Depart this instant, sir, or I shall have you turned out."

"I do beg your pardon, sir," purred Jones, raising his hat with elaborate courtesy. "No harm intended." He spun about and tipped Mary a wink. "Good day, laddie."

James merely glowered and kept moving. "Now, Quinn."

Like a good little errand boy, Mary turned to follow him. But even as she trotted after James, a new idea whisked through her brain and her head swiveled to watch Octavius Jones's retreating figure. Medium build. Damn. He was definitely not the party who'd broken into the site on Monday night.

Just at that moment, Jones twisted around and caught her frowning at him. A broad grin broke across his face and he reached into a pocket, took out a coin, and flipped it toward her in a high, showy arc. Reflexively, she caught it—then cursed herself for doing so. She couldn't have done anything else in Mark Quinn's persona. But as the coin changed from cool to warm in her clenched fist, she couldn't help but wonder how and when she might be compelled to repay Jones's generosity.

Thirteen

The Agency's headquarters
Acacia Road, St. John's Wood

This was all highly irregular. She'd explained her need to live in lodgings in order fully to inhabit the role of Mark Quinn. She thought Anne and Felicity understood. Yet tonight's summons from the Agency threatened to undermine that effort. As she knocked on the familiar attic door, Mary tried to swallow her temper. She'd gain nothing by sounding cross and frustrated; Anne and Felicity might even read those emotions as indicative of an inability to continue.

"Come in." Anne and Felicity looked the same as ever, sitting in their usual chairs, drinking tea. Although their expressions didn't change, Mary thought she detected surprise nonetheless. Her suit of clothes—her only suit of clothes—was filthy. Street muck clung to her boots and calves in a most unpleasant fashion. She could only imagine how she must smell.

"Good evening, Miss Treleaven; Mrs. Frame." She remained standing; she'd only ruin any furniture she touched.

"Good evening. We called you here this evening, Mary, to ask how you're faring. Not in terms of the case, although we look forward to a full report, but in the persona of Mark Quinn."

Mary swallowed hard. It was uncanny: as though they'd somehow witnessed her shameful breakdown the previous night in the alley. "I'm fine, Miss Treleaven. It's been difficult, occasionally, as expected. But I'm managing to stay in the role and to survive very well."

Anne remained silent. She probably wasn't attending to the words at all, thought Mary with a surge of anxiety. She was listening for tone of voice, gauging her expression, watching for telltale physical signs of distress. But thanks to Anne and Felicity, Mary was trained to pass all these tests. She kept her tone even, her expression thoughtful. Didn't stare too long at either manager. Allowed herself to sound concerned but resolute.

"Are you able to eat and rest?" asked Felicity.

"Adequately. Not well, but it's a short-term assignment."

"And the emotional consequences of your return?" This was Anne speaking. "Your project of confronting your childhood: is that not taxing?"

Mary was silent for a moment, tasting the swell of confusion that threatened her every time she woke or fell asleep, in each half moment she forgot herself, in her transitions from Mark to Mary and back again. And there was that episode in the alley, after she'd visited Jenkins . . . her stomach twisted at the memory. "Taxing" was an utterly inadequate word for such hell. But Anne's gray eyes still were fixed upon her, steady and grave. "I've found I'm capable of managing."

Silence, during which the three women looked at one another. There was no indication of what Anne and Felicity thought, or what silent communication passed between them. Finally, Anne nodded. "Very well. Before you report, is there anything you need? Food? Drink?"

"A bath?" Felicity grinned.

Mary laughed. "The bath would be cheating, and I'll get some food on the way out. But I wanted to ask you about John Wick's home life. Could you send someone to take a look at the house? Find out what his family's like? We'll need to know more of his character in order to understand the reason for his death."

Anne nodded. "A good point."

"I need a look inside. A conversation with Mrs. Wick. Basically, as much of a portrait of the dead man as I can get. I can't manage that as a boy."

"It sounds as though you need a firsthand look. Why not go yourself?"

Mary stared. "As myself?"

"Or as a lady. Let's say, a well-to-do lady on a charitable mission. Take the widow a basket of goods, sweep into the house, cross-examine her." Felicity's eyes were bright. "She could hardly say no."

That much was true: well-meaning ladies often invaded the homes of the poor, arrogantly certain of their welcome as generous benefactors. "But my role as Mark Quinn . . . and the funeral's tomorrow; I've got to be there, too, and there's work tomorrow morning. . . ."

Anne consulted her watch. "We can organize the visit for this evening if we begin immediately. And if you're willing to drive, Flick."

Felicity nodded and rose. "Of course."

As Anne and Felicity swept from the room, Mary watched with an uncomfortable sense of helplessness. Much as she wanted to poke about Wick's house, this certainly wasn't what she'd had in mind. She wasn't sure she could change roles so quickly. Hadn't a clear idea what she was looking for. Didn't like the idea of interrupting, then resuming, her life as Mark Quinn. Yet Anne and Felicity were correct: this was the most effective way to do things. And—her conscience wriggled here—it meant she could have a bath! A hot, glorious, sudsy, middle-class bath.

As run by Anne, the Agency was ferociously efficient. Ten minutes later, Mary was immersed in a steaming tub. As she scrubbed, Anne sat behind a folding screen and listened to her report. Mary began by describing her struggle to be accepted on site, from her own blunders about reading and speaking too well to Harkness's cultivation of her as a charitable project to her utter lack of experience — unconvincing even in a so-called boy of twelve.

"Just as I feared," muttered Anne when Mary paused for breath. "It's a field about which we know next to nothing."

"Miss Treleaven?"

"I do beg your pardon, Mary. Pray continue."

"I haven't learned a great deal in my time on site. However . . ." Mary heard the whisper of Anne's pen making notes on the other side of the partition. The jottings were minimal at first. She explained the tea round and Jenkins's small side profit, which elicited a quiet huff of amusement. But when Mary mentioned Reid's meager collection for the widow Wick and Keenan's reputation as a man "always on the take," the pen scratchings accelerated. By the time she described the break-in, its aftermath, and the appearance of Octavius Jones, Anne was scribbling furiously.

"Since Jones knows Jenkins by name, I'm inclined to think that Jenkins fed him information. I'll check that the next time I see Jenkins — tomorrow evening, I hope."

"Good." There was a final burst of writing before Anne said, "This Keenan character seems almost excessively villainous."

"Jenkins would certainly testify to that." Mary briefly described his flogging and her near escape. "Which reminds me, Miss Treleaven — what does Harkness know about my role on site?"

"Nothing, of course." Anne sounded surprised at the very question. "Is there anything apart from the flogging that makes you wonder?"

"He's been very kind to me; unusually so. I can't decide if it's because he suspects something or whether he has his own agenda or whether he really is deeply paternalistic toward his workers."

"Perhaps he's merely being a good Christian." There came the whisper of pen against paper again, but now it was leisurely—more like doodling than note taking. "It's rather unusual, of course, but he's very active in his church—one of the more evangelical denominations, I understand. Have you anything else to report?"

There was one more subject she ought to broach: the reappearance of James Easton. But even as she opened her mouth to speak, Mary found herself creating excuses. His appointment was already public knowledge. She'd no evidence that James even recognized her. If he didn't, she kept reminding herself, it was all for the best. But she was reluctant even to voice that utterly humiliating fact. "No."

"You must be hungry."

"Constantly," admitted Mary. She stood in the tub, tipped a final bucket of warm water over her head, then wound herself into a large towel. "Although tonight I'd rather have a bath than a meal."

"Fortunately, you needn't choose," said Anne with a small smile.

The table was neatly laid for one. Mary lifted the silver dome and sighed with delight: roast chicken, vegetables, potatoes, and, for pudding, a wedge of lemon tart. All the same . . . "Isn't it getting rather late? I ought to set off soon."

"Sit and eat," said Anne sternly. "You can't behave like a lady if you're half-starved."

Who was she to argue with Anne Treleaven? The only difficulty was in remembering her table manners, now that she was faced with her first good meal in several days. One of Mark Quinn's inelegant habits had become almost ingrained.

While Mary ate, Anne moved quietly about the room, assembling the things they'd need to complete her transformation: fine muslin underclothes, dark silk gown, brocaded shawl, and deep bonnet. Mary's skin tingled as she watched Anne arrange a few extra items on a side table. It was at times like this—bruised, footsore, yet brimming with excitement—that she particularly loved working for the Agency.

It didn't take her long to dress. The crinoline was enormous—the sort that required one to enter rooms sideways—and she practiced swishing it about for a few minutes. At first it was odd to wear her own boots again, and then it was a pleasure. Much to her surprise, the dress fit beautifully, and she looked at Anne. "But how . . . ?"

Anne merely smiled. "Sit down so I can arrange your hair."

Mary stifled a grimace. Her straight, slippery hair resisted buns and chignons at the best of times. Now, cropped short, it was less ladylike than ever. When Anne produced an unfamiliar item, a small roundish net stuffed full of horsehair, Mary resigned herself. It took two racks of pins but when Anne was finished—and she wasn't gentle—Mary's hair was smoothed back into a passable bun, with the false roll of hair anchored just where her own finished. Once the bonnet was in place, it looked surprisingly natural.

"Will I do?" asked Mary, draping the shawl over her shoulders and picking up a heavy wicker hamper.

"Of course."

Outside the house, a good-size carriage awaited. The coachman seemed unfamiliar to Mary—at least until he climbed down from his perch and took the basket from her with a broad wink. Mary's eyes widened and she bit back a gasp. Felicity Frame did, indeed, make a convincing man.

"Where to, ma'am?" The driver's voice was a supple tenor.

"Er—Ayres Street, by Southwark Bridge. Please." She climbed into the carriage, feeling more awkward than she had in ages. So they were to maintain their roles all the way.

As they bowled southeast at a smart pace, Mary settled back on the padded bench, basking in the subtle scent of her own clean skin, a full stomach, and the soft caress of muslin and silk garments. Even after only a few days as Mark Quinn, such daily comforts felt deliciously luxurious. Their return also brought a strong sense of déjà vu. These things were hardly novelties, but she remembered a time when they had been. Several years ago, when Anne and Felicity had first whisked her away from a death sentence and out of gaol, she'd never known daily baths, citrus fruits, or feather beds. Indeed, she'd been poor and hungry for so long that eating three meals a day seemed astonishing and excessive.

But the most difficult part of Mark's life was not labor or filth or hunger. What Mary found grueling was the sense that Mark would never get ahead, never gain a rest, never be at ease. His meager wages bought him just enough food and sleep to survive. There was no possibility of saving money and thus no hope for any sort of change or rest. And as the case of Jenkins showed, any illness or accident was disastrous—not just for the boy concerned but for his extended family as well. This was the bind she too had felt during her childhood. As a young pickpocket and later, a housebreaker, she had acquired her money in daily scraps and infrequent windfalls. What she didn't spend was liable to be stolen from her in turn. And all the time, there was the need to keep her head down, keep her real identity a secret. It was an exhausting life, for she was constantly on the alert, always on the defensive. And except for the heady rush of danger that came with each theft, it was a lonely, joyless existence. It was perhaps understandable that when caught red-handed, she hadn't felt her life worth saving. But Anne and Felicity had.

The carriage halted and Mary blinked. Her eyes were moist and she dabbed them hastily with a handkerchief—another luxury. It took her a moment to return to the present, and it was only when the carriage door clicked open that she felt fully a lady once more. And what a lady!

She descended to the pavement with mincing steps and allowed Felicity to hand down the hamper. "Wait here," she said in the general direction of the carriage.

"Very good, ma'am."

The house was a narrow two-story strip of brick in the middle of a row, made conspicuous by the large, slightly wilted black bow fastened to the door knocker. As Mary rapped on the door, she heard voices inside fall silent.

A small, tousled boy opened the door and gaped up at her.

"I've come to see your mother," said Mary in a carrying voice.

As she'd expected, at the sound of her voice a young woman came hurrying toward the door. "Don't keep the nice lady waiting, Johnny. Let her in; there's a good boy." She bobbed a curtsy to Mary. "Please to walk in, ma'am."

Mary allowed her gaze to travel over the woman and the contents of her house. The sitting room was clean and sparsely furnished, and someone had tried to ornament it with a bunch of white wildflowers arranged in a cracked mug. Despite its plain appearance, it was a large and fairly costly-seeming house for a laborer—even a skilled one like Wick. But the most noticeable feature of the room was the number of children in it: four at a glance, plus the boy by the door. "You're Mrs. Wick?"

The young woman bobbed again. "Yes, ma'am." She was about twenty, fair-haired, and so very thin that she appeared almost translucent. She had recently had a colossal black eye, which was now fading to a greeny-yellowy color. "If—if you come to see the body, ma'am, it ain't here. I ain't had many callers, 'cause of the ink—the ink—" She stumbled to a halt.

"The inquest?"

"Aye, that's the one, ma'am." Something inside Mrs. Wick's dress shifted and Mary blinked: there was a sixth child, an infant, cradled to her breast. She blushed and smiled at Mary's expression. "My youngest, Robert. He's over a year, now, for all he's so tiny."

Mary bent forward to look at the baby, a bald, wizened little man suckling away, oblivious to her inspection. She had no idea what to say: he wasn't pretty or well grown or alert or any of the usual things one complimented in babies. "And this is your eldest?" she indicated the boy who'd let her in.

"Aye, that's John, named for his father. He's rising seven. And the others are Katy, Michael, and Matthew—twins, they are—and Paul. But won't you take a seat, Mrs.—er, ma'am?"

"Fordham. Mrs. Fordham. Thank you." Mary sat in

the chair indicated, the only solid one in the room, and smiled at the children. The children stared back. They looked ridiculously alike, with their mother's round eyes and defenseless expression.

Paul let out a sudden, thin wail, and in response, a deep voice came from the back of the house. "No call for cryin,' little Paul. Tea's ready now." This confident pronouncement was followed by the opening of the interior door—the kitchen door, Mary now saw—and a man entered carrying a tray. He halted, midstep, at the sight of Mary. Surprise, embarrassment, alarm all flashed across his face. His still-bruised face.

It was Reid.

Reid, the bricklayer.

Reid, with whom she'd gone round site yesterday, collecting donations for the widow Wick.

The silence was broken by Mrs. Wick's nervous half sob. "What must you think of me," she asked Mary, "my husband not yet buried and another man in the house? But it ain't what it looks like, honest it's not. Ain't that right, Robert?"

Reid blushed comprehensively, and his hands shook as he placed the supper tray on the table. Despite his guilty look, he faced Mary with a certain awkward sincerity. "Indeed it's not, ma'am. I'm a mate of Wick's—we're both bricklayers by trade and worked the same gang—and I just come around this evening to give Janey—I mean, Mrs. Wick—a hand with the young 'uns. It's a powerful hard time for her just now, burying her husband and looking after all them little ones."

It took a moment for the facts to penetrate Mary's frozen façade of calm. Fact: Reid's given name was the same as the baby's. Fact: he was on sufficiently intimate terms with Mrs. Wick to be frying eggs, unsupervised, in her kitchen. Fact: he didn't seem to recognize Mary. It was this last that refused to register for some time.

Something of the adults' tension inhibited the children, too. They were a quiet brood by any standard, but now their round, pale-blue eyes grew even wider, and the twins shoved their right thumbs into their mouths with sudden, simultaneous jerks. At last, Mary roused herself. Reid hadn't recognized "Mark." That was the main thing—the only thing—that mattered, just now. Everything else could wait.

"Your supper's growing cold, children," she said, relinquishing her chair, and was pleased at how natural she sounded. "You must be hungry."

John, the boldest, nodded. He now made a dash for the table. "Fried eggs!" That lifted the strain, and the rest of the children moved toward Reid, clearly ravenous.

Mrs. Wick smiled nervously at Mary, as though checking to see whether she'd been forgiven. "They call him Uncle Rob, the children do. He's a real blessing to our family." Sudden tears glistened in her eyes. "I don't know what I'd have done without him, this past week."

Mary nodded, and suddenly it didn't matter what the

state of affairs was between Reid and Mrs. Wick—not for the moment, at any rate. "It's always a blessing when friends and neighbors come together in difficult times," she said in affected, pompous tones. "And that is why I've come, too." She drew Mrs. Wick to a quiet corner of the room and unpacked the hamper: a little basket of eggs, a boiled ham, a seed cake, a slice of butter wrapped in paper, an ounce of tea, and, right at the bottom, a length of black crepe.

"Oh, Lord." Mrs. Wick's eyes welled up and she began to cry in earnest now. "I never seen such a basket, Mrs. Fordham, never in my life. It's too good of you." She wiped her eyes on a corner of her apron. "And the children—" She turned pleading eyes to Mary once more, seeming to look up at her although the two women were roughly the same height. "Of course, they don't get such splendid teas, hardly at all; only it was Robert's idea to give them a treat, and they been so grieved. . . ."

Mary felt acutely uncomfortable. She was glad to give things to Mrs. Wick, of course. The widow certainly seemed to need them. But such extravagant gratitude for what were, truly, only small things? Why shouldn't the Wick children have fried eggs for supper every night of the week? It was wrong that they couldn't afford it.

"Janey." Reid's quiet voice broke through Mrs. Wick's anxious flutterings and her head instantaneously swiveled toward him.

"Yes, Robert?"

"I'll be going now. They's two eggs keeping hot in the pan for you, and you're to eat them both, hear? No giving them to Johnny or them greedy twins."

She blushed faintly and glanced at Mary. "Two eggs? But I couldn't . . ."

"You can, and you must." He turned courteously to Mary. "Evening, ma'am."

She nodded graciously and watched him take leave of the children, bidding them be good for their mother's sake. It was impossible not to admire the compassion he showed them. As Reid let himself out of the door, he glanced once more toward the back of the room, his gaze swerving toward Jane Wick as though by compulsion. Guarded as his expression was, Mary couldn't help but see the longing and tenderness in his eyes.

She was almost sorry to observe it. There was no way this man was a casual, drunken pub brawler. That, combined with his passion for Jane Wick and his affection for her children, meant that his bruises were significant. They'd been fading on Monday, so the fight had taken place perhaps a week ago. She wondered if Wick's body had also borne evidence of a fistfight.

Mrs. Wick, whose attention had wandered to her children, passed a weary hand over her forehead and yawned. The languid gesture pulled her dress tight against her body—her thin, narrow body—and the slight swell of her lower belly. Mary's gaze was riveted once more. On a woman that gaunt, such a belly could mean only one thing; even she knew that. It might not be Reid's baby, of course. But odds were it was, and that was more than sufficient motive for violence. It was enough even for murder.

The door clicked shut behind Reid and Mrs. Wick smiled at Mary, meek and conciliatory. "Forgive me, ma'am. I'm sure I don't know why I'm so weary these days. It's in my bones, like."

Mary murmured something about trying times. "Have you family close by? Someone to help with the children?"

She shook her head. "I ain't from London; it was Wick as wanted to work here, and what could I do but follow? I was right sorry to leave Saffron Walden."

"Have you thought about what you might do? Go back to Essex, perhaps? Or at least send some of the children?" A better-off relative might even offer to raise one of them for her.

"I don't rightly know, ma'am. It's all so sudden, and Wick not yet buried on account of that ink . . ." She made a helpless gesture.

"What do you do for work?"

"Straw plaiting, ma'am."

So that was why her hands were so callused and scarred. They were the hands Mary herself ought to have had, the better to pass as a builder's assistant. "And you find time to plait straw, with six children in the house?"

"Aye, ma'am. Katy's a wonder for looking after the little ones, and Johnny's old enough to help in his way.

Wick had his trade, but it's powerful hard to keep a family of eight even on a bricklayer's wages, ma'am, and a working man's wife has got to help in any way she can."

"Very proper," said Mary. "You must both have worked hard, indeed."

Mrs. Wick nodded. "Oh yes, ma'am, poor Wick worked hard enough for his wages. Why, they's nights he ain't come home till nine, ten, nor even eleven o'clock! A working man's life is a hard one, they say, and it were so for Wick."

Nine or ten o'clock, from a building site? From the pub, more like. Mary looked critically at Mrs. Wick's bruised eye, still swollen and slightly distorted. They were an oddly discolored pair at the moment, Jane Wick and Robert Reid—and it was almost certainly thanks to the same, dead man. "And was Wick a good husband to you?"

Mrs. Wick flushed defensively. "I hope you'll pardon my saying so, ma'am, but if a man's so hard-worked, he's often weary."

But not too weary to beat his pregnant wife. Mary's mouth twisted in disgust, but there was no point in pressing the issue if Mrs. Wick was only going to defend her husband's brutality. And what would such an admission prove? Only that Wick was like thousands of men across England. "I ask," she said in a conciliatory voice, "because I wonder what else I might be able to do for you. What do you need, Mrs. Wick?"

A prouder woman would have refused at this point. A

pragmatic one would have made a request. But Jane Wick merely shook her head, uncertain. "I don't rightly know, ma'am, for all you're so kind . . ."

"The funeral's tomorrow?"

"Yes, ma'am, and there's my mourning to finish. I been that busy, I ain't yet put the bodice to the skirt."

"Who will watch the children?"

Three sharp raps on the door interrupted them.

Mrs. Wick looked anxious once again. "I ain't never had so many callers," she said apologetically. "Johnny, do you answer that; there's a good boy."

Johnny left the table still chewing, a hunk of bread-and-butter in one hand. The hinges were rather stiff, and he had to pull on the door with his body weight in order to open it. What he saw on the other side caused him to gasp, let go of the doorknob, and drop onto his bottom with a thump. His bread-and-butter tumbled to the floor, and he made no move to retrieve it.

"Good evening, young man," said a low masculine voice. "Is your mother home?"

For the second time that evening, Mary froze with a combination of panic and disbelief. But this time, it was much, much worse. This time, she had no hope at all of going unrecognized.

This time, the man was James Easton.

He hadn't thought himself all that terrifying to look at. But judging from the little boy's expression, he was the bogeyman himself. It was rather late to be paying calls, of course, but he couldn't help that. He needed to build a picture of the dead man in his head. Was Wick the sort who'd flout safety precautions while in the belfry? Or was he a steady, cautious sort whose fall was inexplicable except by violence? Part of the answer lay here, in his home, and the Wick family would just have to believe that he wasn't a tax collector, bailiff, or worse.

"Well, lad?" When the child continued to gape up at him, James glanced past him into the house. And what he saw made him stare, too.

Two women stood at the center of the room, interrupted in deep conversation. One was pallid and emaciated—obviously the widow Wick, surrounded by her enormous brood. The sight of the other made his pulse kick hard, the blood rush to his head, his hands go weak.

Mary advanced toward him, a complicated expression in her eyes. "Mr. Easton," she said in a high, affected voice. "How very kind of you to call on the Wick family, too. You remember me, of course: Mrs. Anthony Fordham, from St. Andrew's Church."

He stared at her for a long moment, then swallowed. "Mrs. Fordham." His voice was rusty, but at least words were coming out. "What an unexpected surprise." Belatedly, he managed a clumsy bow.

"Wholly unexpected," she agreed emphatically, inclining her head. The long, dyed-blue feathers in her hat swayed each time she moved. "I've just been having a conversation with Mrs. Wick—woman to woman, you know—but I shan't detain her any longer. I'm sure you have business to transact."

"Hardly business," he protested. He wasn't sure he liked the sound of that. And he certainly disliked the voice she was using as Mrs. Fordham. But she wasn't attending. Instead, she turned back to the young widow and murmured a few rapid sentences. Mrs. Wick nodded, apparently rather bowled over—by Mary? By the sudden stream of do-gooding callers? By life in general?—and bobbed a string of curtsies, nodding all the while.

The sitting room was narrow. On her way to the door, Mary passed so close that her wide skirts brushed his trouser leg and he caught the fragrance of her lemon soap. He inhaled gently, surreptitiously.

Mary bowed once again, a faint flicker of mischief in those hazel eyes. "Good evening, sir."

"Allow me to help you to your carriage."

Slight alarm flared in her eyes. "How kind of you, but it isn't necessary."

Alarm. He could deal with that. He rather liked that. "I insist." He turned to Mrs. Wick, who was watching with dazzled confusion. "If you could be so kind—two minutes' indulgence . . ." James turned back to Mary and offered his arm, his eyes daring her to flee.

She looked as though she'd rather walk with the devil himself, but she placed her extreme fingertips on his right sleeve. He clamped them in place with his left hand, and her eyes widened. Still, she said nothing. The moment the door closed behind them, he expected her to wrench free.

Instead, she stopped demurely on the pavement. "Thank you, sir. This is my carriage just here."

He pressed down on her gloved hand, wishing he could feel her skin. "What are you playing at, Mary?"

"I beg your pardon?" The voice was still Mrs. Fordham's, but there was a slight quiver at the end that he quite enjoyed.

"I think you'd better tell me what you're up to." He paused, looked into her eyes. "Both here *and* on site."

Her eyes widened.

He grinned.

"I—I must be on my way." She glanced at her coachman, a young fellow who watched them with undisguised interest.

James scowled at him, and he merely smirked in response. Insolent. "Well?"

"Did you follow me here?" The voice was all Mary, now—not Mark, not Mrs. Fordham. He'd not realized how much he'd missed hearing it.

"Answer me first."

She glanced toward the carriage again. "We haven't time right now."

"So out with it."

With a sigh, she tried to pull her hand away.

He curled his fingers around hers and gripped hard—hard enough to hurt.

"Carter!"

The young coachman hopped down from his seat. "Yes, Mrs. Fordham."

James promptly relinquished her hand. "Until tomorrow, Mrs. Fordham."

She didn't reply. But he caught a glimpse of her expression as she mounted the steps to the carriage, and it was both worried and cross. Good.

At least there, they were even.

Fourteen

The early hours of Thursday, 7 July

The Agency's headquarters

The drive back to the Agency was swift and tense—on Mary's part, at least. She couldn't see Felicity, perched atop the carriage, but her imagination was vivid. She saw herself shamed, scolded, sacked. And she had little to say in her own defense, except the stupid-sounding "He didn't seem to recognize me." How could she have been so naive as to hope that? So foolish as to conceal James's presence from the Agency?

Once in the attic office, though, the conversation took an unexpected turn. Rather than reprove Mary, Anne sighed. "I must confess, I worried about your ability to blend invisibly into a building site."

"I thought we did well, considering the pressing nature of the assignment," said Felicity smoothly. A trifle defensively.

Almost without pause, Anne asked Mary, "Have you any suggestions as to how you might explain yourself to Mr. Easton now?"

Mary nodded slowly. "I have an idea. . . . Not an especially good one, I'm afraid, but it's plausible."

"Wait a moment," drawled Felicity, leaning forward. "Even with a beautifully turned, utterly plausible background story, we're rather missing an opportunity here." Both Mary and Anne turned to her with some surprise. "This is the second time you've encountered James Easton. He was rather helpful to you during the Thorold case, was he not?"

"He was." Mary cursed the warmth in her cheeks that must signify a blush.

"And he's certainly curious about your current activities. Even I could see that."

Mary nodded, remembering the smirk on "Carter's" face as she and James bickered on Mrs. Wick's doorstep.

"I think no matter how perfectly you performed as Mark Quinn, he would always have recognized you. He probably knew you straightaway, but was keeping silence for his own reasons."

"I expected him to know me. But when he didn't let on, I thought it best to leave it alone."

"And he's just returned from India. This isn't the sort of small job he'd normally bother with."

"That's right."

"Clever, discreet, and underemployed." Felicity made an elegant gesture with her hands. "Why not recruit him to work for the Agency?"

"What?" gasped Anne.

Mary stared. It was either the best or the worst suggestion she'd ever heard. It might be both.

"Of all the absurd, impulsive, inappropriate schemes!" Anne nearly spat the words. "How utterly nonsensical!"

Bright flags of color appeared on Felicity's cheeks. "How so? Easton demonstrates all the traits we seek in candidates."

"He's . . . why, he's—"

"Male. Is that the problem?"

"Well, it's certainly a problem for the Agency. We were founded on the Scrimshaw Principle: women, who are undervalued and underestimated at every turn, have the advantage when it comes to intelligence work."

"I'm well aware of the Agency's history," said Felicity. "But in this case, Easton has the advantage. He has experience of building sites and a position of authority."

"That's because we had no business accepting this case! We strayed outside the Agency's area of expertise, and this confusion is the consequence. James Easton, whatever his virtues, can play no part in the usual work of the Agency."

"The 'usual work of the Agency,'" drawled Felicity, "bears reconsideration. The current case demonstrates that perfectly. If we cannot accept work—interesting, well-paid, important work—we ought to question our self-imposed limitations. Male agents may be just what we need in order to grow as an organization."

"The current case is not just beyond our scope! It is inimical to our aims."

"Please!" interrupted Mary, standing awkwardly. Anne and Felicity stared at her, startled. They seemed to have forgotten her presence entirely. "I must return to Lambeth. I've a decent story to tell James Easton for the moment, until you—until a decision is made."

Anne swallowed and said, in something approximating her usual tone, "It's very late, Mary. Why don't you stay here until morning? It's quite safe for you to do so."

Mary nodded reluctantly. She had already compromised her seamless existence as Mark Quinn. James Easton had destroyed her cover. It seemed she had nothing to lose by staying one night in her old bed, here at the Agency—while it was still the Agency she knew.

Thursday, 7 July

A long evening, a fierce quarrel, an impending confrontation. Given these three, sleep for Mary came only toward dawn, and she was nearly late for work as a result. Running the last few hundred yards into Westminster, she dodged round a gent in a badly ironed suit, realizing only at the last second who it was.

Octavius Jones tipped his hat to her with a flourish.

"Hello, laddie!" he called loudly. "What have you for me today?"

"Nothing, sir."

"Come, now—a clever boy like you? Tell me something. Anything."

She backed toward the site entrance, step by slow step. "Er—funeral's today, sir."

"You won't get paid for that!" he said with good-natured contempt. "Tell me something that's not public knowledge."

"I don't know what you mean, sir."

"Well, tell me this: what's the new engineer got to say about site safety?"

The wooden fence pressed up against her shoulder blades, but still Jones advanced. It was far from subtle, his trick of standing too close in order to pressure one, but it was effective nonetheless. "Still working, sir. Hasn't told me aught."

"And in all the time you've spent with him, you've surmised nothing?"

Mary wrinkled her brow. "Sur-what, sir?"

"Surmised: Observed. Guessed. *Reckoned*."

"There'll be a reckoning, but not the sort you had in mind," said a caustic voice behind them.

Mary squeezed shut her eyes. Rescue and trouble at the same time.

"I told you to clear off!"

"Mr. Easton!" Jones had his party voice on. "What a

pleasure to see you again; I don't believe we were properly introduced yesterday."

"We never shall be. Now, get off my building site."

"Would it be overly pedantic of me to point out that we're not, in fact, inside the building site?" Jones grinned at James's expression. "I don't suppose I could interest you in giving us an exclusive, sir. No? A pity. Well, I must be off. You mustn't blame young Quinn for talking to me, y'know—I waylaid him, not the reverse. Well, cheerio, then."

The sudden hush as Jones sauntered away was entirely in Mary's head. The street itself was as raucous as ever, but her primary awareness, as she followed James through the site entrance, was of his uncharacteristic and ominous silence. She remembered perfectly well what he'd said yesterday: if he caught her talking to Octavius Jones again, she would be disciplined. He hadn't then let on that he'd recognized her, of course. But she doubted that would make the slightest difference.

James marched into the tower entrance without a glance over his shoulder. Mary followed meekly. It wasn't as though she had a choice. As soon as they were alone, she blurted out, "I can explain."

He didn't seem to hear her. Instead, he stared hard at a spot a few inches over her head and said in a low, taut voice, "Tell me, who the hell are you, really?"

She opened her lips to reply, then paused. It was an excellent question—and right now she had no idea how to answer him. She was Mary Quinn, of course. But also Mary Lang. Secret agent. Orphan. Ex-thief. Ex-teacher. Englishwoman. Half-caste. And she was none of the things she'd represented to him in the past. He had every right to be livid.

"You can't even tell me that?" His voice was bitter. "At least answer me this: is there really a Fordham?"

She blinked, startled. "No. Of course not."

The tension in his jaw eased a little. "And Jones—he's really a journalist?"

"Of sorts; he writes for the *Eye on London*." This wasn't what she'd expected. James's lines of questioning were usually focused, rational. These questions made no sense, unless he was actually jealous . . . and that seemed more like a preposterous hallucination than lucid observation.

"Were you following me last night?"

That, at least, gave her ground to stand on. "How could I have been? I was at the Wicks' house first."

"You could have anticipated where I was going."

"For that matter, you could have followed me." The possibility had cost her some sleep that night.

"Assuming I knew who the hell you are." His words were bitter, but his tone less acid. He was looking at her now, those dark eyes trying to read her mind. "What the devil are you doing on a building site in boy's clothing, Mary? If that's even your name."

"Of course it's my name." It was the only part of her identity she could honestly share with him.

"Well, that's a start, I suppose."

She bit her lower lip. "Do you really want to know why I'm here?"

He made an oddly helpless gesture. "Who wouldn't? Don't you think I feel like an ass? You saved my life last year; you pulled me out of that damned Lascars' refuge. But you don't even trust me enough to tell me what you're doing now."

She hadn't thought about his feelings—not in that way. But he was right. She could at least offer him a coherent, reasonable explanation for her presence here. It was a long way from telling the truth, but it might satisfy him for the moment, even if doing so made her feel wretched. Spying was all very well. She loved disguise and acting and all the covert skills in which she'd been trained. Yet she hated this sort of duplicity, lying to someone whom she—

Mary cut off her train of thought. She couldn't afford to pursue it. And James was, after all, still waiting for an explanation. It was time to produce her story. "I—I'm researching a book." The words sounded foolish the instant they left her lips, but she could hardly backpedal now. "Investigating, I suppose you could say." She paused, waiting for his reaction, not meeting his gaze. When he didn't reply, she stumbled on. "It's about the working poor in London. Whether it's possible to make ends meet on a laborer's wages, and the daily details and textures of an errand boy's life. How they live, really. It's why I'm here right now, as Mark Quinn, and also why I was at Wick's house, nosing about in the guise of a rich, charitable lady."

James's eyes widened as he listened, but unlike many others, he always listened in silence. He was intent on her every word and when she stopped—she couldn't bear to string out the lie—he let out a long, low whistle. "Never dull, are you?"

She smiled crookedly. "That's quite a compliment, coming from a man who's just returned from India, survived malaria, and been appointed to this safety review."

He waved his hand impatiently. "But I'm just a stick-in-the-mud professional man. What you're doing is really radical! I mean, Henry Mayhew does those interviews of poor Londoners in the *Chronicle*, of course. But for someone, especially a woman, actually to live the life? That's original."

She cringed. As though she hadn't felt fraudulent enough without his excitement and admiration. And what would she do when he asked to read her work in progress? Then, with a pang of regret, she remembered she would no longer be in contact with James at that point. This was a cover story to protect the assignment. Once it was over, she would have to take care not to run into James again if she valued her work as a secret agent. "I'm not sure whether it'll work out. . . ." she demurred.

"I've wondered about the life of an errand boy. How do people treat you?" A new thought occurred to him, and he frowned. "You must often be in situations that are dangerous for a lady."

"Oh . . ." Despite her best intentions, Mary found herself warming under his protective scrutiny. "I manage."

"I'm sure you do." He looked her up and down, slowly, carefully, and she felt a deep, tingling blush begin at her toes. It was all very well running about in breeches when others supposed you male, but now she felt distinctly underdressed. "Trousers become you," he murmured.

"Had—" She cleared her throat. "Hadn't we better get to work?"

He grinned. "The correct response, when one is complimented, is 'Thank you.' You've not forgotten your manners already, young lady?"

"That's not the sort of compliment one pays to a lady."

"I'm so sorry. I don't think the etiquette manuals cover this sort of situation." He leaned in close, his lips all but grazing her neck, and inhaled. "Mmm. You smell good, too."

She nearly choked. Took a step backward, until her back met cold stone. "Th-thank you."

"That's better. May I kiss you?" His finger dipped into her shirt collar, stroking the tender nape of her neck.

"I d-don't th-think that's a good idea."

"Why not? We're alone." His hands were at her waist.

Her lungs felt tight and much too small. "Wh-what if somebody comes in?"

He considered for a moment. "Well, I suppose they'll think I fancy grubby little boys."

At that she burst out laughing, and the shift in mood lent her strength to push him away slightly. "I've another question: when did you recognize me?"

He released her with visible reluctance. "Immediately, of course."

"But you didn't let on! Why not?"

He grinned, a little shyly. "No. I thought I'd see how things unfolded."

"So you might have completed the review and disappeared, all without saying anything?"

"Would you have been disappointed?"

"Answer my question first."

"Of course not. I was just choosing my moment. And you?"

"Oh, I'd have been deeply disappointed in your intelligence."

"Is that all?" He laughed.

She smiled. "Perhaps."

"Any more questions?"

"Yes. Are we to do any work today?"

"Have you become duller since we last met?"

"Yes," she said primly.

His charming grin flashed again—illness hadn't changed that, at least—and then he turned serious. "I suppose the next order of business is to inspect the belfry."

As they ascended, their pace gradually slowed from brisk to measured—imperceptibly at first, then unmistakably. Mary glanced at his face and was unsurprised to see his cheeks flushed and a slight frown between his eyebrows.

He caught her looking. "Don't tell me you're tired."

She shook her head. "I'm fine."

Another thirty steps and his breathing was distinctly audible: measured, but with a breathless edge. Mary risked another quick look and again, he immediately noticed her concern. "What?"

"What d'you mean, 'What?'"

"Why d'you keep staring at me?"

Fine. If that's how he meant to play it. "Perhaps I'm just admiring your Roman profile."

He smirked. "'Roman' is a nice euphemism for broken nose." They climbed another dozen steps. "A nose you helped to shape," he reminded her.

She grinned at the recollection of their first fight—a fistfight. As the shorter, weaker party she'd lost, of course, but she'd held out for a decent length of time. "Anybody as high-handed and arrogant as you are ought to expect the occasional broken nose."

He snorted with amusement, which immediately led to a fit of coughing. It wasn't an ordinary sort of cough, but a prolonged, wheezy hacking which halted their progress. His face turned scarlet, he steadied himself against the wall, and eventually he sank down to a crouch on the steps. Mary put out a hand toward him; he swatted it away impatiently.

As the coughing subsided, his breathing became somewhat easier. "Phew." Fishing out a handkerchief, he mopped a light mist of sweat from his forehead. He attempted a smile, but his eyes were watering. "You were saying?"

She couldn't remember and didn't care. "Is this an aftereffect of malarial fever?"

He shrugged. "Suppose so."

"It's not something new — like pneumonia, or bronchitis?"

"Certainly not," he said with a scowl.

"But it's made worse by overexertion?"

"Stop fussing."

"A couple of questions is hardly fussing. I just wondered whether you're ill."

"You're not my mother."

"Thank God for that."

He glared at her and pushed himself to his feet. She could see the effort involved: he moved as though all his limbs were weighted down. "I'm fine."

"Ooh . . . very convincing."

"I'm not going to spend all day arguing in a stairwell. Are you coming up or not?" Without waiting for a reply, he resumed the climb. This time, however, he was gripping the handrail.

Mary stared up at his receding form. He *was* thin; from this angle, it was obvious that his suit was too big—the jacket hanging loose from broad shoulders, the trousers roomier than was fashionable. He must have lost a great deal of strength as well as weight. She followed him meekly for another dozen steps or so, then said in a conversational tone, "We're less than one-third of the way there."

"I know."

It was a slow ascent, and when they reached the landing at the one-third point, he stopped to wipe his forehead and neck again. She stood quietly, unsure what to do. Showing concern or offering advice would doubtless result only in the same mulish denial. Not that she was in a position to criticize; it was a trait she recognized in herself. So she simply leaned against the wall and didn't look at him.

James's breathing, rapid and shallow, was the loudest sound in the room. The belfry was still some two hundred steps above them, the artisans and laborers in Palace Yard several stories below. The rough brick was cool against Mary's cheek, and she closed her eyes for a moment, letting her thoughts drift. Bricks—mortar—Keenan—thrashing. Her eyes popped open again, and she glanced around the landing, seeing it properly for the first time. It was surprisingly spacious, apparently designed as a sort of resting place, although there was no seating yet. After this point, the stairs seemed to narrow and—yes, of course . . . why hadn't she thought of this before?

She whirled around to address James. "Has anyone said what Wick was doing in the belfry?"

His eyes were pinched shut, as though against pain. "No." Then, with a certain reluctant curiosity, "Why?"

"Look at the next flight of steps: the walls are built of stone. If that continues, there's no reason for a bricklayer to have been working up there."

His eyes snapped open. "That continues all the way up?"

"We'll see. But none of the brickies works this high up."

He nodded, animation returning. "Certainly. And the glaziers should be able to give a fair account of how they left things that night." He looked warily at the narrow staircase curling upward, out of sight. "Er—perhaps you ought to go up ahead of me."

"I have a better idea: lean on me as you go up."

He seemed nonplussed. "But—I—you—"

She took his hand and set it on her shoulder. "Like a walking stick; so."

He jerked his hand away as though scalded. "I can't!"

"Why? Because I'm female?"

"I can't just *use* you as a *prop*. . . ."

"Of course you can; think of me as a twelve-year-old boy named Mark." She captured his hand and replaced it. "I'm fairly strong for my size, you know."

He recoiled once again. "That's hardly the point."

"I thought the point was to get to the top of the stairs,"

she said, not bothering to hide her impatience. "How else are you going to manage that?"

"I'll just have to try harder."

"Ooh, yes—sheer stubborn stupidity should certainly carry the day."

They glared at each other with genuine irritation. Then, after several long moments, James sighed ruefully. "Pot and kettle, eh?"

She offered him a half smile. "I'd be the same if our positions were reversed."

"I know."

There was an awkward pause and then he said, "Well. Shall we?"

He followed her up the first few stairs, his hand barely resting on her shoulder. As they ascended, Mary felt him begin to lean into her frame. It was subtle at first, mainly on the step up. With each story gained, though, the weight of his hand became heavier, his breathing more labored. Their pace slowed, and eventually, he began to rest every few steps.

"Don't worry," he rasped when they came to one such stop. " 'S not contagious."

"I know."

"Desperately unfit. Been on bed rest for months."

She nodded. He must have been gravely ill; James wasn't the sort to tolerate bed rest unless he was actually too weak to crawl.

"Soon be back to normal."

Incredible—the most arrogant man alive was actually apologizing for his weakness. Not directly, of course, but the sentiment was there. She was half-afraid to think of what it might—or might not—signify.

They climbed. And climbed. And continued to climb. It was a shock, finally, to round a curve into a large room filled with dazzling light. Mary squinted and blinked, and as her eyes adjusted, she realized she was looking at a wall of glass and wrought iron—a vast mosaic with each pane of glass thick and pearly bright, the smallest of them about the size of her head. They were beautifully ordered, pieced together in a balanced, intricate circle. As she tilted her head back to take in the full pattern, she gasped.

It was the back of one of the clock faces! From the ground they appeared flat and white, like painted surfaces. But seen from behind they were astonishingly luminous, refracting and softening the stingy yellow-gray daylight into something quite unearthly. She stared dreamily, forgetting where or who she was. When she came to with a start, she had no idea how long she'd been entranced. Half a minute? Half an hour?

And there was still so much to see. A long table at the center of the room supported a sprawling engine, a complicated tangle of gears, cranks, and shafts that drove the clock. It was surprisingly quiet; it didn't tick, in the manner of a wrist-watch, although there was the constant whisper of well-greased metal parts turning one against another.

The final flight of steps, numbering perhaps fifty, took them up to the belfry. There, suspended from an enormous framework in the rafters, were the bells; the reason they'd climbed the tower. All of London remembered the embarrassment and disappointment the previous year when the great bell was first tolled. There had been a glorious parade in which "Big Ben" was brought to New Palace Yard, drawn by sixteen white horses. But soon afterward it had cracked and was taken down, broken up, and recast. Its replacement—still dubbed Big Ben—had been installed. But given the recent question of site safety, it was James's responsibility to inspect everything once more before it could be rung.

The four quarter-bells were enormous, judged by human scale. But they, in turn, were dwarfed by Big Ben. From Mary's perspective, this massive central bell was a dark cave large enough for several people to hide in. She blinked and instinctively stepped back, out of its span. It ought to be firmly fixed in place, of course, but James's very presence here suggested otherwise. And there was something sinister about the bell, too—this metal beast that had cracked, been melted and recast, and raised again only to witness a man's death.

A strong breeze wafted through the belfry, and Mary moved toward its source: the huge open arches, one on each side of the tower, which allowed the weather in and the sound of the bells out. What she saw made her gasp and instinctively steady herself against the stone half wall: the city sprawled before her in all directions, vast and miniaturized at the same time. It was recognizably London—the buildings, the cobwebs of streets, the rowdy bustle that rose, almost visibly, from the place. But it was also London as a toy village; an exquisite map. Viewed from here, all the familiar monuments were scaled down to the size of her fingernail yet retained every detail. A slight dizziness consumed her as she gazed out over the rooftops, reluctant even to blink lest the magical sight dissipate. She had never seen the like before and doubted she would again.

Glancing at James, she saw her own expression reflected in his face. He smiled at her and she could see he would have spoken—something tender, something intimate. She collected herself. It was too dangerous to play with James this way. It wasn't fear just for her cover as Mark Quinn but for her entire existence as a secret agent. She stepped back from the ledge, reeling. It wasn't the height at all, but he didn't need to know that.

"How on earth was the bell raised?" Her voice sounded overbright.

He looked at her. Hesitated. Then said, slowly, "Pulley systems and manpower. Straight through there."

"There" was a square opening, perhaps eight feet wide. Mary peered inside. It appeared to run the height of the tower. "Is this for ventilation?"

"Yes—the central air shaft. The bell nearly didn't fit,

but I don't think the original designers had any idea how large it would be."

She nodded. "It must have been an enormous task."

"It took days, with teams of men working in shifts. But you know all this, don't you, Mary? As part of your background research?"

She shrugged. "It's better to hear it from someone knowledgeable."

"And to fill silence, when you'd rather avoid conversation?"

She couldn't meet his gaze. "I need to understand this job fully. And hadn't we better get on with things?"

Fifteen

For someone of her age, Mary's experience of funerals was slight. There were always funeral processions in the streets, of course: immaculate hearses drawn by glossy black horses and followed by a train of crepe-swathed carriages. Depending on the cost of the funeral, there were often mutes—paid mourners—marching stolidly beside the hearse and precarious heaps of hothouse flowers about the polished coffin. There were humbler funerals, too—perhaps a hearse pulled by a single horse, with only a couple of carriages following. Although such a display was considered meager, the cost could still bankrupt a working family, consigning its survivors to the workhouse. This happened often, yet the tradition continued. The poor, especially, were reluctant to forgo in death what they could not afford in life.

Some enjoyed taking notes, totting up the cost of a dozen long-faced mutes plus six dozen forced white roses. Mary was not among them. Her mother had refused to give up hope for her father, lost at sea, and rejected any ritual that presumed his death. And when her mother's own turn came, a few short years later, they hadn't had the means for a coffin, let alone a funeral. She'd been shoveled grudgingly into a pauper's grave, the site marked only by a pathetic wooden cross made by Mary herself—back when she thought such things carried significance. So she'd lost both parents and seen hundreds of funeral processions in her life, but had somehow escaped attending a funeral service. It was thus with some trepidation that she slipped away from the building site and toward Southwark. Although the inquest had been adjourned, still awaiting James's safety report, the coroner had seen fit to release the body. That was fortunate. Although this July was cool, unlike the heat wave last year that led to the Great Stink, it was still midsummer.

The street on which the Wick family lived—for how much longer, now that its breadwinner was dead?—looked grimy and diminished in the presence of the rather splendid hearse. To this were hitched a pair of black mares, their bridles a suitably dull black, and an oddly jaunty headdress of black feathers atop each horse's mane. Behind the hearse waited two large carriages. The door of the house stood open, its crepe bow renewed and enlarged for the important day.

The neighbors were all at their windows, of course—she could see curtains twitching all up and down the street—but none would take note of a nosy lad behaving like a nosy lad. The Wick house was already full of women, she could see that much, wearing somber colors rather than mourning. Friends and neighbors, then, who wouldn't attend the funeral itself but were there to help with that formidable pack of children. Mary found a spot on the corner that afforded a good view of the house and its approach, and settled in there.

She hadn't long to wait. In half an hour or so, a small company of men made their way down the street, walking in single file at a dignified pace. Their leader was a tall, angry-looking dark-haired man whose black suit, a good deal too small, stretched painfully across his broad back: Keenan. Reid followed in somber gray, his fair hair slicked down with pomade, which made it appear much darker. The hod carriers Smith and Stubbs were, like Reid, not in full mourning.

At the door, Keenan hesitated before stepping inside. He had the air of a man about to enter a new place, where the only thing he could be sure of was danger. It was odd, considering what great friends he had been with Wick. Or so one assumed. Mary realized that Keenan alone, in the brickie gang, seemed affected by the loss of Wick. Reid had his own motives, of course: his obvious affection for Mrs. Wick meant he was still the prime suspect in any theory of Wick's death involving violence. But the hod carriers seemed little moved by the man's death—outwardly, anyway. It was possible that in private they were deeply shaken while maintaining a brave façade. But the marked contrast between Keenan's black mourning and the other men's Sunday suits suggested otherwise.

The door closed behind them. After another half hour's delay, it swung open and the four men reappeared, this time shouldering the coffin between them. They marched smoothly, in step, as though they'd rehearsed this precise maneuver with care. Perhaps they had; perhaps it was the unintentional result of their laboring together every day. They transferred the coffin to the hearse with a minimum of fuss, placing it on something of a dais surrounded by bunches of greenery. Fixed to the top of the coffin was a small arrangement of white roses in the shape of a cross.

Coffin in place, the men returned to the doorway of the house but this time remained outside until the widow Wick came into view. Mourning dress made her appear paler and thinner than ever, and even from Mary's distance it was clear that she was feeling unwell. She took a few faltering steps, then paused. The sight of the coffin, mounted on the hearse for its final journey, seemed to make an impression upon her. She stared, eyes wide, mouth working. A moment later, she sank soundlessly toward the ground.

Reid caught her before she fell, his arms flashing out to raise her before the other men had even noticed her distress. Keenan's habitual scowl spasmed with strong emotion—anger?—then smoothed out into a carefully impassive expression. He waited while the neighbors revived Mrs. Wick with fans and smelling salts, taking her from Reid's arms and supporting her wasted frame against their shoulders.

Then, another attempt. The girlish widow set her face, clenched tight her black-gloved fists, and walked to the first carriage, where she was helped up by the hired attendant. Following respectfully, the four men climbed into the second carriage. And that was that. Within a minute, the entire procession was under way.

Following the funeral train was rather more awkward than it sounded. To begin with, the hearse and carriages moved at a glacial pace, much more slowly than other vehicles and pedestrians. There was the difficulty, too, of showing proper respect. Most people turned to acknowledge the passing of the hearse, hats removed and heads bowed. At the very least, they stopped their activity, whether furious or lackadaisical, for the minutes it took the hearse and carriages to pass. And through these motionless tableaux, Mary had to move. It was as well that she was still dressed as a child, a boy who couldn't be expected to behave properly or empathize with the scene he was witnessing. All the same, she worried about drawing attention to herself. She was bound to be recognized if spotted by one of the bricklayers, and didn't like her chances of explaining herself to Keenan yet again.

Had it been raining, her task would have been easier: general vision obscured, pedestrians skulking beneath umbrellas. But this afternoon, the dirty gray skies only pressed down upon the rooftops, promising rain at some unspecified time to come. The horses plodded on, enforcing a relative quiet in the streets through which they passed. Even in Southwark Bridge Road, where the breadth of the avenue dwarfed the coffin, the hearse, its followers, and, by implication, its entire significance—even in such a busy road, there was a discernible slowing of activity. Such general courtesy would be rather gratifying if the mourners were the sort to take note of such matters.

Eventually, the procession wound its way into narrower streets once more. When it halted before a small Methodist chapel, Mary realized with some surprise that they were only a few streets from Wick's house. Apparently, the procession had been largely a matter of form, to satisfy the desire for proper rites—or perhaps to squeeze some value from the expensive hire of a hearse and two carriages. But they were now outside the church nearest the Wick house. From what she'd learned of Wick, he hadn't been the church-going type. But perhaps his widow was: any woman burdened with such a family would surely have need of prayer.

Mary watched with genuine interest as the attendants prepared to let down the carriage steps. Although ladies did not view funerals, being too delicate, too emotional, too easily undone, to witness such scenes, working women were different—at least according to popular wisdom. If Mrs. Wick was strong enough to prepare her husband's body for burial, she was capable of attending his funeral.

However, only the bricklayers stepped onto the pavement, solemnly straightening their Sunday suits, and shouldered the coffin once more. Instead of carrying it into the chapel proper, the four men walked it around the building toward the graveyard. Their smooth progress faltered at the gate. One of the hod carriers—Mary couldn't tell which, from behind—seemed to waver a little, and the coffin bobbed slightly, its floral wreath slipping to one side. There seemed to be some hasty muttered conference among the pallbearers, during which Reid glanced back toward the carriages, an anxious expression creasing his face. Then, with renewed solemnity, they marched forward once more.

It wasn't until they passed through the gate that Mary saw the cause of this disturbance: a portly figure in a dark suit, clutching an umbrella. He stood beside the open grave, a strange, shuttered expression on his broad face. She couldn't cross to their side of the street without becoming conspicuous. But she could see that no words passed between Harkness and Keenan, despite the compounded rage on the latter's face. The four men placed the coffin on a sort of table erected for the purpose, then spaced themselves widely around it, allowing for a meaningful gap between them and Harkness. As an attempt to make the group seem larger, this failed dismally. It was pathetically clear that few cared to see John Wick into the next world.

The minister, trotting neatly down the walk with a

bible clasped between his hands, seemed struck by the sparseness of the gathering. He slowed and peered for just a moment before resuming his sedate pace, his somber expression. As he cleared his throat to begin, Reid glanced fleetingly toward the carriages once more. He couldn't have seen Mrs. Wick. It was only a nervous reflex, suppressed the very instant it was enacted. But Keenan scowled at him nonetheless.

The service was brief. A short speech, an even shorter reading—New Testament, judging from the open place in the book—and no hymn. In rather less than ten minutes, two attendants were expertly looping lengths of rope about the coffin and slowly lowering it into the open grave. The four—no, five—mourners watched the first shovelful of earth drop onto the casket, damp and clumpy. There was no echo, of course, but it looked as though there ought to have been. After a suitable pause, the gravedigger tugged his cap and nodded once. This was the point at which the affair ended, leaving him to his solitary task.

The bricklayers seemed to understand this. But Harkness, his eyes fixed on the grave, didn't seem to notice the brittle atmosphere of expectation surrounding him. His gaze was fierce in its sightlessness, his thoughts clearly miles from this ugly bare graveyard in south London. The seconds stretched out endlessly. It was a full minute before Keenan's low growl, audible even to Mary across the street, shook him from his meditations. With a rattled look, Harkness murmured something—three syllables, four at most. Mary was practiced at lipreading, but the combination of Harkness's fulsome beard and the angle of his stance defeated her here. All she knew was that it wasn't the traditional "God bless you." A moment later, without looking at the bricklayers, Harkness turned on his heel and marched away.

Expressionless, the four men watched him go. Now that both Wick, their comrade, and Harkness, their common adversary, were gone, they seemed rather at a loss, as though requiring an external reason to stay united. They left the graveyard in a shuffling, disorganized manner far removed from their earlier, almost-martial discipline and scrambled into the waiting carriage for the return journey. They didn't retrace the route of the formal procession, instead returning directly to the Wicks'.

Mary considered what she'd just seen. An expensive but otherwise minimal funeral for a man whose death few seemed to regret. Confirmation of Reid's tenderness for Mrs. Wick. Harkness's seemingly extraordinary attachment to a dead bricklayer, in the face of bristling suspicion from the man's friends and colleagues. It didn't amount to much, put like that. Yet something about the charged atmosphere—something unspoken but lurking behind all those carefully composed expressions—was very wrong. There was a storm coming. An explosion of some sort. And she still couldn't tell where from.

It seemed daft to stand outside Wick's house, where the funeral tea was just beginning. She ought really to return to the building site. Yet she continued to loiter at the street corner, watching the bricklayers and Mrs. Wick—helped down from the carriage by Reid, who'd brushed past the waiting attendant—reenter the house. The female neighbors would be inside, preparing food and keeping the children calm. The meal could go on for ages yet. All the same, Mary prepared herself for a long wait. She could justify it rationally, of course: additional mourners, those who couldn't afford to forfeit an afternoon's wages, might turn up. They might, in turn, lead to additional knowledge of Wick's character. But beyond all that, something like blind instinct told her to wait. And so she did.

It was a good three hours and nearing dusk before something happened, but that something was even more dramatic than she'd imagined. A handful of friends had indeed rolled in through the late afternoon, and the babble of voices and clinking of crockery had increased in volume. But suddenly, there came sharp, distinct voices raised in anger. It was a genuine quarrel between Keenan and Reid, and it escalated for several minutes, despite placating noises from others—mostly female and, Mary guessed, not Mrs. Wick. It was truly raucous now: a vicious-sounding scrap, male voices barking and snarling like savage animals, that made passersby turn and stare in brief wonderment.

A few minutes later, the front door burst open, tearing off one of the hinges, and two bodies tumbled out, already locked together in passionate rage. Mary stepped back, tucking herself neatly behind a lamppost. The gesture was totally unnecessary. Neither Reid nor Keenan was likely to notice if Queen Victoria herself came strolling down the narrow street.

It was a fight in earnest, no mere display or posturing but a battle between two men who had passed from trust into hatred. Keenan was the larger man and ought to have had the advantage. But Reid fought with grim determination. He seldom missed an opportunity to land a punch, and each blow was placed with care and strategy.

The battle ended only when Mrs. Wick ran out of the house, stumbling slightly as she came, and dived between the two men. "Stop! Stop it!" she cried, a desperate expression on her narrow, pale face.

The two men reared back in shock, as though dashed with cold water.

"You call yourselves friends of John's, and this is what you do? You come to his house and you fight like dogs, a-shaming me before the neighbors?" She was quite breathless and held one hand protectively over her belly. "How dare you?"

Reid opened his mouth to protest, to explain, but a sharp gesture from her stopped him midbreath. Keenan scowled at the road, panting but otherwise silent.

The three figures stood like statues in the dusty road, oblivious of all around them: of the neighbors, young and old, peering out doors and windows with avid hunger; of the friends in Wick's house, urging them inside; of the frightened tears and babble of the children, clamoring for their mother. All this they ignored.

Finally, Mrs. Wick spoke in a low, trembling voice. "You got no call to be a-quarrelling over Wick's money. It was his money, and now it's mine, and I'll spend it as I like. *You*—" She stabbed a finger at Keenan, who stood there, sullen and stolid. "You mind your own business. You got your wage and the other money besides, a bigger share than Wick ever got, I daresay, and I ain't never said a word. And *you*"—she rounded on Reid, who flinched as from a blow—"you got no call to speak for me." She was panting as she finished this speech.

By now, Reid and Keenan each had something of the disciplined schoolboy about them, one surly and unresponsive, the other shuffling his feet and not daring to meet her gaze.

Mrs. Wick folded her arms, a gesture both protective and defiant. "Get thee gone." When the two men only gaped stupidly at her, she stamped her foot. "Go on! You got no right to be here, a-spoiling everything and teaching the children your bad ways." Reid looked at her, wounded as a puppy, but she stuck out her jaw stubbornly. "Go, then, the both of you!"

In silence, Reid and Keenan made their departures. Keenan moved with care, planting each foot squarely before transferring his body weight—a walk very unlike his usual gait. He must have had a great deal to drink. Reid followed mechanically, unable to stop glancing over his shoulder to where Mrs. Wick stood, arms folded. After a minute, though, he shook his head angrily and sped up, swerving neatly around Keenan and disappearing down the street.

Mary let out a long, shaky exhalation. She'd not realized she'd been holding her breath. Her fingers, too, tingled from being clenched tight. That was what she'd waited to see. What "other money" had the widow meant, precisely? It was clear enough now that Keenan, Reid, and Wick were all "on the take"; possible, too, that the hod carriers were involved. No wonder Keenan was slow to engage a replacement for Wick. It wasn't a simple matter of finding a competent brickie; it meant finding someone they could trust.

Someone bent.

Someone like them.

Sixteen

Mary's final stop this evening was Peter Jenkins's cellar. As she picked her way through the stinking cesspools of Bermondsey, the air grew thicker and more humid, coating her throat with dust. The weather-beaten door was slightly ajar tonight, and no one answered her knock. She rapped again, then pushed the door open. "Hello?"

No reply. Inside was still and quiet, sticky and fetid. She let her eyes adjust to the dim light before advancing. Still nobody. She made her way to the cellar hatch, half holding her breath. The hatch was already propped open, and she stared down for a moment into the cellar's murky depths. "Jenkins? You there?"

Again, no reply. With a sigh, she prepared to climb down the rotting ladder. She hoped that this would be the last time. The Academy should surely help Jenkins's father meet the cost of clean, safe lodgings. Her foot was on the top rung when somebody shrieked in her ear, "Get out of my house!"

"Gah!" Mary jumped, nearly tumbling down the ladder. Something swiped at her face—something foul and prickly—and she batted it away, spitting in disgust. It was the straw end of a broom.

As it clattered to the floor, she saw the hunchbacked old woman who'd opened the door to her last time. She was clearly terrified, and now she flew at Mary, gnarled claws seeking to tear out her eyes. "Get out! Get out!"

"I knocked!" shouted Mary, twisting away from those cold, crooked fingers. "I'm here to see Jenkins!"

"Get! I ain't got naught to steal, nohow!"

"I'm not here to steal! Nobody answered when I knocked!"

Eventually, the old woman stopped her feeble attack, exhausted. "Young man," she croaked, a terrible, helpless expression on her face, "I ain't got nothing. You see for yourself. There ain't nothing for to take."

Mary shook her head. "I'm not a thief," she said again, enunciating clearly. "I'm here to see Peter Jenkins."

"Eh?"

"Peter Jenkins!" shouted Mary. She pointed to the cellar. "The boy!"

The old woman shook her head. "Ain't nobody lives down there, lad."

"Peter Jenkins lives there," insisted Mary, "with his family."

The old woman shook her head again. "The lad Jenkins moved out yesterday morn. Took the babies with him."

"Where did he go?"

The woman shrugged. "Somewhere better, I suppose. Ain't much worse out there."

Mary privately agreed. "You don't know where he went? Was it nearby?"

"He just up and went. Didn't say nothing."

That couldn't possibly be good news. Yet . . . "What about his father? Did he go, too?"

"His pa?" The woman looked at Mary, confused. But her eyes were clear and alert, and her mind certainly didn't seem to be wandering. "He ain't got no pa."

"Yes, he has. He's a joiner or something, isn't he?"

She shook her head. "He ain't nothing. Jimmy Jenkins been dead these past two years."

Friday, 8 July

Coral Street, Lambeth

Despite her concern for Peter Jenkins, Mary slept better that night than she had since arriving at Miss Phlox's. It was a combination, she decided, of exhaustion and experience. Even Rogers's bed-shaking snores hadn't spoiled her rest. Once he'd left the room, she swung her legs over the side of the bed and stretched sore muscles. Did she have time for a wash? She investigated the amount of fresh water in the jug by the washstand and had just decided she did when the door banged open and somebody staggered into the narrow room. It was Winnie, the maid. She was lugging a mop and bucket.

At the sight of Mary, Winnie's eyes widened and she blushed fiercely. "P-pardon," she managed to say after a few seconds. "I thought—I didn't—I never knew you was in here. You ain't come in for a couple nights."

Mary shrugged. "Sometimes I stay with friends."

Winnie nodded. She was staring at Mary again, in that fixed way of hers, and showed no signs of leaving.

Mary began to pull on her boots. Apparently, any sort of wash would have to wait.

"Where?"

"What d'you mean, 'Where?'"

Winnie's gaze was fixed on the floor, which she mopped with careful, vigorous strokes. "Where do your friends live? Limehouse? Poplar?"

It was hardly a subtle approach; everyone knew that east London had significant south Asian and southeast Asian populations. Mary had spent all week dreading this moment. But now that Winnie had finally found the courage to ask, however clumsily, it seemed foolish to dissemble. "No," she said. "In St. John's Wood." Winnie's expression—what she could see of it—was carefully still. "They're not Chinese, although my father was."

Winnie's head snapped up, delight stretching her normally downturned features into an eager smile. A rapid-fire string of questions, all in Cantonese, poured from her lips.

This was the bit Mary hated, and no small part of the reason she always dodged questions about her race. "I'm sorry," she said, shaking her head. "I don't understand you."

Winnie's mouth fell open in an expression of dismay so foolish it was difficult not to smile. "You don't understand your own language?"

"No," said Mary firmly. She had no intention of entering into explanation or apology.

"But your father—he did not teach you?"

"He's dead."

"And your mother . . . ?"

"Dead. And a *gwei lo*." That was about all the Cantonese she knew. And she'd got the inflection wrong.

"Ohhh . . ."

The pity in Winnie's voice was both moving and irksome, and Mary was glad for a reason to leave. She shrugged on her jacket and said, "I mayn't be back tonight." The last thing she wanted was Winnie creating an opportunity to question her further.

She stalked from the lodging house in a bitter mood. People were so damned nosy, so obsessively intent on categorizing and classifying. She would forever be plagued by that question or variations thereon, and there would never be a satisfactory way to answer. If she was untruthful, it was a denial of her blood. If she met the question directly, she became an object of pity or a lesser species; a mongrel. The only reasonable solution was to do the very thing she'd done for years: keep her head down, often literally, and avoid the issue entirely.

For the thousandth time, she wondered what her father would have done. He'd been a brave man, a clever man, highly regarded in their little community. Mary had learned, just the previous year, that he'd perished trying to uncover a truth; ironically, the details of his life and death were so lost to her, she didn't even know what about. But when she'd made that limited, all-transforming discovery, it had affirmed her resolve to work for the Agency.

To uncover truths.

To serve the truth.

To live a life worthy of her father's approval.

The jade pendant he'd left for her—the only thing that had survived the fire at the Lascars' refuge, and her sole memento of childhood—was curled safely in a drawer at the Academy. It was her most precious belonging. There still remained the problem of how to reconcile that pendant, a talisman of her Chinese heritage, with her equally powerful desire to bury entirely the question of her race. But she would have time enough to think of that once she was Mary, just Mary, again.

Seventeen

Palace Yard, Westminster

It was an odd, sluggish, unbalanced sort of morning, with heavy air pressure and little prospect of the much-needed storm. Keenan didn't turn up for work at all, to general puzzlement and Reid's poorly disguised relief. It was less certain how Harkness viewed this absence. He ought to be livid, demand an explanation, discipline such a sloppy foreman. But nothing in Harkness's treatment of Keenan so far made this likely. If anything, Harkness seemed to avoid looking in the brickies' direction altogether in order to avoid the fact of Keenan's absence.

The site engineer seemed to have had a bad night: he was waxy of complexion and the half-moons beneath his eyes were a deep purple, rather than the usual greeny-gray. He had a habit of rubbing his fingers through his beard when anxious, and today there were times when he appeared to be grooming himself like an ape, so frequently did he rake the hair on his chin. And there was the nervous twitch. Always that twitch. Certainly Harkness was suffering. But the untimely death of one unpopular worker would never explain the extent of his anxiety. No: his concerns were clearly much larger than any sort of petty crime or disciplinary problem on site.

The new Houses of Parliament were notoriously unlucky. One of its designers, the brilliant A. W. N. Pugin, had died some seven years before, and its architect, Sir Charles Barry, was said to be unwell, made ill by the strain of working on the palace. Now, with blame being redirected toward the site engineer, Harkness certainly had cause to look and feel unwell: a building twenty-five years behind schedule, a budget swollen to several times its original estimate, a dead bricklayer, and a safety review that might implicate him as the man responsible for these problems. Taken together, Harkness's difficulties made the *Eye on London*'s fanciful "curse of the clock tower" seem almost rational.

Mary was among the last of the laborers to depart Palace Yard at the dinner hour. She'd been working steadily with James, making notes, taking measurements, generally being a good little errand boy. Now, as she trailed the narrow file of men through the entrance gate, her attention was snagged by a distinct change in Reid's posture. This morning, he'd been tense and reluctant. When Keenan hadn't appeared, he'd turned watchful and wary. Now, though, he was alert and purposeful, moving with an athlete's deliberate grace toward the site entrance. And from the expression on his face, he wasn't thinking about his dinner.

He was so preoccupied that he left without cleaning his hands. Reid's careful hand washing was the subject of some chivvying from others, and was something about which he was particular. Each day, before dinner and before going home, he splashed his hands and forearms liberally with water from the rain barrel and dried them carefully on a threadbare towel hanging from a rusty nail. But today he glanced neither at the rain barrel nor at the two hod carriers with whom he normally ate.

Mary followed him to a busy coffee shop across Parliament Square from which wafted an intense aroma of hot pastry. Inside, twenty-five or thirty men were wedged into a space intended for half that number. They seemed content with their lot nevertheless, tucking into enormous platefuls of food: pie and peas, pie and potatoes, pie and pie . . . Her stomach rumbled fiercely.

She slowed her pace just outside the shop. Its open windows vibrated with boisterous conversation and sharp barks of laughter, these deeper sounds ornamented with the bright clatter of forks. Among this relaxed bunch, Reid's single-minded intent was only too evident as he picked his way through the crush of bodies, promptly disappearing from view.

Mary prepared to wait. She crossed the street and bought her dinner from the outdoor stall that looked nearest to clean: a hot potato, still in its jacket. There was nowhere to sit, of course, but she didn't mind. She quite liked to lean against lampposts, lounge on walls—manners severely discouraged in young ladies but essential to street urchins. The dinner hour was at its peak now, with working men and women dining according to their budgets. Those with the most money went to coffee shops like the one Reid had chosen, where one could sit down to a hot cooked meal. Public houses appealed to those who preferred to drink their sustenance, downing a few pints of ale with, perhaps, covert bites of a smuggled-in slab of bread-and-butter. There were also the bakeshops, which sold pies and other savories to be eaten elsewhere—"elsewhere" meaning the street. Cheapest of all were the street vendors, like Mary's potato woman, with her tumbledown stall and hoarse cry of "'Ot-pitaaaaaaytoes, nice 'n' 'ot!" One could buy slabby boiled puddings, elderly scraps rolled up in pastry, or even fried things—chunks of anonymous fish, for example—according to appetite and budget.

There were those who couldn't afford the street stalls, of course. If they waited until day's end, a generous coffee-shop owner might offer them a handful of scraps—trimmings, kitchen sweepings, anything that couldn't be resold another day. Or they could take matters into their own hands and, as a friend from Mary's vagabond days put it, "make their own prices." It wasn't difficult to pinch food, especially with an associate. Confectioners were easy, since they put yesterday's goods out on tables to entice passing trade. And loose fruit was as good as windfall. But hot wares were trickiest, since they were kept covered, and Mary never outgrew her yearning for cooked meals. Even a badly roasted potato, burned outside and grainy at the core, was better for being warm.

She finished her potato, which was not burned, and contemplated a second course. But the dinner hour was passing fast and the coffee shop across the road emptying of customers. They strolled to the door, those men, sleepy and replete, and stepped onto the pavement with an air of awaking from a pleasant dream. It was time to take another look.

The first man Mary recognized was Octavius Jones, sprawled easily at a corner table in a high-backed chair, an open notebook before him. This must be his favored coffee shop, the hive of gossip he'd mentioned in the *Eye*. Sitting across from Jones, with his back to the window, was Reid. She stopped and permitted herself a good, long look. Reid leaned toward Jones, as though forward momentum might help his concentration. His narrative was clearly of import; the man was practically vibrating in his chair. In contrast, Jones's posture was casual. He had a pencil in hand but wrote nothing, asking only an occasional brief question. Neither man looked at the other; both were entirely focused on the story flowing between them.

Mary would have given much to know what that was. While it would likely appear in tomorrow's *Eye*, that might be too late. It was already Friday; Wick was buried, and the inquest was waiting only for James's report before returning a verdict. Without more concrete information, the Agency would be unable to challenge that decision, if necessary. However, for the moment she had seen all she could.

As she began to slip away, something in her movement, slight as it was, caught Jones's eye. He glanced up, eyes widening, body going completely still for a fraction of a second. Then his gaze sharpened in recognition and he grinned at her through the glass, not the least bit put out to catch her spying. Indeed, he raised his thick glazed mug to her in a mocking toast. Reid, already twitching with anxiety, spun round instantly. His eyes were wild, suspicious—and, when they lighted on Mary, incredulous.

She stood, dumbstruck. The best thing she could do was to move on and assume that Reid saw only a nosy little boy. But she couldn't shake the notion that in his eyes, in that look of startled recognition, he'd seen something else. Someone else. Not Mrs. Fordham, necessarily; it needn't be that specific. But Reid had seemed to look at her anew just then, and she was worried what that might mean.

Eighteen

Palace Yard, Westminster

"Where d'you think you're going?"

It was astonishing, the effect James had on her heartbeat. "Er—home?" A glance about showed they were nearly the last people on site.

"Wrong. You're dining with me."

"Like this?" She looked down at her dusty clothes, mud-caked shoes, grimy hands.

"Well, you could come home with me and have a bath first." There was a distinct leer in his voice.

She blushed from toes to hairline. "Your brother would have fits."

"He would," he conceded. "I suppose, then, we'd best go elsewhere."

"Where?"

"Don't look so alarmed." He grinned. "I was thinking of my office."

"But your brother—"

"Won't be there; he keeps gentleman's hours. And even if he were, he'd not look twice at a scruffy little boy."

This was the opportunity she'd been wishing for . . . so why was she hesitating now?

"This is hardly the time to come over all ladylike . . ."

"Don't be ridiculous," she snapped, her feet beginning to move of their own volition. "What's for dinner?"

He grinned with satisfaction. "No idea. But it'll be good."

It was an absurdly short distance from Palace Yard to the offices of Easton Engineering in Great George Street—a matter of perhaps three hundred yards. And one of the freedoms of being Mark was that she could stroll quietly beside James through the sticky streets, dusty and weary at the end of a day's work, without attracting a single questioning glance. As he'd promised, the offices were deserted, but for a pair of clerks preparing to leave. James nodded to them casually. They returned the greeting, clearly accustomed to his irregular hours. Neither did more than glance at her.

Once they were in his private office, James pulled out a chair for her and she sat, amused. The first time she'd visited him here, he'd been rather hostile. But then, so had she.

"Dinner won't take long," he said. "It comes from a pub around the corner."

"D'you always dine in the office?"

He shrugged. "I like to work late."

She looked around the room. It was tidy, extremely so. Quite unlike the last time she'd seen it. "What are you working on right now, apart from the safety review?"

"Oh—I'm just sorting through old papers, getting ready for the next job." Was that a blush? "Makes a change, having time to do that sort of thing."

So he was underemployed. She wondered if it was because of his health or whether the firm itself was short of contracts.

"So—"

"I suppose—"

They'd spoken simultaneously.

"Sorry—you were saying?"

"Please—carry on."

Their words collided again, and he grinned. "Ladies first."

"Even one such as I?"

"The most interesting sort there is."

She couldn't hold back a smile. "You've learned the art of fine-sounding nonsense since we last met."

"Oh, I always had it."

Moments ticked past. The smile lingered on her lips, in his eyes. It seemed enough—more than enough—simply to sit, saying nothing.

Eventually, though, he leaned forward. "Mary."

"Yes?" Weary as she was, she hadn't felt this awake for days. Weeks. Months.

"Are you . . . ?" He hesitated, trying to frame the sentence just right.

A double knock on the office door made them both jump.

"Come in," said James, sitting back hastily.

"'Evening, sir." A young, coppery-haired barmaid entered carrying two trays, one stacked on the other. She advanced confidently and set the trays on the desk. "When the order come in for two dinners, I thought it were a mistake." She giggled, and her green eyes flicked momentarily in Mary's direction before returning to James. "I thought, ain't one of Mrs. Higgs's portions big enough for a hungry gentleman?"

James's smile was rather sheepish. "Good evening, Nancy."

Nancy?

"And you's early tonight," she chided him, laying a place before James. "I weren't expecting for to come for a couple hours yet." It seemed to Mary that she was leaning forward quite a lot more than necessary, the better to display ample cleavage in a low-necked shirtwaist.

"Er—" James cleared his throat. "Nancy, meet my young associate, Mark Quinn. Mark, this is Nancy of the Bull's Head."

"Charmed, I'm sure," cooed Nancy, flashing her dimples at Mary. Before Mary could reply, she turned back to James. "Double-thick mutton chops, just as you like 'em, with French beans and tatties and all. And your Mr. Barker didn't say about a pudding, but I know as you're partial to the fruit crumble so I brung it, too, and a jug of cream."

"It smells wonderful. Thank you."

Nancy's swift hands dealt out the dishes. Once she'd distributed the food and drink, she stood back and surveyed the desk with satisfaction. "I s'pose, being as your lad's here, you won't be needing company with your dinner tonight?"

"Er—no, thank you."

She gave a good-natured pout. "I'll come for to clear away in an hour, then, sir."

"Very good."

Tipping them a wink, she tucked the trays under a strong, dimpled arm and sashayed toward the door, skirts swaying in an imaginary breeze. For a full minute after the door closed behind her, there was perfect silence. Mary stared hard at the feast laid before her. It looked appetizing and substantial and utterly luxurious, but she suddenly wanted none of it.

James cleared his throat awkwardly. "Well. Smells good," he said.

"You've already said that," she said acidly. Even as she spoke, she knew she was being childish. What did she care what James did with pretty barmaids? But she couldn't seem to stop herself. "It's no wonder you like Mrs. Higgs's cooking."

There was an expression she didn't like in James's eyes. It looked suspiciously like satisfaction. "The cooking, among other things," he said casually. "I often nip over for a pint in the snug."

She would not rise to the bait. "I'm sure you do," she heard herself say.

"It's a friendly pub," he drawled, brandishing his knife and fork. "Quiet. Select. And very friendly. Or have I said that already, too?"

She poked a slender bean with more force than necessary. It was perfectly cooked, and she resented this, too. "I'm sure it's very pleasant."

"It is."

"Good."

"Very welcoming."

"I get the point."

They ate in silence for several minutes, and despite her resentment, Mary discovered that she was ravenous. Table manners, she decided, were an affectation invented by those who'd never been hungry.

James took his time, cleaning his plate. It was no small achievement, as Mrs. Higgs's portions were indeed enormous. When, at long last, he was done, he sat back with a sigh—a smug sigh, thought Mary—and took a deep draft of beer. "Aren't you glad you came?" he asked, his eyes gleaming over the rim of the tankard.

She pushed aside her lingering resentment. This was no time to behave childishly. "I suppose it depends," she said, "on what we discuss and how we decide to proceed."

He examined his pint with care. His voice was carefully neutral as he said, "Tell me what you're thinking."

She was prepared for this, at least. "It seems to me that we'd do well to share information. Whatever you learn about site safety can be helpful to me, in my attempt to understand life as an errand boy. And in my role as Mark, I've noticed and overheard a few things that may be useful to you."

"Such as?"

"After Harkness stopped Keenan from thrashing me on Monday, Keenan all but threatened him. Said he'd not forget the incident, as though planning some sort of revenge."

"Hmph." James pondered for a moment, then leaned forward and fixed her with a look so intent she began to blush. "Now, what about you?"

"Wh-what d'you mean?"

"Well, you seem rather intent on a partnership here. Teamwork. Whatever you care to call it. That's new for you. And you'll pardon my saying so, but you don't play well with others. I believe we established that the last time we tried to work together."

Mary swallowed hard. "You're right. I didn't think through some of my decisions on the Thorold case, and I ought to have shared more information with you."

He feigned surprise. "An admission of imperfection? How unlike you, Miss Quinn."

"Pot and kettle, as you said earlier."

"True enough, and thus even more reason you ought to be resisting a partnership rather than proposing one."

He was right: she needed his help more than he did hers this time. She sat for a moment in silence, steeling herself for the confession, and then sighed. "All right. You want the real, humiliating reason I need to work with you again?"

"You're terrible at flattery, as well—did you know?"

She ignored that. "The men don't trust 'Mark.' He's too well spoken, too inexperienced, too—well, too not one of them. They're very guarded when I'm about, and while I've managed to pick up a few bits of information, it's nothing like what I'd hoped."

"Ah. Finally, we have the ugly truth: you need me."

"I need to share information with you. I need to learn about building sites from you. You don't have to make it sound so . . ."

"Oh, just admit it: you need me. You can't survive without me. I'm your greatest—no, your only—chance for success and true happiness."

She snorted. "If that's what you choose to tell yourself."

His grin was brilliant, annoying, endearing. "You'll admit it soon enough."

"So we're agreed?" she demanded, suddenly impatient.

"Of course," he said calmly. "I knew it would come to this all along. I'm quite looking forward to it."

"But you—you still made me—the apology—" She groaned with frustration. "Sometimes I think I hate you."

"You don't," he assured her.

She said nothing. He was correct, once again.

"So . . . you said Keenan threatened?"

"Very clearly. And Harkness didn't respond."

"That may have been the wisest course of action; the man's deeply unsavory."

"Like his former associate Wick?"

"It's true that nobody seems to regret him much."

"When you add together Mrs. Wick's banged-up face, the late hours Wick kept outside the home, and the fact that he was good mates with Keenan . . ."

"You get quite a scoundrel, with no short list of suspects. Just the sort of man almost anyone would like to push off a tower."

"What about Reid?"

"What about him?"

"I forgot—he was gone by the time you turned up." She explained about Reid's presence at Jane Wick's house the night they'd both called on her. "And his face was bruised on Monday last, as though he'd been in a fight."

"He's completely banged up now. Perhaps he's always getting into fights."

She shook her head. "I think not. He's a careful man, a responsible one. I think fighting two men in one week—the second was Keenan, yesterday evening—is significant in his case."

"So you think his first fight was with Wick, over his wife? In the belfry?"

"Quite possibly. Either that or the fight led directly to Wick's fall."

James was silent for a moment. "It's certainly the likeliest theory. I'll ask the coroner about bruises on Wick's body. Anything else you've observed?"

"It's of less import, but there's a great deal of muttering on site."

"Yes. The joiners and the masons are concerned with petty theft. It seemed quite small-scale at first—a handful of nails here, a fraction of a load of Anston stone there—but their complaints are adding up. It's a serious drain on resources."

"Is widespread pilfering unusual?"

"It varies according to the site and the caliber of the laborers. It has to do with management, too: a well-managed site led by a respected engineer will suffer fewer losses."

"When talking among themselves, the men have scant respect for Harkness. I've not heard anybody say anything positive about him."

James frowned, as though pained. "I know. They've told me much the same thing." There was a pause, and he said slowly, "Widespread theft could affect site safety. . . ."

"How so?"

"Well, theft on the scale the foremen suggest would seriously affect the materials budget. Perhaps Harkness is economizing on other fronts."

Mary could practically see him jotting the note in his head: *Check site budget*. "Are they clever thefts?"

He considered that. "Well, they're fairly small ones. The sort that could be attributed to a larger number of people all taking things independently."

"But you think otherwise."

"They're also quite similar. Not opportunistic; it's more as though . . ." He considered for a moment. "It's as though someone's carefully skimming a small percentage of all the materials, like a levy of some sort."

"The word *levy* suggests a sense of entitlement. . . ."

"And it's much too early to attribute motive, of course. But yes. It's as if someone's carefully taxing each of the materials in kind."

"Each foreman is in charge of supervising the unloading of his trade's materials."

"Yes. That's what makes it difficult to understand. It can't be happening at that level."

Mary leaned forward. "Keenan and Wick have a reputation for being 'always on the take.' Suppose they're behind all the thefts and are skilled at making them appear petty to a casual observer?"

James paused, frowned again, shook his head. "Possible. Have you any proof?"

"No. But if it's the case, proof must exist."

He nodded, filing that away for future reference. "But all this is a long way from site safety practices. Or life as a working-class errand boy. How are you finding things?"

Excited as she was—by James's news, by their new partnership, by his very presence—Mary found it difficult to suppress a yawn. Through watery eyes, she saw James grinning at her. "Exhausting," she admitted.

He nodded. "I can well imagine. Especially since it's your first taste of that sort of life."

She could have corrected him there. But that itself would have involved a carefully guarded set of halftruths. "I'm sorry, but I must go. I'm so very tired."

"At least allow me to give you a lift back."

She half laughed at that. "That's very kind of you, but it wouldn't do at all."

"You can't be worried about propriety at this late stage."

"Not propriety; realism. I can hardly arrive at my lodgings in a fine carriage, can I?"

He looked startled. "You're no longer at that girls' school?"

"What—Miss Scrimshaw's? No, no, no; that would be cheating. I'm in cheap lodgings, in Lambeth." She laughed outright at his expression. "You look utterly scandalized."

Still no spoken response from James, although his eyes said plenty.

Mary decided not to mention her new bedmate with the pungent socks; the poor man might never speak again after that shock. "The landlady's all right. Bit of a skinflint, but it's quite safe. No brawls so far." She rose and settled Mark's battered cap on her head. "And you've already given me an unfair advantage, with a lovely big dinner like that. I ought to've had half an inch of bread-and-butter, and considered myself fortunate at that."

He shook his head. "You. Are. Extraordinary."

By this time, her hand was on the doorknob; she turned and grinned. "That ought to sound like more of a compliment than it did." She tipped her cap and had the satisfaction of seeing a faint smile. "See you tomorrow, sir."

Nineteen

Saturday, 9 July

Palace Yard, Westminster

Saturday was a double occasion for workers, being both a half day and the weekly payday. Despite the heavy weather oppressing all of London, Mary felt a sense of excitement permeating her labors that morning, conscious that come one o'clock, she would be free for a precious day and a half. Free to think. Free to pursue some of the questions that nagged at her.

At one o'clock sharp, she felt a general exhalation ripple around the building site. Men downed tools, packed up their satchels, and streamed toward the site office in easy-moving clusters of two and three. Instead of the usual charge for the gate, they formed a relaxed, meandering queue, greeting one another with nods and grunts and the odd jocular comment. For the first time since Mary had been on the site, she felt a sense of community, of common expectation.

Harkness stood just outside the door to his office, a pair of spectacles balanced low on his nose. They lent his round, pallid face a rather scholarly air. Before him stood a small table with a wide, shallow metal box on top. Peeping out from the top of the box were rows of tall, narrow manila envelopes. As the men stepped forward, one at a time, Harkness handed each a pay packet and made a check mark on a separate sheet of paper.

Some of the men bobbed their heads or muttered something courteous before jamming the envelope into a pocket. Others stepped to one side and, quite openly, tore open the packet to count their wages before slouching away. It was a slow process, with Harkness checking each man's name twice before relinquishing his money. His movements suggested a distinct reluctance in the act, as though doubting the men's competence or entitlement. And, Mary supposed, from Harkness's perspective as a teetotaling evangelical, wages spent in the pub were worse than money lost or differently squandered; drink itself was a vice, and a begetter of further evils.

And, no doubt about it, the men were going to the pub. There was a buzz of holidayish anticipation in the air: men calling out to one another, slapping one another's backs. They were also less hostile toward her. One of the stonemasons even slowed as he passed, saying, "Going down the air?"

She blinked stupidly at him for a moment. But just as he was about to turn away, she found her voice. "Y-yes. I mean, thank you." Air. Hare. Hare and Hounds, of course.

He looked slightly bemused, but nodded. "Right. See you there."

She was the last to receive her pay packet, appropriately enough, as she was the newest laborer. By the time she presented herself, Harkness was rubbing his eyes wearily but he dredged up a kindly smile for her. "And how did you find your first week, Quinn?"

"Very interesting, sir." Behind Harkness, in the relative dimness of the office, she noticed James for the first time. He was leaning over a paper-logged desk, examining a large, dark blue ledger. He glanced up, as though he could feel her gaze upon him, and flashed her a lightning grin. It was difficult to keep a straight face, but somehow she managed to say a plausibly Mark Quinn good-bye to Harkness before, like the other laborers, stuffing the envelope in her jacket pocket and going to the pub.

Much to her satisfaction, the Hare and Hounds was nothing like the Blue Bell. It was far from elegant, but its general atmosphere was of noisy merriment rather than sodden despair. Looking about, she could understand why working men and women enjoyed the institution of the public house. The Hare had wide, well-worn benches and tables, adequate lighting, plenty of conversation, and most important, good beer. This last was evident from the number of pints of ale she saw on tables, as opposed to measures of gin. It was a much more comfortable place, Mary reckoned, than a lot of laborers' homes, and it offered company as well.

Her workmates—strange to think of them that way—were already established at a corner table, deep into their first round. It was a tightly packed scrum, and few of the men noticed her approach. Those who did merely stared at her, their gazes somehow both challenging and uninterested. The stonemason who'd invited her was in the corner. Perhaps it was logical that she was shyer of the men here than she was on site—in her place, doing her job, trying to remain focused. But she was still at work here, too, she reminded herself. The thought gave her courage.

"What are you drinking?" she asked the men nearest to her.

The chap on the end turned at that. He'd been facing away, cradling his face in the hand nearer Mary, and she now realized, as their eyes met, that it was Reid. An arrow of panic shot through her, but it was much too late to back down. She forced herself to look diffident.

He was visibly startled to see her but after a moment, said, "Mine's a Landlord's Finest."

Apparently, what was good enough for Reid was good enough for the rest. Mary made several trips to and from the bar and on her last, the men on one bench scooted down to make room for her. Apparently, buying a round was the quickest way to acceptance. She only wished she'd thought of this five days ago.

Sticking her nose in a pint pot was an ideal way to observe people, and from where Mary sat, she found herself learning in ten minutes as much about labor relations as she had all the rest of the week. Although the men tended to sit in the same corner of the pub, they still held very much to their trades. The masons sat together, beside the joiners, who passed the occasional remark with the neighboring glaziers. The brickies were the exception, being represented only by Reid, Smith, and Stubbs, but that was certainly for the best—Keenan's presence would have destroyed everyone's enjoyment. Together, the men were friendly enough, and the beer did the rest. The joiners, as Mary had expected, were the boisterous core of the gathering, trading gossip and shouting ever ruder jokes down the table with a view to making the new lad blush.

As the afternoon wore on, Mary found it difficult to imagine a time she'd felt uncomfortable around these men. It was almost as unlikely as their being suspicious of her. Here in the pub, they were all mates. Good mates. They'd been mates for absolutely ages. They joked about the teetotal tea break, complained about Harkness, about the slow progress of work on site, even about the new engineer.

"Now you," said Reid, leaning across the table and fixing her with an intent, if slightly glazed, look. "You knows all about the new gent. Posh fella, ain't he?"

Mary's most recent pint of ale churned slowly in her stomach. "Not so posh," she said slowly, her beer-fuddled brain scrambling to chart the conversation ahead. "Only like Harky, I'll bet."

Reid shook his head with slow conviction. "Swanker than old Harky, that one. *I* know."

"What do you know?" demanded the man next to Mary.

"He called to Wick's house one night after work. Gave Janey Wick a right fright—she thought Wick was in trouble again, for all he's well dead."

"If a bloke could get into trouble when dead, John Wick's the one!" snorted a third. A few men rumbled with polite amusement, but most were intent on Reid's tale.

"Anyways, this gent calls round to Wick's, says to Janey as he'd like to see the body, polite like. And Janey says, 'Well, it ain't here; that there coroner's still got it and he won't say as when he'll give it back.' And Janey, right, she's that upset about it 'cause of the funeral being the next day, and she's got to wash it and dress it and all, and this here chappie—this Easton—tells her not to worry and he'll see what he can do.

"And Janey's thinking, 'My eye you will, all you lot say that but you don't do nothing, and whyn't you get home and leave me alone, anyways.' And blimey, if the next morning a blasted great carriage don't turn up—nine o'clock of the morning remember—and these two chaps bring in Wick's body, all polite like, saying 'Yes, Missus Wick,' and 'No, Missus Wick,' and all!"

There was a general ripple of surprise. "Did he say

how he done it? Easton, I mean." This was the man beside Mary, again.

Reid shook his head and took a long pull of beer. "Didn't say nothing, just left his card and said if she needed aught else, to ask him."

Someone else gave a sly, knowing chuckle. "Got his eye on the widow, eh? Bet she's paying him back for his trouble right this minute."

Reid looked around indignantly. "She ain't doing nothing like that; she's a good girl, is Janey Wick." From the looks of suppressed mirth around the table, it was obvious that Reid's passion for Mrs. Wick was an open secret. "That's why I'm telling you," he persisted; "that Easton's a right posh gent. Fancy Harky doing anything like that for a poor little widow, with all his hymn singing and tea drinking!"

The conversation moved on, the characters of James Easton and Mrs. Wick being of only passing interest to the other men.

But Reid wanted to keep talking, and he buttonholed Mary across the table. "You ain't done building work before." It wasn't a question.

"No," said Mary. She offered him the same explanation she'd given Harkness: orphaned, no money for an apprenticeship, living in lodgings.

"You been to school," said Reid, his brow creasing.

She nodded reluctantly. "For a little."

He ignored this. "'Cause after I seen you yesterday,

looking in the window, that Mr. Jones—Octavius Jones"—he sounded out the given name with care—"said you's a right clever little fart, and for to watch myself around you."

Beer made her bold. Rather than cringing and trying to minimize herself and her story, Mary grinned broadly. "You got so much to watch?" A flash of panic crossed Reid's face and she added, hastily, "You, like, the ghost of the clock tower, or something?"

He relaxed. "Not me, laddie. But that Mr. Jones—I reckon he knows what's what."

So he was sounding her out. Trying to work out what she knew. "Suppose he must, writing for the newspaper and all."

Reid nodded, his eyes never leaving her face. "Keeps a sharp eye on that site."

"I don't see him round that much."

"He's got his ways."

It was like a game of cards with high stakes. Each trying to push the other closer to a confession, while both tried to keep their own secrets. "You mean, like paying people to tell him stuff?"

Reid exhaled slightly. "Yeah. Like that."

"I ain't told him nothing yet," she said candidly. "Does he pay as good as he says?"

"Oh—naw. I dunno. I ain't got nothing to tell." But he flushed at this and unconsciously pushed a hand into his trouser pocket. Presumably, that's where Jones's little bonus was tucked. "I got no secrets." It was the most unconvincing denial Mary had heard in some time—so incompetent it made her wonder anew at Reid's involvement with crooks like Wick and Keenan. Or whether she was meant to inquire further.

"Keenan does," she said boldly, draining her tankard.

Reid looked sly—or perhaps that was just the effect of the cut under his eye, which made him appear quite raffish. "Maybe."

"He talks to Harky like he's the boss."

"Mmm."

"And him and you and Wick, you're all up to something."

Reid blushed, half-ashamed, half-defiant. "I don't know what you're on about."

"'Course you do." She paused and leaned forward slightly. The other men paid them no attention; this was a perfect opportunity. "Tidy lot of money it pays you, too."

He gaped at her, his beer-pinked cheeks slack and quivering. Panic made his round blue eyes even rounder. "That bit ain't me!" he yelped, drawing a lazy glance from his nearest neighbor. "I never meant it to go that far," he muttered, leaning toward her.

"But you know," she persisted, encouraged both by the expression on his sensible, naive face and by the booze. "You know, and you told Octavius Jones."

"I got to piss," he said, and stood abruptly. As he pulled his hand from his pocket, a twist of paper tumbled out, bouncing onto the bench and then to the floor. Reid's anxiety was such that he didn't notice: a moment later, he was through the back door into the alley, which served as a generalized chamber pot. Mary slipped the paper into her own pocket and, when Reid reappeared after a few minutes' absence, accepted the offer of another pint.

As though mention of him had conjured his real presence, the pub door swung open and Keenan himself walked in. Reid, halfway to the bar, blanched and steadied himself against a table. He stood still, waiting.

Keenan looked to be in his usual foul mood. He'd been at work that morning, though uncharacteristically quiet, and Harkness had made rather a point of ignoring him. He'd not been reprimanded for his unexplained absence yesterday. Now his gaze settled on Reid, and although the pub was dimly lit, he narrowed his eyes. The silence between them was rich with accumulated tension. Finally, Keenan said in a low tone, "Let's take a walk."

Reid gulped and stared at him. He'd been drinking swiftly, downing two pints to Mary's one, and the beer seemed to have fuddled his brain. Or perhaps it was the expression on Keenan's face.

Keenan twitched impatiently. "Have a heart, man—I ain't like to kill you." It was a poor choice of words, and Reid's face blanched. His fingers tightened around the tankard in his fist. Then, as if thus reminded of its presence, he lifted the drink to his lips and drained it in one swallow. His eyes were wide and wary, and the ruddy color of his cheeks seemed to sit atop his skin like a painted mask. Then, setting the pot on the nearest table, he followed Keenan out of the pub like a man going to his death.

Mary gave them a full half minute's lead before standing to leave. Suddenly, the world tilted sideways, the faces of the men around her blurring and warping crazily. Her knees buckled. She clutched at the table for support. Something solid struck her hand, making her knuckles ring. What the devil . . . ?

A large hand grasped her shoulder roughly and she flailed against it. He mustn't feel her back. He mustn't know. Something smacked her bottom, hard, and she struggled again, uncertain now which way was up. What was wrong with her eyes? Blood roared in her ears. She gasped for breath. It was like drowning on dry land. She was still on dry land, wasn't she? At that, all the liquid sloshing around her stomach began to roll and churn. Oh, no. Not that.

The pressure continued against her bottom, flat and hard and impersonal. Not a man, then. Slowly, she became aware of a general sort of guffawing. Gradually, the world resolved into a blur of likely browns, yellows, and skin tones, eventually coming into focus. She was in the pub, of course, sitting on the same bench, surrounded by the same laborers.

The pounding in her ears quieted.

Queasiness receded.

She found herself taking long, shaky breaths.

"You look fit to faint," chortled one of the joiners.

The man next to her released his grip on her shoulder and grinned. "You ain't much of a drinker, eh, sonny?"

Sonny. She was relieved to hear that.

"It's the sitting down what does it," said another sagely.

"Aye," agreed another. Then began a chorus of advice, all just a few pints too late. It seemed that she'd committed two beginner's errors: she'd not eaten before coming to the pub, and hadn't known that suddenly standing up could transform the sensation of merry ease to that of fall-down drunkenness.

This was all helpful. And when she tried again to stand, slowly this time, the room rocked only a little, although the floorboards were damned uneven. Funny. She'd not noticed that earlier. She took a cautious step, then another, and a third, before bidding her new mates a friendly good-bye. Next came the pub door, which swung open with hazardous ease; she stumbled into the street, but that was certainly the fault of the door, which banged loudly behind her. At least now she was outside, where the rich and complex smell of London's streets could help to clear her brain.

What time was it? There were few street vendors about, so she was in the lull between the early ones closing down and the late ones opening up. Late afternoon or early evening. There was some passing traffic, too—

carriages and whatnot—but they were moving at a smart trot. In fact, even the pedestrians seemed to be moving quickly: men in suits, still conducting business, and laborers, footsore and intent on getting home. Only a few of the poorer sort of prostitute idled along, halfheartedly angling for customers. One blew her a kiss and shrugged a not very come-hither shoulder, then laughed unkindly at her startled response.

The suggestion of movement: it stirred something in the back of her mind. There was something she had to do . . . but she couldn't, for the life of her, recall what it might be. Never mind. She had a good walk ahead of her. Likely as not, she'd remember along the way.

Twenty

On the road from Palace Yard to Bloomsbury

James was deeply perturbed. His request to inspect the project's financial records, which he'd thought a matter of form, had been met by Harkness with prevarication, procrastination, and finally, reluctant accommodation. Once he'd gained access, James expected to spend an hour; instead, it had consumed his entire day. Now, sprawled in the carriage on his way home to Bloomsbury, he stared sightlessly out of the window, considering the unpleasant suspicions he'd entertained all week. They were fast becoming certainties.

He was in no rush to return home. On a Saturday afternoon, George would be out, and the prospect of being alone in the large house was rather daunting. It would only mean more brooding about this damned situation of Harkness's and what, if anything, he could do about it. Going home also brought him one step closer to the evening's duty: a dinner party at the Harkness home. He'd accepted the invitation some days ago, more from duty than with pleasure. But given today's events, neither he nor Harkness could possibly be looking forward to the meal. Indeed, the only thing that prevented his fabricating an excuse and canceling at the last minute was his own ludicrous sense of hope. If he could dine with Harkness, if he could look his father's old friend in the eye, things might not turn out as dire as they promised.

These were his thoughts as the carriage drove along the northern embankment, rocking gently on its springs. He stared moodily at the streetscape. The threat of rain still pressed down on the town, making the air thick and sticky, the skies a weary gray. His eyes focused on a figure trudging unsteadily up the street. It tacked a bizarre course from lamppost to pillar-box, stepping with excessive caution, as though afraid of slipping and falling. The figure was instantly, subcutaneously familiar: the last person he'd expect to see in such a plight, but the first he'd recognize anywhere, in any circumstances. He rapped on the carriage roof, two solid thumps, and they slowed to a plod alongside the staggerer.

Slight. Rather grubby. Very rosy cheeks.

James smirked. He couldn't imagine a better diversion. "Lost your way?" he called through the open window.

Her head whipped round, causing her to stumble. It took her a moment to focus on his face. When she did, however, it was with a transparent delight that turned his heart to water. "You!"

He beamed like an idiot. Any sort of clever quip was now impossible. "You look as if you need a lift." The carriage slowed very gradually and came to a halt. Barker carefully averted his face as he opened the door and let down the steps, but James could well imagine his carefully arranged expression of distaste.

Mary's upturned face, framed by the carriage interior, looked small and slightly perplexed. "What are you doing here?"

"Going home. Climb in."

She put one hand to her forehead, as though trying to remember something.

"Still worried about propriety?"

"No . . ."

"The authenticity of your disguise?"

She frowned. "I—well, I suppose . . ."

"Oh, stop dithering." He leaned out, grabbed her by the upper arms, and hauled her bodily into the carriage, steps and propriety and authenticity be damned. Tense with surprise, she was light, and yet his own weakness startled him. A year ago, he'd not have thought twice about the effort; today, he required all his diminished strength to lift her. Nevertheless, he managed to plop her beside him on the bench with only a small thump, and by the time she stopped sputtering and giggling, they were away. "Phew. You reek of ale."

"I thought you liked ale."

"I do." He cupped her face in his hands and kissed

her soundly on the lips. She made a small sound of surprise and her hands came up, as if to push him away. Instead, they settled on his chest and relaxed there, and she returned his kiss with sweet enthusiasm. Beneath the malty ale she tasted delicious, familiar. But it was better than last time, infinitely so, and what he'd intended as a single embrace unraveled into a long string of kisses.

Deep.

Hypnotic.

Luxurious.

Kisses that threatened to blot out the world.

Time passed, in some arbitrary fashion. He became aware of it only very gradually as a cessation of movement, an unexpected stillness. With some surprise, he realized the carriage had stopped. More specifically, they were in the lane behind his house in Bloomsbury.

"What's wrong?" murmured Mary. Her voice was languorous, remote.

"We're—" He cleared his rusty throat. "We're at my house."

"Oh." She tensed, then swiftly untwined her limbs from his. There was an awkward pause, which they broke simultaneously:

"I ought to go."

"Won't you come in?"

Her eyes widened, and he realized how it must sound. "For a cup of tea. Or a chat. Or—I mean, I didn't have anything in mind. In particular. I only meant, there's no reason for you to go."

She passed one hand over her hair, looked down at her boy's rags. "I don't think I possibly could."

"George isn't home," he said eagerly. "It's only me."

She leaned over to the window and sized up the house. "You must have servants."

He looked surprised. "Of course. But they don't talk."

She looked amused. "Much *you* know. Servants always talk."

"Does it matter what they say?"

"I—" She seemed unable to explain.

James thought he understood. "I know: you're still a young lady, despite the costume. But you're also half-cut, and I absolutely refuse to take you back to a rough lodging house in this state."

"I'm not that drunk," she said indignantly.

"Well, I hope you're not utterly foxed; that wouldn't be very complimentary to me. But you'll stay until you're sober." He couldn't help grinning. Her surprise was so very readable, when normally he struggled to guess what she thought.

It was a curious experience, bringing Mary home. He found himself excessively aware of the daily surroundings he had generally ceased to notice: the rattle of his key in the lock, the stiff springiness of the doormat beneath his boots, the way his voice echoed in the high-ceilinged hall. James stood aside to let her enter, but she hung back, looking about the garden with a frank curiosity he found impossibly endearing.

The house was fragrant with beeswax polish and baking. Mrs. Vine, the family's housekeeper of some thirty years, stepped into the hall. "I've been expecting you these last two hours, Mr. James," she said, examining his face with critical eyes. "Though you don't look so worn-out as I expected."

He smiled. "That's the first nice thing you've said to me all week."

She clicked her tongue impatiently. "Go and tidy yourself, for heaven's sake. The scones aren't getting any warmer." Her gaze shifted to something behind him and, while her features didn't move, her voice turned formal and courteous. "Shall I lay a place for this young man in the kitchen?"

With a calm he didn't feel, he said, "Actually, Miss Quinn will take tea with me." He sensed, rather than saw, Mary tense behind him. "Mrs. Vine will show you where you can, er, wash your hands."

Not a muscle moved in Mrs. Vine's face. She merely nodded and said, in that same neutral voice, "Please follow me, Miss Quinn."

James watched them go. Mrs. Vine sailed ahead, tall and regal, while Mary followed three steps behind, quieter than he'd ever seen her. He wasn't at all certain he'd done the right thing in bringing her here. What on earth was happening to him? A kiss or two was one thing; what had passed between them in the carriage quite another. She had no right to overturn his world so easily and perhaps not even realize she'd done so. And here he was, inviting her into his private domain. It wasn't wise to allow her so much insight into his life when he scarcely knew anything beyond her name. But it was much too late for such caution now.

Mary followed the Amazonian housekeeper up two broad flights of stairs, struggling with equal measures of disbelief and amusement. The disbelief was at being here, in James's house, the private expression of the man. He was such a guarded character, and this suggested a new degree of intimacy she was reluctant—even afraid—to consider. The amusement was more straightforward. Mrs. Vine, charging ahead, was a perfect music-hall servant: hatchet-faced, razor-tongued, and the rest. She'd probably served the Eastons since James was a wee fat baby (impossible to imagine!) and didn't even blink when James brought home a scruffy little boy who turned out to be a woman.

The beer was beginning to wear off. She was certain of that, if little else. Her limbs and movements were much more her own, she was fiercely thirsty, and she had a desperate, cramping need to pass water. How many pints had she drunk—two? Three? More than she'd ever had before, that was certain—and she'd thought she was being so careful. Evidently, she still had everything to learn about men, whether they were hardworking laborers or arrogant gentlemen.

Mrs. Vine paused on the second-floor landing. "I hope I'm not presuming too much, Miss Quinn," said the housekeeper in her formal, public voice, "but would you care to perform a more thorough toilette?" At Mary's mystified look, she added, "I could draw you a bath . . ."

Mary ought, she knew, to have been mortified. What must this woman think of her, tumbling into the house with James, filthy and disheveled and demanding food and a bath! Instead, Mary could think only about the magic word *bath.* "Oh yes, please," she said rather fervently. "If it's not too much trouble . . ."

It was an absurd thing to say. Baths were trouble, plenty of trouble, what with the boiling of water and hauling it up three flights of stairs, never mind taking the slops back down and laundering the towels. But the corners of Mrs. Vine's mouth seemed to suggest majestic approval and Mary soon found herself in a special room designed just for bathing. It was a rather swanky idea, the separate bathroom with its glazed tiles, piped-in hot water, and self-draining tub, and she was rather amused by the notion of James as a bath-obsessed modernizer.

As her second bath in the space of a week, it was a thorough betrayal of the authentic worker's life. Baths ought to be infrequent luxuries for Mark Quinn, not regular affairs, and they ought to occur in shallow tin tubs by the kitchen fire, never in purpose-built temples to cleanliness. But this afternoon, Mary didn't care; she'd never reveled so much in soap and water in her life. On climbing out, she found that Mark's grimy clothes had vanished from the other side of the privacy screen. Laid out in their place were a fine linen nightshirt, immaculately pressed and fragrant with cedar, and a light dressing gown. They were much too big for her, the nightshirt billowing around her ankles and the dressing gown trailing on the floor. James's familiar scent settled around her, warming her and making her shiver at the same time. She felt bold and scandalous; almost fallen. Exactly the sort of woman she'd never been.

She brushed her hair—an odd sensation, the bristles scraping her bare neck. And then Mrs. Vine appeared to conduct her downstairs once again. The stark formality of the drawing room—James and George were not, apparently, devoted to knickknacks and cushions—made her curl a little into herself. Much of her awareness was focused on the two flimsy layers of fabric that swathed her body, her only barrier against nakedness in this unfamiliar masculine domain.

James was reading a book, his long legs unfolded over the length of a sofa, but he leapt to his feet when she entered. For once, there was no acerbic comment. Instead, he looked almost shy. "Mrs. Vine will bring tea shortly."

Mary sat gingerly in the space he indicated, beside

him on the sofa. "She must think it so strange, my arriving in boy's clothing and having a bath and her providing fresh things, and a nightshirt at that!"

"I imagine the nightshirt is the only thing I have that comes even close to fitting. And even that buries you."

"Well, perhaps you ought to keep a stock of women's clothing on hand, just in case."

He grinned at that. "D'you plan on returning often? Or are you trying to work out how often I entertain half-naked young ladies?"

She blushed furiously. "Neither!"

"Really? Because it sounded like one or the other, to me."

This was the James she knew. Despite his teasing—or rather, because of it—she was suddenly much more at ease. "I'm sure you meet any number of half-naked young ladies, but daren't bring them here for fear of what your brother would say."

"Extraordinary. That was meant to be your cue to fly into a jealous tantrum."

"I thought I'd already covered that the other night at your offices."

"I suppose you rather did. You're not worried about Nancy anymore?"

"No." She truly wasn't. At this moment, in his presence, it seemed ridiculous that she ever had.

He'd had a wash, too, and removed his tie and jacket. She'd no idea whether this was to put her at ease in her undressed state, or whether he expected to undress further. The idea made her tremble, although she wasn't afraid. Not in the usual sense, at least.

"Your hair." He touched the shining strands. "Were you sorry to cut it?"

She shook her head, a tiny movement, lest he withdraw his hand. "I didn't think about how it felt. It had to be done."

"Will it take long to grow back?"

"I don't think so. It grows so fast."

"Mmm." His fingers slipped down to explore the curve of her neck. "This is a weak point in your boyish disguise, you know."

"What—my neck?" Even her disbelief sounded breathless.

He smiled. "Too long. Too slender. And"—he leaned down to plant a light kiss on her collarbone—"not nearly grimy enough."

She exploded with laughter. "Is that a complaint?"

Mrs. Vine entered, balancing a heavy tray. She set it down and turned to Mary. "I beg your pardon, Miss Quinn, but in preparing your trousers for laundering, I found this in your pocket. Do you wish to retain it?"

"This" was the twisted paper she had filched from Reid that afternoon; the thing she'd been trying to remember before tipsiness and James pushed all logic and strategy from her mind. She seized it with an overloud "Yes, thank you!" Her horror must have been evident on her face. But Mrs. Vine remained as carefully expressionless as ever, merely inclining her head before leaving the room with swift, noiseless steps.

"What is it?"

In reply, she unfolded it carefully. It was a small, battered envelope, its edges dented and smudged with use. "It fell out of Reid's pocket at the pub this afternoon."

"It fell? Or did you help it?"

She grinned. "No, I didn't steal it. But neither did I restore it to him." She turned it over and pointed to the dark pencil marks that seemed to grow from one corner of the envelope. They formed a simple design of tall, narrow triangles, every other one of which was shaded in. "Is this familiar?"

James swallowed hard. After a frozen moment, he nodded with obvious reluctance. "It completes the circle."

"Does it?" She hated the expression of misery on his face.

"Of course it does," he snapped. "It wouldn't convict him in a court of law, but those marks—they're inarguable. Harkness is always drawing them when he's thinking with a pencil in hand. They're all over the accounts ledger and his working drawings, and now they're here. This envelope is proof that he's connected with the bricklayers' thefts."

"Reid may have pinched it."

"What would Reid want with an old envelope? No, never mind that. Think of it the other way: Harkness's involvement explains how the bricklayers could steal so much for so long."

She was silent. The envelope markings showed clearly enough that it had passed from Harkness's hand to Reid's, at the very least. It wasn't a pay packet, so that could safely be ruled out. And it was a dainty piece of stationery—much too small to contain architectural drawings, for example. She smoothed the envelope under her fingers. It had never been addressed, never stamped—and that was logical enough, since who would trust illicit information to the penny post?

As she stared at this bit of evidence, a new sense of dismay rose within her. If Reid and Keenan had become reconciled this afternoon, Keenan would now be aware that she, too, knew about their scheme. And even if Reid and Keenan were still at odds, Keenan might have extracted the information from Reid. Mary had no doubt that he was ruthless enough to turn on his friend and colleague, perhaps even to use violence to gain his end. Either way, a dangerously angry man would be after her. And she doubted that Harkness would be present to rescue her this time.

She shivered. This was her fault. Her own foolish, overconfident doing. She ought never have tried to press Reid for information. What had got into her? And her inner voice immediately returned the answer: it was more that *she* had got into the pub. The beer had emboldened her, and the sociable ease of the place had given her license to utter things she'd never have dared on site. What had she done?

"What's wrong?" James's voice was sharp with concern.

She shook her head.

"Tell me, Mary. You must."

"'Must?'" Ah: the authoritarian aspect of his character. She'd nearly forgotten.

"Yes, 'must.' Things are different now, between us." He seized her hands and shook them, but gently. "We both feel that now."

She looked into his eyes for the briefest of moments, and their expression made her tremble. She was exultant, blissful, terrified, and half a second later, utterly in despair. Only her emotions were true here: everything between her and James was still a lie. And she would never be able to tell him the truth about herself. Not without betraying the Agency and the women who had saved her life and made everything possible for her in the first place.

"Mary."

Her name again, on his lips. The very thought of it made her want to weep, but she hadn't the luxury. Instead, she drew a deep breath, nodded, and told him of her confrontation with Reid. She could reveal that much. When she'd finished, she glanced at his face again, reading the concern—no, alarm—she saw there.

"We must report this to the police."

"Report what? That I accused a man of theft?"

"That a man with a violent temper, whom we strongly

suspect of theft, may have cause to do you harm. You're too clever not to see that whatever Reid knows, Keenan soon will."

"The police can't do anything about that. What d'you propose—having a bobby trail me about the site on Monday?"

His lips tightened. "You're not going to site on Monday."

"There! Again!"

"What?" He was genuinely mystified.

"Ordering me about, as if I'm a dim-witted child."

"I don't think you're dim, much less a child."

"But you've just told me what to do."

"I've just told you the *sensible* thing to do!"

"But that's just it—you're *telling* me!" Could they have a lovers' quarrel when they weren't truly lovers? It seemed so. "You've no right to make decisions for me."

His jaw tightened. "This isn't about rights; it's about common sense."

"So you're saying that if our positions were reversed, you'd accept my command not to go to work on Monday?" Her temper was rising fast, but at that moment she didn't care.

"There's no need to be theoretical about this. The difficulty is what it is."

"And you are what you are!"

"Pray tell," he drawled, coldly angry now.

"Arrogant, high-handed, and controlling!"

"Rather that than arrogant, impulsive, and irresponsible."

She flung herself up from the sofa and stalked around the room. "It's my life, not yours! Can't you understand that?"

"What I understand is that you'd rather risk your safety on Monday than admit I'm right."

"Untrue! You may well be right about Keenan, but I don't agree with your method of dealing with it. And I certainly won't permit you to give me orders simply because—because—"

He'd risen when she did, as a gentleman ought. He stood now with his arms folded across his chest. "Go on—say it. 'Because . . .' "

Here she floundered, unwilling to articulate just how she felt about James. Unable to assume that he felt the same way, now that he was staring at her with those cold, angry eyes. As she struggled, her sense of righteous indignation began to seep away, leaving only despair. It didn't matter how this argument ended. Suddenly, she felt bone weary. Deep behind her temples, a headache was blossoming. "Because," she said wearily, "you're concerned for my safety. I know that, and I am, too, and I'll not be cavalier about it. But I refuse to go to the police just yet."

He was silent for a long moment. Then he said, "What about Monday?"

"I've not decided."

"What do you propose to do now?"

"Well, what about working out the precise nature of the link between Harkness, Keenan, and Reid?"

Instead of replying, he pushed the tea tray toward her and said, "Will you pour?" The familiar rituals helped to smooth things between them: tea, cream and sugar, sandwiches, cakes. Once their hands were occupied with small matters, it was easier to pretend that their thoughts were, too.

"We might be jumping to conclusions about Harkness," said Mary at last, when it seemed that James intended to stare into his teacup forever. "As you said before, Reid might have filched the envelope from his desk."

He nodded slightly. "But if Harkness is truly innocent, I don't understand why he hasn't reported the thefts. Or sacked Keenan and Reid. He's involved with them, and it seems personal."

"Well, he does seem to feel a sense of responsibility toward the men. Toward Mark Quinn, for example— trying to teach as well as employ."

"True." James crumbled a scone with his long fingers. "So perhaps he's trying to lay a trap for them, or persuade them to give up their bad ways?"

"Possibly. All I'm saying is, why not try to learn more about their connection before assuming the worst? If you report your suspicions to the police and Harkness turns out to be blameless, you'll never forgive yourself."

"Neither will he," he said with the faintest of smiles.

The clock on the mantel chimed six o'clock in silvery tones. Both looked at it, then at each other, with surprise. "I'm dining at Harkness's home tonight. I might learn something there." He drained his teacup, set it down decisively, and flashed her a charming grin. "Care to join me?"

"Wearing your nightshirt?" She laughed.

"Oh, you won't need it."

"I beg your pardon?" She felt the blush wash over her in a swift, comprehensive wave.

"Tut tut, Miss Quinn — not as pure of mind as a young lady ought to be."

"You must be terribly disappointed."

He laughed aloud at that, a sound of pure joy. "Never less so in my life."

Another great roll of warmth rippled through her body and she couldn't stop smiling. "Go on, then — how am I to join you this evening?"

"As Mark Quinn, of course. I'm surprised you had to ask."

Twenty-one

Leighton Crescent, Tufnell Park

The Harkness home was a broad, blocky villa in Tufnell Park, part of a tightly packed estate built a decade before. Viewed together, the houses reminded Mary of nothing so much as a row of false teeth plonked into a field. Or perhaps that was simply her jaundiced eye. Despite tonight's promise of adventure and discovery, she was exhausted. And even after a large dose of willow-bark powder, her headache continued to swell, pounding against her temples in time with her footsteps. Her mouth was dry and thick. Either she was falling ill or these were the aftereffects of too much drink. Perhaps there was something to Harkness's teetotaling gospel, after all.

She pulled her cap lower over her eyes and considered the house before her. Despite the lingering dusk, for it was not yet eight o'clock, the house was brightly lit, as for a party. A neat row of carriages lined the street just outside. The first-floor curtains were still open, and ladies and gentlemen in evening dress paraded back and forth before the large windows. As she strolled past the house, a fourth carriage drew up and disgorged a stout mother-and-daughter pair. They were quite spectacularly alike, from their bulging eyes to their jeweled silk slippers. Although the evening was far from cold, each had a stole wrapped about her neck, the fur slightly wilted in the humid evening.

The mother frowned at the house. "Well, I suppose it's not a bad size—but, my dear! The location!"

Mary paused to watch as a footman opened the door to them. The hall blazed with gaslight, and she received a fleeting impression of plenty of highly polished ornaments before the door closed once again. Quickening her pace now, she walked to the corner of the road and turned into the back alley. Even if she hadn't known which house was Harkness's, it would have been evident from the extraordinary level of light and noise emanating from its grounds.

The hum of conversation floated out of the first-floor windows, punctuated by barks of masculine amusement and the occasional bright squeal. At times, this was nearly drowned out by the clatter and half-panicked exclamations of servants on the lower levels. As Mary stopped to listen again, there came a smash of crockery and a cry of dismay, followed by ugly haranguing and then, perhaps inevitably, the wail of a slapped woman. Nearer her, the stable was alive with the whickering of horses and the rustle of hay, and even the quiet whistling of a man at work. He had by far the best job this evening. The atmosphere in the house was clearly fraught; she could tell even from here.

The noise and chaos were to her advantage. She'd been worried about gaining access without lock picks or a skeleton key; people were generally so careful about keeping doors and windows locked. But tonight, the first window she tried slid up quite easily. She found herself inside the darkened breakfast room. The door had been left ajar, and in the corridor, feet pounded swiftly up and down with rather less grace and discretion than was generally desired. One could almost measure the distance between the private and public spaces of the house by listening to the point at which the footsteps slowed, the hissed instructions ceased, and a harried expression was undoubtedly smoothed to a mask of impassive calm.

This was all very well, thought Mary, crouching behind the door, but if the servants didn't stop scampering past, she'd never be able to leave the breakfast room. The clock on the mantel, a squat thing heavily embellished, ticked off the minutes. Five. Ten. A quarter hour. And then came a different sort of stampede—languid of pace, brightly chattering—down a staircase near the front of the house: the guests going in to dinner. Another five minutes and through the wedge of open door, Mary saw a pair of footmen bearing soup tureens, moving with perfect sangfroid—a denial of the frantic scurrying she'd witnessed earlier. When the dining-room doors closed,

Mary peered out into the hallway. Empty. She had a good interval while this course was served. If she didn't move now, she'd be caught in the changeover between soup and fish.

The corridors were wainscotted in dark wood and papered in a smudged floral design that looked a peculiar greeny-brown by gaslight. The house, so far, seemed a testament to someone's violently rich tastes: ornate rosewood breakfast table and chairs, enormous tiered chandelier in the entry hall, walls jammed with paintings in gilded frames. Mary's eyes widened as she noticed a suit of armor—an actual suit of armor!—standing sentry by the broad staircase. It seemed a far cry from Harkness's rather puritanical posture on site. She walked on, wide-eyed. Surely this faint, stirring queasiness owed as much to the decoration as to all that beer this afternoon. . . .

Fortunately, there were only so many places to locate a study in a house like this. In rambling, aristocratic homes, one could wander forever before finding the correct wing, let alone the study door; in the slums, one might become thoroughly lost in the rabbit warren before working out which families shared which rooms. But in square bourgeois houses like this, thought Mary, the study was generally—*here*.

The doorknob turned easily in her hand, and not a moment too soon. Far down the corridor, she heard an approaching half shuffle, half scurry. A servant retrieving or delivering something. Quickly, she slipped into the room, closed the door behind her, and turned the key. It took a while for her eyes to adjust, and in those few seconds she had a sudden, vivid recollection of her first meeting with James. In the dark. In a study. In a wardrobe. She shivered slightly, and the room suddenly felt cool. Her headache, though, was beginning to lift.

She had a candle stub and a box of lucifers in her pocket. Though the single small flame seemed meager after the yellowy glare of the rest of the house, it was enough. And as the details of the room became visible, she was thoroughly startled. She'd expected a study to match the rest of the house: a cacophony of the most expensive and oppressive furnishings one could buy. What she saw, instead, was a room as austere as a monk's cell. No Turkish carpet, no wallpaper, no vases or figurines or paintings. Just a wide, slightly battered desk and a few mismatched filing cabinets. There was nothing here to make the room comfortable. Not so much as a cushion on the upright desk chair.

Harkness's office at the building site was essentially a haystack of rumpled papers that threatened to subsume the furniture. Here, today's *Times* lay folded at one corner of the desk and there were no other papers in sight. Mary shivered again. There was something pathetic about the contrast, as though Harkness spent little time here, or as though a ruthless domestic routine had purged the room of his personality. And yet . . .

As she looked about the room in amazement, Mary

realized that this room did indeed belong to Harkness. This was the study of a man who denied himself wine, who did his clumsy best to help his workers do the same (regardless of whether they wished to), who wanted to help Mark Quinn better himself. The blotter on the desk was covered in those black-and-white triangles, layer upon layer of them, a testament to the fidgety frugality of the man who worked in that space. She stood there in wonder, simply staring at the room for a few minutes. Then, across the hall, the dining-room door clicked open and the burble of conversation grew loud. Despite its showy decoration, the walls in this house were thin.

Right. Time to start. Her first act was to unlatch the window, in case she should need to make a rapid exit. After that, however, her momentum faltered. Somehow, she was loath to inspect Harkness's filing cabinets, to sift through his personal correspondence. This wasn't the first time she'd felt these sorts of scruples: she'd struggled before with the notion of prying, but always managed to justify it because she was trying to do right, to uncover truths. But tonight, in this sad, bare cell, she found herself suddenly in doubt.

It wasn't that she thought Harkness blameless. He was certainly linked to Keenan and Reid, and if he was trying to combat their thefts, he'd chosen a very strange and indirect method. He was much more likely to be cooperating with them. But there was something tragic about this study.

Mary felt that she'd somehow stumbled onto a distressing personal secret just by entering the room.

Nevertheless, she was here, and this was her task. The desk drawers glided smoothly, rather to her surprise. She'd half expected them to be stiff with age and disuse. The top drawer held the usual bits: pens, pen wipers, an extra bottle of ink, the rules and T-squares and protractors of the architectural draftsman. She opened the other drawers: writing paper. A handful of loose penny stamps. A postcard from Margate from someone signing herself "Hetty." A file of newspaper clippings about the clock tower (favorable mentions only). And, finally, in the bottom drawer, the things she'd been looking for, stacked neatly one on the other like presents.

Checkbook and register.

Bankbook.

She paused to listen to the dinner party under way. The rumble of polite conversation swelled and ebbed like a tide, interrupted occasionally by laughter. One man had a high, yipping, nasal sort of laugh that sliced through the rest, through the walls of the house, so that Mary felt as though she were seated next to him at table. She wondered who that might be, and whether he would ever be asked back. She wondered how James was faring, as a reluctant guest at the Harkness table. She wondered—

She hadn't time to wonder and abruptly opened the checkbook. Harkness wasn't a man for writing checks except to cash, and if the monthly sums were surprisingly large, they were also fairly consistent. Although . . . Mary flicked back a page or two in the register. There had been a steady increase in the amount of cash Harkness had required over the past year. Increased household expenses, she supposed; the cost of supporting a large family. Or perhaps the redecoration of the house or new clothing for all the family. The Harknesses certainly seemed to enjoy shopping. Although the numbers seemed high to her, Harkness might have private means to supplement his salary.

The bankbook, however, told a different story. The last entry, dated perhaps six months earlier, showed Harkness to be two hundred pounds overdrawn. Two hundred pounds would be—what? A third, or even half, of his annual salary. It was certainly more than most men earned in a year, and much more than Peter Jenkins could ever hope to see in his lifetime. And there were no further entries showing it as paid off.

She began to rifle through the remaining drawers now in earnest, looking for other documents. If Harkness had gone into overdraft six months ago and not repaid the money, there would be other loans. Loans from family members or friends, loans from banks, perhaps even a loan from the sort of private moneylender who served only the desperate. All her reluctance had fallen away now, and she had to force herself to slow down. To search methodically. To handle only what was necessary. After all, one couldn't scrabble quietly.

In the end, she found only a memorandum book. It was large and quite empty, with the occasional appointment ("Dr. Fowler, 11") or family anniversary ("Amy's birthday") recorded. But as she flicked through the pages to July, a genuine sense of urgency surged through her veins. The last remaining page in the book was Sunday, 10 July: tomorrow. It, too, was blank. But every following page had been torn out. According to Harkness's diary, there was no future. She stared at the book, possible interpretations flooding her brain. It was clearly the end of something: the end of his involvement with Keenan's gang? But apart from that obvious starting point, there was no sign of what he intended.

She stood and stretched muscles stiff from long crouching. As she did, a squiggle at the edge of the blotting pad caught her eye. It was so unlike all the other marks on the pad: a looping, dramatic flourish that stood out in contrast to Harkness's tense, scratchy penmanship. It looked like somebody else's handwriting, yet it was the only indication that a second person had used this blotter. She bent to inspect the ink mark, frowning. Ran a finger over it, mentally reversing the letters. At that, her eyes widened. Good Lord. Could it be? It seemed rather far-fetched, but it was certainly possible. Yes.

Although it was a large risk, she tore away the edge

of the top sheet of paper, removing the mark in question, and slipped it into her pocket. She turned to leave, then had a second thought. From the stationery drawer, she carefully withdrew a single sheet of writing paper and pocketed that, too. Another rumble of laughter erupted from the dining room, that same hyena laugh making goose bumps rise on the back of her neck. As she eased out of the study window and dropped quietly onto the shadowy garden, Mary hoped that James enjoyed at least part of his evening here. For what she was about to suggest to him would certainly spoil his night.

Twenty-two

That laugh! That piercing, grating, hysterical *yipping*. James had seldom heard anything like it, and certainly not from Harkness. The man had always been sober. Earnest. Pompous, even. And now the sound of his mad laughter rang ceaselessly in James's ears as he and Barker drove through Tufnell Park, on the lookout for a small lad in the dark.

Mary was at the meeting point they'd arranged, a few yards from a quiet-looking pub in Leighton Road. She'd been all for somewhere less noticeable—a park or a church, say—but James had prevailed, saying it would be easier for her to blend in near a busy shop front. He'd not dared admit he was worried for her safety in a dark, deserted park. She was a tricky, stubborn proposition, Mary Quinn, and despite his anxiety, at the thought of her, a deep excitement stirred within him.

"Good dinner?" she asked as she climbed in. The carriage, which hadn't entirely stopped, now accelerated smartly toward Bloomsbury and home.

He shrugged. It had been a good meal, as far as food was concerned, although the total absence of wine and spirits had been strange indeed. The sweet, fruit-flavored drinks accompanying the meal had made it seem like a children's party, and eating Stilton without a glass of port was rather pointless. "I'm worried about Harkness. He seems to have gone completely around the bend."

Mary's eyes grew round. "The mad laughter—that was Harkness?"

James nodded. "Telling desperately poor jokes and then laughing at them. His wife hadn't the faintest idea what to say or do, and neither did the rest of us."

"Any idea what . . . ?"

"What made him behave like that? Well, he wasn't tipsy, that's certain."

"The pressures of the building site . . ."

"They're not new. He's been on that job for years now." She was silent, then, looking at him with concern in those luminous eyes. He felt a sudden impulse to bury his face in her neck and weep. Instead, he looked out of the window, concentrating on the gaslamps as they whizzed past. Each light was surrounded by a gauzy yellow halo that vanished when he blinked. "His behavior. The account books. Everything points to his guilt, doesn't it?"

For answer, she fished in a pocket and, with an apologetic look, offered him something. "I also found these."

He took the items with some puzzlement. They didn't look like much: a long strip of thick blotter paper, much used and reused; a blank sheet of writing paper. As he studied the scrap, though, the sinking dread that had attended him all evening came into sharp focus. His stomach rolled queasily, and he cursed under his breath. "You tore this from his blotter?"

She nodded. "I'm sorry."

"Why should you be?" he said fiercely. Turning his attention to the blank sheet, he stroked the watermark with tingling fingertips. "Confirmation," he said softly.

It wasn't a question, but she nodded nevertheless. "It could be an accident. . . ."

"The first commissioner's signature neatly blotted on Harkness's pad—that's an accident?"

"He could have called on Harkness," said Mary quickly. "Borrowed his desk to write a letter."

"He could have borrowed a sheet of paper, if it comes to that."

"That's true," she said slowly. "It would be simple to verify a visit to Harkness's house."

Abruptly, he crumpled the page he'd been holding so carefully. "False hope. If the commissioner was in such a rush to appoint me to the safety review, he'd never have driven all the way out to Tufnell Park to write a letter.

He'd have done so from his office, beside Palace Yard. No. This is clear evidence that Harkness forged my letter of appointment. And if he's forging letters from the Committee of Works, God only knows what else he's up to." He looked at Mary's reluctant expression and groaned. "Oh, Lord—you've more to say, haven't you?" Mary's gaze dropped toward his hands, and he wished she'd look up again. As much as he hated this conversation, it was easier when he could see her eyes.

"Tell me about Harkness," she said quietly.

James paused for a moment. "A friend of my father's. A decent engineer, but not a brilliant one. Devout Christian. Wife. Children—four, I think, about my age and younger. Bit of a clot, but well meaning, and a sound man." His mouth twisted. "Or so I thought."

"Has he money? Or rich relations?"

James shook his head, mystified. "Don't think so. He's always made a virtue of being a professional man, not an idle aristocrat. You know."

"So he's unlikely to have a private income."

"Just what are you suggesting, Mary?"

Her gaze was still averted, slim hands clasped tightly against her knee. "What did you think of his house?"

"What is this?" He grasped her arms and tried to make her look at him. "What are you insinuating?"

"I'm looking for motive," she said calmly, not the least frightened of his explosion. "Tell me what you thought of his house. Its contents. The decorations."

He looked at her blankly. "It was just a house. A bit oppressively froufrou, but Mrs. Harkness has always been like that. A dozen lace doilies where none is needed, that sort of thing. Bad taste isn't criminal."

"But the cost of their furnishings . . . didn't you notice? All the faux-medieval statues and carved wooden furniture and gold-plated everything? What about the dinner service and the candelabra? Could an engineer's salary pay for all that?"

James frowned. "I don't shop. I don't know the cost of things."

"Trust me, James—they're dear. Even if rented or bought on the cheap, the contents of that house are worth a small fortune because there's so bloody much of the stuff."

He closed his eyes for a long moment and listened to the silence in the carriage. Beyond it, there was the *clop* of horses' hooves, the racket of carriage wheels on cobblestones, the swelling sounds of the town as they neared the city lights. Just now, the quiet within was more oppressive than all of these. "So we have motive: greed."

"Or desperation." Mary's voice was careful, gentle, as she made her point. He almost wished she'd be brutal about it. "Harkness's study was entirely different: bare, uncarpeted, underfurnished, and utterly uncomfortable. Doesn't that suggest a man who disagrees with his family's expensive tastes?"

James considered. "His children have large allowances. Son at Cambridge, daughters at finishing school.

And Mrs. Harkness was spattered with jewelry, now that you mention it."

"So we've a man trying to accommodate his family's desires. . . ."

"And failing. On his salary, at least."

"But it seems rather forced on him. The study, at least, suggests that Harkness doesn't share their tastes and would live differently, given the choice."

James felt a sudden, deep weariness. "Every man has a choice."

"But if it means denying his family, or making them unhappy . . ."

"Then it's his responsibility to do so," he said severely. "A man must live by his values. Especially when he's as public and do-gooding about them as Harkness was. Is."

There was a silence. Then Mary placed a hand on his and said softly, "It's a fine philosophy. But perhaps he realized what was happening only when it was too late. He's clearly a man under enormous pressure—his behavior at dinner, for example."

"Why are you so intent on defending him?" asked James, suddenly irritable. "We're talking about a man whose greed compromised the safety of a building site, who may have caused the death of one of his laborers, all because he wanted some gold-plated candlesticks."

"What if he didn't? What if Wick jumped, or was pushed by Keenan or Reid, and the compromises Harkness made didn't have a thing to do with Wick's death?"

"Then Harkness is still morally culpable. And when I turn in my safety review, the authorities and the world are going to conclude the same, no matter what excuses you concoct."

She withdrew her hand swiftly. Sat back, shoulders straight, spine erect. "I'm not excusing anything, just searching for the real cause of Wick's death. And perhaps a little compassion is in order here, as opposed to . . ."

"Go on. You may as well say it."

"Unbending sanctimony."

"You would condone his actions? Theft? Endangering men's lives owing to inadequate equipment, and God knows what else?"

"Of course not. But no man—no person—is perfect." She looked at him for a long moment, but her expression was shuttered. "Except, perhaps, you."

There seemed nothing else to be said.

Twenty-three

Sunday, 10 July

Gordon Square, Bloomsbury

She was angry with him; that much was clear. But he couldn't remember what he'd done, what he'd said, what she'd expected. He couldn't see her face, only her slim back as she walked rapidly away. They were in a park of some sort—a field, perhaps—he couldn't tell—he'd no idea where—and night was falling. He tried to keep up, to speak to her, but no matter how fast he ran, she remained ahead, always ahead. How could she move so swiftly?

He called after her, but she didn't hear. And he kept on chasing, stumbling. He was gasping for air now, each breath stabbing his lungs, and the air around him was hot, so very hot and sticky, like the stifling, blanketing heat of Calcutta. He heard the whine of a mosquito in his ear and then another, and it was too cold in England for mosquitoes, he knew that, so Mary must be in India, which meant that he, too, was back in India. . . .

The mosquitoes whined on, looming close, then

receding in great swoops. He didn't have a net. Foolish to sleep without a net. But he was walking, wasn't he? Not sleeping. Couldn't be sleeping. He was covered in sweat, shirt sticking to his back, lungs aching with the effort, and Mary was no longer in sight, the meadow was gone, and those damned mosquitoes began to cackle, to giggle hysterically, louder and louder, even when he stopped his ears it didn't go away. If only it would stop . . .

"Mr. James."

Why couldn't someone—anyone—make it quiet?

"Master James!"

Anybody at all?

"Jamie! Jamie-lad!"

Rough hands about his head. He swatted at them irritably, but they persisted, those hands, doing something to his head, smothering him. And that voice kept repeating his name, his name—his childhood nickname.

He struggled against the assault. "Stop! Stop it!"

"I'll stop," said a voice with cool clarity, "once you wake up."

With a shudder and a gasp, he was suddenly awake, blinking in the pale glare of what passed as daylight in London. He looked about. He was in his bedroom, of course. It was bitterly cold. And two pairs of eyes stared down at him: Mrs. Vine and George.

"Who called me that?" he demanded. He had a sour taste in his mouth.

"What—Jamie? I did," said George.

"I hate being c-called Jamie. D-don't do it ag-gain." Damn his chattering teeth. Why hadn't they laid a fire if it was so cold?

"Yes, I'd say he's himself again," said George to Mrs. Vine. He heaved a dramatic sigh. "More's the pity."

"You were hallucinating, Mr. James." She placed a cool hand on his forehead. "Feverish. I knew it."

"N-not feverish. F-freezing."

"Chills," she said matter-of-factly, sweeping a hand over his sheets. "And night sweats, too."

"Oh, Lord—it's a relapse, isn't it?" said George, beginning to pace the room. "I'll send for the doctor. He warned you against this, James."

"Don't b-be an ass. I'm n-not having a relapse. I just need a fire."

"It's July, not November."

"It's still f-frigid. A fire, please, Mrs. Vine."

She shook her head gravely. "Not with that fever, Mr. James. You're too warm as it is."

He threw back the bedclothes in a gesture he knew to be pathetic and childish. "Then I'll make it myself." Each leg was weak and felt heavy as lead. The rug beneath his bare toes prickled and burned, and when he tried to stand, his thigh muscles buckled. "Damn it."

Mrs. Vine shifted him to the center of the bed as if he was still eight years old. "Wiser to lie down, Mr. James. I'll send up a pot of willow-bark tea."

Why was she always right? He glared at her retreating

back. Then as it disappeared through the door, he shifted his attention to George. "Why are you still here, then? I thought you went to church with the Ringleys."

"When Mrs. Vine heard you shouting in your sleep, she thought I'd better know about it."

"I—what?" Suddenly the room was stiflingly hot, and he threw off the bedspread. "What did I say?"

"A lot of nonsense about wine and forged letters and hyenas." George's mouth broadened into a sly, rosy smile. "Or did you mean wine-drinking hyenas who are also skilled forgers?"

Remembrance came flooding back with a speed that took his breath away. Or perhaps that, too, was a symptom of malarial relapse. "I—you'd not believe me if I tried to explain." He needed to be alone. To think. His temples throbbed with a vicious headache. "I'm sorry you missed the Ringleys, old man."

"Don't worry. I'll call on them this afternoon. If you're feeling a bit better by then, of course."

"I'm sure I will be." The tea tray arrived, and James eagerly gulped down a cup of the bitter brew. "You've not really sent for Newcombe, have you? The man's a perfect quack."

"He's an excellent physician," said George with reproof. "You just don't like his advice."

"'Lie in bed all day and play cards. One guinea, please.' It's the same in every case—just that the rest of them are old ladies, and so they enjoy it and think he's a genius."

"Well," said George wearily, "malarial fever hasn't improved your temper, at any rate."

James was wrong about Dr. Newcombe, who did indeed recommend complete bed rest but charged one pound ten shillings for this advice, as today was Sunday. Yet this verdict pleased George, especially as James offered not the slightest protest.

"You know," said George, popping into James's room on his way out to the Ringleys', "it's a great load off my mind, knowing that you value your health and want to look after it. I was always against that Indian venture, you know, and it's done us no good as a company. But once you're completely recovered, we can look forward to bigger and better jobs right here in jolly old England. Cheery-ho!"

James offered him a sarcastic wave, the value of which was lost as George returned the salute with pink-cheeked good humor. As the bedroom door closed on his brother, James lay back against his many pillows encased in fresh new linens. He drank two cups of willow-bark tea. And then he rang for writing paper, pen and ink, and a portable desk.

Sunday, 10 July

Noon

My dear Harkness,

Having completed my review of the safety of the St. Stephen's Tower building site, I should like to present my findings to you before their submission to the first commissioner of works tomorrow. I shall call upon you today at your earliest convenience.

Yours sincerely,

J. Easton, Esq.

He composed this letter swiftly and without hesitation and dispatched it by messenger. Then, arranging a second sheet of paper before him, he dipped his pen and let it hover over the page for a long time. He made several tentative pen strokes, all without putting nib to paper. Frowned. Flung down the pen, then took it up once more. Changed his mind yet again. Ten minutes, then twenty, ticked by. Finally, with a groan of frustration, he packed up the writing table. It was senseless. Some things simply couldn't be written.

Twenty-four

Coral Street, Lambeth

Reid. She had to find Reid—and quickly. Last night, she'd not got as far as telling James about the memorandum book; they'd fallen out before she'd had a chance, and she'd no specific idea how to interpret it, anyway. But it left with her a sense of urgency and the conviction that whatever Harkness envisaged happening would take place today. Whatever Harkness and the bricklayers were doing, Reid was the key. He was the least hardened, the most remorseful, the most malleable. His love for Jane Wick meant that he had the most to lose. If she could persuade Reid to confess, that was the Agency's best chance of solving this case. Otherwise, they would be forced to rely on any scraps of evidence Harkness and Keenan failed to destroy.

Mary left by the front door—one of Miss Phlox's rules was that lodgers had the privilege of the front door on Sundays only—and set off down The Cut toward the baker's. Collecting a message from the Agency was awkward on Sundays, when so many businesses were closed. But it wasn't impossible. A small alley ran behind the row of closed shops, and with a glance over her shoulder—not that she expected to see anyone—Mary turned into this narrow passage. The baker's dustbin had, of course, been tipped over. Unsold goods were used by the baker's family, but things they deemed inedible—stale crusts, floor sweepings, weevily flour—were still prizes for the very poor, who scavenged through the bins at dusk. Mary had often seen fistfights break out over the privilege of digging through the scraps. In her long-ago childhood she herself had fought, more than once, over a carelessly discarded bun or trimming.

Beside the back door, the third brick in the fourth layer from the ground was loose. Prising it from its place, Mary ran her fingers around the gap it left. Frowned. Swept the space again. Odd. There'd been a message every day so far. She examined the brick carefully, then the wall, and finally, on hands and knees, sifted the loose earth below. Still nothing. And no indication as to whether it simply hadn't arrived or had been intercepted. Damn, damn, damn.

She had to find Reid, somehow, and didn't much like her choices right now.

James was out of the question.

She could return to the Hare and Hounds and try to trace Keenan's route of yesterday. But, her fear of Keenan aside, such a project seemed foolish in the ever-changing city streets, and anybody still at the Hare would be in no condition to remember anything short of a riot, and perhaps not even that.

Her only option—waiting passively for Monday morning—was impossible, given Harkness's mysterious deadline. But at the very least, she could send another urgent message to the Agency. Accordingly, she began to walk toward the Pig and Whistle, a newish public house less than a quarter of a mile from Westminster.

She stalked, at first, at her usual brisk pace—modified, of course, to accommodate Mark's boyish bounce and slouch. But as her irritation cooled, she slowly became aware that something felt wrong. Someone was watching her. Following her, even. She could see nobody likely in front or beside her. Yet . . .

On the Baylis Road, she slowed her pace. Her pursuer remained behind. She continued to stroll, considering who might be following her. James? Unlikely, given the way they'd parted last night. Besides, today he had to finish his report and struggle with his conscience: work enough for any Sunday, without his tagging after her.

If not James, then her pursuer was Keenan—a thought that chilled her even before she acknowledged it. Her chances of evading him were low. She was in a part of London that she knew only moderately well. It was neither raining nor particularly foggy. And, in truth, she was bone weary. Late nights, high tension, and a bedmate who snored hard enough to shake the foundations of Miss Phlox's flimsy house: this was not a recipe for rest. If she was going to face a pursuer, Mary reasoned, she had better do so in this peopled street. Especially if it was Keenan.

She spun about before she could think better of it. Looked straight into a pair of eyes not five yards behind her. Dark eyes. Familiar eyes. After a long, incredulous moment, Mary found her voice. "Winnie? Why are you following me?"

The girl was quaking, her cheeks a solid pink. "I—I'm sorry." She tried to gather herself, without much success. "I—I only—I thought—"

"You thought what?" Mary all but shouted her question. Then, at the look on Winnie's face, she moderated her voice. "I'm sorry. I didn't mean to frighten you." Now there was irony: the prey apologizing to the stalker. But Winnie still didn't reply—only stared at her in a timid, spellbound way, her color deepening from pink to red. "You surprised me, that's all," Mary said as gently as she could manage.

Winnie nodded. She fidgeted with her sleeve, summoning the courage to say something. She was no longer wearing her usual dress, a brownish affair that was too short in the sleeves. Today she was in Sunday best, a bright, stiff blue that suited her ill. "You going to see your friends?" she asked in a small voice.

"Yes." Mary hoped this wouldn't take long. Perhaps she ought to play the callous, cocky boy after all. Gentleness could swallow up another half hour.

"In St. John's Wood?"

"Maybe. I got lots of friends, you know." She glanced around, as though in a hurry.

"I suppose you have."

But Winnie looked so forlorn that Mary relented. "You can't follow me about, Winnie. It ain't safe."

"I weren't following! I wanted—I was going to ask—" Here, she drew a deep breath and rattled out a speech so quickly that Mary scarcely caught it. It was clearly one she'd been rehearsing for some time. "Would you like to come to Poplar with me, for Sunday dinner, at our house? It's always proper food, Chinese food, not like all that muck at Miss Phlox's, and my mother, she's a wonderful cook, and my father, he's home on shore leave, and—oh, I think you'd like it ever so much. It'd remind you of—well, of home, and all that."

For one incredulous minute, Mary thought she might be dreaming. Or perhaps it was a nightmare. The idea of Winnie's Sunday dinner—a Chinese family, a Chinese meal—made her stomach twist with a complex stab of fear, resentment, inadequacy, jealousy.

Stupid Winnie, who invited strange boys to her family's home.

Hateful Winnie, who had a family to go home to.

Smug Winnie, who thought her family so superior.

Lucky Winnie, who had a family at all.

Mary looked at the girl's pink face, her hopeful, timid eyes. And the knowledge of what Winnie had in Poplar—a mother who was a wonderful cook, a father who'd come home from sea—made Mary go cold and numb. "Can't. I've got things to do."

And she spun on her heel and walked away.

She was crying. Again.

Mary ducked into another alley and tried to staunch the flow. Sometimes it felt as though she'd never stopped. But rather than calming her feelings, the luxury of privacy—even in a smelly back alley—seemed to stir up even more, and she began to bawl outright. Curling herself into a ball, she huddled against a dusty stone wall and wept. For her mother, dead and gone. For her father, lost and forgotten. And, mostly, for herself. For Mary Lang, the mixed-race child, daughter of a Chinese sailor and an Irish seamstress. For the sweetness of her childhood, while her parents lived, and then for its horror, after they died. For the fact that she'd once belonged, and the knowledge that now she never would again. Winnie hadn't deserved such rudeness, but she would also never understand just how privileged she was.

Mary cried as she hadn't in years. Perhaps as she never had. And even as she wept, she understood that this couldn't go on. This was her last such indulgence—a farewell of sorts. Because after these minutes of weakness, she must let go of her Chinese identity. She would deny it, protect it, conceal it at all costs, because the truth was simply too painful and too dangerous. There was no room in English society for half-castes, and her choice was simple: either deny her Chinese blood or be forever limited by it. The last thing she wanted was to be defined solely by her father's race—and so she would have to sacrifice it entirely.

It was a crude choice, a hateful one. But it was better to choose than to have her fate thrust upon her. Gradually, her sobs eased. Tears dried up. She wiped her face as best she could, using the inside of her jacket. Then she took a deep breath, embracing the fetid smell of the river as a means of concentrating her attentions. And she set out once again for Westminster.

Twenty-five

On Sunday mornings, the Pig and Whistle had the aspect of a busy church: clean and polished, and all within gathered for the same purpose. Most tables were occupied by quiet clusters of three or four, while a number of solo gentlemen leaned against the bar, meditatively sipping beer. The landlady, a rosy, bosomy woman in a ribboned cap, polished imaginary smears from the bar.

Mary gave the coded greeting. "Half an ale for a thirsty lad, missus."

The landlady directed her round to the end of the bar and provided her with not only half a pint of ale but also a scrap of paper, a pencil stub, and enough privacy so that only an excessively nosy neighbor might observe the spectacle of a small, shabby lad writing a note with considerably less difficulty than one might expect of that sort of boy.

The note was in a simple code—easy to memorize and quick to decode, using a replacement key that rendered it a simple string of numbers to the uninitiated. Mary's message was terse: *Suspect H in league with K, R. No evid yet re W. Pls advise*. Having written the note, she drained her half-pint. Before she could ask, a new drink was placed before her and the old mug removed, along with the note. "You drink that nice and slow, lad," said the landlady firmly. "That's a fine ale for sipping, not gulping."

Mary followed her instructions. She'd never been a great beer drinker but she was rapidly growing accustomed to its complex, bittersweet flavors. On a diet that meant she was eating less than ever before, in a job that required more physical labor than she was used to, she recognized in her daily pints an important form of nutriment. Harkness was off his rocker, trying to ban his workers from beer. How else could they find the energy to work?

A large hand clapped her on the shoulder. "Don't you look comfortable," drawled its owner.

She nearly bit her mug in surprise. There, smirking down at her, stood Octavius Jones. His other hand was curled around a pint pot and he perched on the stool beside hers, his sleepy green eyes narrowed in amusement. Amusement and . . . scrutiny.

Mary tried to control her panic. He'd not watched her write that note; she'd been careful about that. He must have appeared afterward, during or after the removal of the message. All the same, his eyes had a knowing glint that she didn't like. "Mr. Jones," she said in her gruffest boy's tones.

"Young Quinn. What a surprise to see you in my local on this stinking Sunday. You know, I've been thinking about you. . . ."

She shifted uncomfortably, as any boy would at such a declaration. "I ain't done nothing wrong."

His hand still lay on her shoulder and when she shrugged, he didn't remove it. He elevated an eyebrow—something he'd clearly practiced in a mirror for just such an occasion. "I wouldn't dream of suggesting such a thing. No, no, no," he said authoritatively, as she knocked back the rest of her ale and made to stand. "Another pint for me, Mrs. Hughes, and the same again for my young friend here. We're just going into the snug."

"Can't, sir. I got to go."

"Stay and have another, do," he said, his voice still easy and sociable. But his hand on her shoulder was heavy now, the fingers digging in hard enough to bruise. "I want a word with you, young Quinn."

"I got nothing to tell you. I don't know nothing."

"Rubbish. We've plenty to talk about."

"You take your hands off," Mary said loudly. "I ain't that kind of boy."

"And I ain't that kind of gent," replied Jones promptly, unperturbed by the heads turning in their direction. "Don't be afraid, young Quinn. It's not your sexual services I'm after."

"What d'you want, then?"

He'd not taken his eyes from hers. "I think," he said very quietly, "you'll find it to your advantage to have that drink with me. *Miss* Quinn."

The landlady set two foaming pints before them and looked hard at Mary. "Everything all right, young man?"

Very slowly, very reluctantly, Mary nodded.

Mrs. Hughes's gaze lingered for a moment longer, but when Mary met it with an even stare, she shrugged and returned to her customers at the other end of the bar.

"I'll talk to you here," said Mary in a low voice. "Not in the snug."

"Suit yourself," said Jones easily. "Though you'd be just as safe there. I'm not in the habit of ravishing the competition."

The competition . . . ? Mary felt a sudden great wave of relief. If that was all he meant, she was in luck. "I wouldn't have thought the *Eye* worth competing against," she said scornfully.

Jones smirked. "Insult me all you like, but I've just tricked you into admitting that you're a reporter, too."

"You didn't trick me," she said, settling into the role now. "I was surprised you saw through the disguise, but the explanation's clear enough. Why else would I be wearing boy's clothes and working on site?"

"Indeed," said Jones, settling himself on the stool

beside hers. "I must admit, you had me fooled until I saw you looking through the window at that coffee shop. That was a dead giveaway."

"Oh—Reid's great tip." She smirked. "The poor sod."

"How do you mean?"

"Are you asking me for information, Mr. Jones? Without offering to pay?"

He grinned at that, rather reluctantly. "I've already confessed that I fell for the whole boy-laborer thing. It's not a bad getup, until you go peering through windows with those curious, adult eyes." His eyes skimmed over her with a detached sort of assessment. "Aren't you going to tell me your real name?"

"You may continue to call me Quinn."

He looked wounded. "Subterfuge is so very wearisome, don't you think? I prefer to embrace the truth, myself—it's only proper for those of our shared profession."

"Surely you're not claiming that Octavius Jones is your real name?"

He grinned. "Beggars belief, doesn't it? But I'm afraid it's so: I'm the eighth son—son, mark you, not child, for I've three sisters—my father never being one for moderation. Tertius, Quintus, and Septimus were my favorite brothers when I was a child."

She laughed. "Now that's a tale."

"It's true! My mother was a gentlewoman of little education and even less common sense who eloped with a ruffian called Jones. Naming us in Latin was her only revenge on my very unsaintly father." His eyes dared her to disbelieve him.

"You must take after your father."

"Naturally." He held his pint aloft. "Well, Miss Mark Quinn, here's to the pursuit of truth—or, in my case, scandal and profit." Without waiting for her to respond, he drained his pint, sighed with satisfaction, and said, "Who d'you work for, then? Never one of the broadsheets; they'd not have a mere weak woman writing in their pages." He tapped his lower lip thoughtfully. "Perhaps one of the more radical weekly mags? I suppose you're a regular hyena in petticoats."

She grinned. "I didn't know trash journalists read Mary Wollstonecraft."

"Only enough to insult her," he replied, good humor unruffled. "But you're trying to distract me. Whom d'you write for?"

"Nobody. I'm researching a book."

He groaned melodramatically. "Heaven preserve us—*researching* a *book*! Of all the idealistic, unrealistic, ninny-ish things to attempt. A book, indeed! And I suppose it's intended as one of those well meaning, authentic reports on the lower orders and their struggles for survival, etcetera, etcetera." He caught her expression and chortled. "I knew it! I knew it! You earnest little dunce! Don't you know that won't sell? You might as well flog those breeches you're wearing; they'll fetch more than your silly *book*."

"Perhaps. But I'd wager that I know a deal more about the death of John Wick than you do," she said coolly.

That brought him up short. "Poppycock. What can you have learned while fetching and carrying and ruining your back on a worker's wage?"

She shrugged and began to climb down from her stool. "What a pity you'll never know."

"Wait!" His hand shot out and grabbed hers. Then, as he met her gaze, he meekly released her. "You're so abrupt," he complained. "Can't we be friendly about this?"

"After you've insulted my research and my proposed book?" She injected a degree of wounded pride into her tone, just to see what he'd say.

"And touchy, too. My dear girl, you'll never be a proper journalist if you don't grow a rhinoceros's hide to cover your skin."

Mary considered the man standing before her. Despite his constant stream of nonsense, he was alert and observant. Now here was a man whose allegiance was clear, it being entirely to himself. He was obsessed with the scandal at the building site. He had connections: if anybody knew what was what and who'd gone where, it was Jones.

And she was desperate. The image of Harkness's mutilated diary was fresh in her mind's eye. Today was the day, and she still didn't know what, where, how, or why. If she'd had the time, she'd have waited for the Agency. But she doubted she could afford to now. "So, why would

I tell you what I know? I've worked hard for the knowledge." She held out her bruised, nicked hands as proof.

"Ah, the age-old refrain: what's in it for me?" Jones ignored her hands. "You know, a proper old-fashioned lady would ask, 'How may I assist you, Mr. Jones?'"

"A 'proper old-fashioned lady' would summon her footman to escort you out by the tradesman's entrance, Mr. Jones."

He cackled with delight. "What a fearsome old tartar you'll be one day. Now. What can I offer you as an inducement to tell all?"

"To begin with, a promise not to publish a word of what you learn until the first of August, or until I say you may—whichever comes first. Second, not to speak about the same until that time. Third—"

"My dear child, those are conditions, not inducements. Tell me what *you* want. Money? An introduction to publishers? A penn'orth of lead-painted sweeties?"

"I was just getting to that," said Mary. She was accustomed to Jones's style now, and obnoxious as it was, it seemed to be growing on her. "I need your help."

"Aha." He leaned forward, his eyes keen. "What sort of help?"

"Finding Keenan and Reid. Today."

"That I can manage," he said promptly. "That all?"

"I also want to know how you think Wick died, and why."

He let out a long, low whistle. "I knew it! I knew we

were after the same thing. You secretive little devil, why didn't you say so in the first place?"

"You'd have sent me packing."

"Of course I would! But I'd have appreciated your foolhardy confidence."

"As you do now?"

He shrugged, turning up his palms. "As it happens, I'm feeling generous today. Also, short of ideas. It's a devil of a problem, isn't it? How did the scoundrel—for everyone seems to agree about that, if nothing else—how did he die?

"It's obvious, of course, that the brickies are robbing Harkness blind. All that 'ghost of the clock tower' business—it's not entirely my invention, y'know. It began as Keenan's thing, to explain mysterious goings-on at night, and the sudden disappearance of quantities of expensive building materials. Although"—he cocked his head to one side—"I suppose it might be true. Many a man perished during the blaze of eighteen-thirty-whatsit that burned the old Parliament buildings to the ground. Only that's not talked of these days. It's all Big Ben and the improving effects of Gothic architecture on the morals of the working class.

"But I digress. Keenan and Reid are filling me with this stuff about the ghost, but all the while there's a big problem in their little gang. Y'see, Reid's fallen in love with Wick's wife—scrawny little sparrow, don't see the appeal myself . . . though, egad, she's fertile enough—

and Wick and Reid are at each other's throats. Keenan's none too pleased with this crack-up, since if the gang splits the profit goes, and who's to say they won't start to talk? So he's at 'em to work things out, and he's the sort of man who means it. I'd not put it past him to push Wick off the tower just to shut him up."

"Why Wick and not Reid?"

"P'raps Wick looked at him wrong. I don't know, but he ain't sentimental, Keenan."

"Wouldn't Reid be more likely to push Wick? Being in love with his wife?"

Jones sighed. "In theory, yes. But he's an anxious, do-gooding sort, is Reid. He'd like nothing better than to marry the widow and raise her brood and go straight for the rest of his life. He's much more likely to wait twenty years for Wick to die, then marry the toothless widow and call it the triumph of true love."

"Hmph."

"Indeed."

"So you're for Keenan."

"Not so fast, young Quinn. There's an additional problem. Wick was a moody, brooding sort—type of fellow who's your best friend one minute, don't know you the next. And he'd been talking back and forth with Harkness."

Mary tried not to look too suddenly alert. "What about Harkness?"

Jones sighed dramatically. "That's what I don't
Wick was sneaking on Keenan and Reid, maybe. C
ing to bring Harky into their little circle—but that don't really make sense: why share out the profit four ways, when you can get away with three? My money's on Wick double-crossing his mates for some paltry reward, for that's the sort of chap he was."

Mary thought fast. The theory didn't account for Harkness's elevated lifestyle, but that might be a separate matter. Perhaps she and James had been too quick to put together cause and effect.

"And now we come to my little conversation with Reid—the one you were so keen to hear." He cackled at the memory. "What a load of poppycock that was. Reid's panicked about something, that's all I know, and he gets hold of me and fills me with the purest nonsense about Wick: staunch family man, devout churchgoer, etcetera, etcetera. When all of Southwark knows he beat his wife to a bloody pulp every night, and her screams could be heard across the Thames."

Mary shuddered. She was only too able to picture that domestic scene.

Jones took no notice. "But the interesting thing about Reid's story is that he's trying to throw blame on Keenan. Not directly, mind you, but Keenan's name keeps cropping up, and it's clear that things are sour between them. The gang's cracked up for good, and Reid wants out, and his first thought is to get the journalist on his side." He smiled pleasantly. "Newspapers are the new courts of law, it seems. Even scandal sheets such as mine."

"So, to clear his own name and place the blame on Keenan, Reid wants you to whitewash Wick's character before the reading public?"

"So it seems. Crude, isn't it?"

"Clever, assuming you believed him."

"People generally assume too much." He signaled to Mrs. Hughes for a fresh drink, then propped his chin on his fist and looked at Mary. "Your turn."

Tailoring her narrative to Jones's swift, casual style, Mary told him about the tea round. Her visit to the Wick home. Harkness's attendance at Wick's funeral. The subsequent fistfight between Keenan and Reid. And yesterday's disappearance of a drunken Reid with a sober Keenan.

Jones listened in complete silence—something she'd not thought him capable of. Then, pursing his lips, he let out a low whistle. "So you're for Reid as the killer. Anyone else we ought to consider? Jolly old Harkness, perhaps?"

Mary kept silent.

"I suppose there's always Wick himself, though I can't think why he'd have done that. Unless the idea of going home to all those brats was suddenly just too much." He pulled a vivid face. "Understandable, really."

"As though he'd nothing to do with the *getting* of all those brats," said Mary indignantly.

Jones twinkled with amusement. "Easy, Miss Radical; I was only in jest. No, much as I hate to admit it, I like your theory better."

"Well, then," said Mary, standing and stretching her legs. They were numb from unaccustomed sitting. "How do I find Keenan and Reid?" She stared at Jones, who studied the depths of his pint with deep concentration. "Or have you already forgotten your end of the bargain?"

"Not at all," he said easily, "but I do wonder if it's not a little irresponsible of me to send you in search of them. Of Keenan, in particular. He's utterly ruthless, you know."

"I know."

"And if he sees through your disguise . . ."

"I don't need you to frighten me; I'm quite capable of doing that myself."

"But you still need to locate him? There's such a thing as overdedication to the profession, you know. Why not have another drink with me and wait to see what happens on site tomorrow? My money's on Reid's murder. Body found in Thames. Keenan captured in daring, high-wire escape."

"That's your plan? To place a bet, then wait and see?"

"Even God rested on the seventh day."

She smiled. "Just tell me where they live. That's all I need from you."

"That's all, eh?" He looked her up and down once again, not the least bit detached or critical this time. "Pity." But he gave her the directions all the same.

Twenty-six

Southwark

It was an enormous, accidental tenement—a pair of houses that seemed to have fallen into each other and thus been prevented from collapsing. One door was boarded over, and none of the ground-floor windows was intact. It was far beneath what Mary expected for a skilled laborer, even one intent on saving money, and her first, angry thought was that Jones had played her false. It was a simple matter, spouting off a random address. By the time she discovered his perfidy, he'd have long departed the Pig and Whistle. Or perhaps he'd not bother. Quite likely if she went back to the pub, she'd find him draped across two chairs, laughing at her credulity.

She stood for a moment on the pavement, irresolute. This was a waste of time. Yet where could she go next but St. John's Wood, to report her failures? As she hovered outside the ramshackle building, a skinny boy hobbled out the door. He moved stiffly and descended the two front steps with the care of an invalid. Mary's eyes widened. Surely not . . .

Yet as the boy turned, he caught sight of her, and recognition flashed across his freckled face. He waved a hand in greeting.

"Jenkins!" Mary sped across the street. "I been looking for you!"

"Well, I didn't know." He tried to sound sullen but couldn't quite control a smile of pleasure. "How's tricks, then?"

Relieved as she was to see Jenkins safe, Mary steered the conversation round to Reid as soon as she reasonably could. Jenkins was utterly unsurprised at the mention of his name.

"Aye, he's a good one, that Reid. He's the reason we live here now." He caught Mary's expression of surprise and grinned his old, knowing grin. "You didn't know? He felt that bad about me losing my place through Keenan, he come and found us in that cellar. He's the one what got us a room in here." He gestured behind.

"Very decent of him," said Mary cautiously. It seemed like a small enough gesture, given Reid's illicit income.

But Jenkins was clearly thrilled. "Decent!" he scolded. "It ain't decent—saintly is what it is. Bloody Harky wouldn't give me even an extra day's wages, for all he's a gent and rolling in money and a teetotaling saint, but Reid's paying for me and the kiddies to live, food and all, on his wages. That's a sight more than decent."

"It's all right for those who can afford it." Mary didn't like Jenkins's new tone of worshipful fervor. Especially not toward a crooked laborer who'd soon be sacked and tried for his part in the site thefts.

"What d'you mean?" Now he was all bristling suspicion again, much as he'd been on the day they'd first met. "What you saying?"

"About the brickies being on the take," said Mary patiently. "You're the one who told me."

Jenkins made a noise of disgust. "I never said that. It's Keenan what's on the take, all the time. Him and Wick; they played Harky blind. But Reid weren't never a part of that. Reid, he's living here now 'cause he can't keep his old digs and us."

She hesitated, unsure where Jenkins's hero worship left off and his canny knowingness began. If Reid wasn't part of the thieving ring . . . "Where's he now, then? Isn't he with Keenan?"

Jenkins looked worried. "I dunno. His room, it's next to ours, and he's always out of a Sunday, at Mrs. Wick's. But he ain't never come home last night."

"He went off with Keenan yesterday."

"He never!"

"I saw them. We all saw them." As she explained Reid's nervous departure from the pub, she watched Jenkins's expression grow more and more worried. The lad was in earnest about Reid's shining character.

"We got to find him," said Jenkins, thoroughly alarmed now. "That Keenan—he's a bad one."

"So everyone says."

"You and me," he said fiercely. "We'll find him. I should've been at the Hare yesterday."

Mary stared, but he seemed in earnest. "D'you really think you could have stopped Reid from going off with Keenan?"

"I could have tried."

"What are you going to do now?"

"I'm going to find him," he said with perfect confidence. "And you's going to help me."

Twenty-seven

Gordon Square, Bloomsbury

James awoke from a feverish nap with his small stock of patience thoroughly exhausted. His head pounded. His skin felt raw and tender, even against the smooth linen sheets. The ticking of his bedroom clock seemed excessively loud, and he stared at it with some suspicion. It read seven o'clock, clearly an error. He was still staring at it when Mrs. Vine appeared with a tray.

"Mrs. Vine, what time is it?"

She glanced at the clock with some surprise. "Why, seven o'clock, Mr. James."

That made no sense whatsoever. "In the *morning*?"

"In the evening, sir. It's Sunday evening, and I've brought you a little supper."

He felt a peculiar jolt. Of course it was evening; dusk was falling. But that meant he'd been asleep for hours. . . . "Hang supper. Where's that letter I've been waiting for?"

"You've not received a letter, Mr. James."

"There must be a letter. When I woke this morning,

I sent a letter by messenger and he was to wait for a reply. Where's my reply?" He heard his voice growing loud and cross, but seemed quite unable to control it.

"The messenger delivered the letter but received no reply, sir."

He swore and threw back the bedclothes. Cold air rushed against his skin, making him shiver. "I'm going out. Tell Barker to be ready in ten minutes, please."

"That's most unwise, Mr. James. Malarial fever's a serious business; you'll injure your health in earnest."

"There's nothing you can say to change my mind."

"Drink a little soup, at least. You must be parched."

"Ten minutes, Mrs. Vine." He opened a drawer and extracted a small envelope of thin, foreign paper.

Her expression remained perfectly neutral. "Very well. Any message for Mr. George when he asks about your absence?"

"Thank you, no."

Barker, too, was reluctant to the brink of mutiny. "You ain't fit to go nowhere. I'll go and ask for the letter meself, Mr. James, but you ought to be resting up."

"I'm not inclined to bargain with you, Barker."

"That fever's got on your brain. Don't play the fool, lad."

"Thank you, Barker. Now, let's be off."

The streets were quiet and the roads dry, but the drive to Tufnell Park was a rackety torture. Each bump of the cobblestones, the steady sway of the carriage, the sharp *clop* of the horseshoes — to James all appeared grotesquely magnified. He was still desperately cold, despite his heavy woolen overcoat. It seemed absurd that people might walk through the streets in light jackets. Despite the very real sensations of fever, however, this was manageable. He could finish his job, even when ill. It was just a matter of being rational.

At Harkness's house, the door was opened by a distracted footman who twice asked for his card after he'd already presented it, then left him to wait in the hall for a long time. He could hear hurried footsteps and the sound of doors opening and closing upstairs. Eventually, Mrs. Harkness came down the stairs. She wore a rich satin gown and, on top of it, a rather pilled and misshapen bedjacket.

"Mr. — ah, Mr. Easton. I do apologize for this confusion. My husband . . . he can't see you just now."

James waited for a few seconds. "Is he unwell?" he asked politely.

"Oh, Lord, I don't know." She tottered as though about to fall but ignored the steadying arm he offered her. "I simply don't know!"

She didn't smell of drink, but he couldn't think what else might cause this sort of behavior. "Have you sent for a physician?"

Her dilated eyes looked at something past him. In fact, she'd not met his gaze at all in the course of this brief, strange meeting. "No, no — no doctor."

It wasn't clear whether she simply hadn't summoned one, or Harkness didn't want one. James found it difficult to control his impatience. "May I see him? Perhaps I could assist you somehow."

Finally, she looked at him. Her eyes were terrified, and shining with incipient tears. "If you could see him, that would be helpful indeed." But she didn't move.

James took a half step forward. "Is he upstairs?"

She shook her head. "No. Not upstairs."

Perhaps she was the one who needed a physician. "Kindly lead me to your husband, ma'am."

A strange, horrid sound emerged from her throat—half shriek, half sob. "Would that I could!" She tottered again and this time began to topple in a slow, stiff way, making no attempt to right herself or to break the fall with her hands. With a swift movement that made his joints ache, James dived forward, arms outstretched. Mrs. Harkness was a tall, ample woman, Harkness's equivalent in build, and he hadn't the strength today to right her. The best he could do was arrest her fall. In this awkward posture—bent double, sweating with effort, arms clasped about the madwoman—he remained until the distracted footman finally returned.

"Quickly!" snapped James. "Help me lift her to a sofa."

The footman blinked once, twice, and then creaked slowly into motion. Between them, they lugged Mrs. Harkness's limp, heavy form upstairs to the drawing room. James found the bell pull and tugged it energetically. "Smelling salts, brandy, and send for a doctor, quick," he snapped at the bewildered-looking maid who answered. "And you"—he rounded on the footman who was in the act of slinking away—"where's Mr. Harkness?"

The footman sidled backward, blinking rapidly. "I'm sure I don't know, sir."

"What d'you mean, you don't know? Is he at home or not?"

"N-no, sir."

"Not at home to callers, or actually not in the house?"

"N-not in the h-house, sir."

James stared at the ninny. "Then tell me where he's gone."

"I—I don't know, sir. He didn't say."

"What time did he go out?"

The man's eyes rolled in his face, unwilling to meet James's gaze and unable to focus anywhere else. "R-round about one o'clock, sir. Just after."

"Stand still while I'm talking to you! Did he take the carriage?"

"N-no, sir."

"A horse?"

"I—I don't believe so, sir."

"What did he say?"

"I—I don't rightly know, sir." The man blinked rapidly as he spoke. He looked like a frightened rabbit.

James sighed. Clearly, his direct approach had addled

the man's wits. "All right," he said, trying for patience. It didn't come easily. "Tell me what happened."

The footman licked his lips once, twice. Swallowed. Then said, "He ain't been himself, sir. Not since last night. And today he got a letter—round about noon, it'd be. And he's in his study, reading it, and he starts laughing. You heard it, sir—that high, loud laugh he was doing last night. And he's half laughing and half crying, and Mrs. Harkness here comes down to him and she asks what's wrong, and he says, 'Everything. Nothing. It is—'" The footman creased up his face, trying to recall. Eventually, he shook his head. "Don't rightly know what he said, sir—it were French, or something."

"Never mind that. What next?"

"And—and he says to Mrs. Harkness, 'I can make this right. Just remember, my dear—I did this all for you.' And Mrs. Harkness is asking what's the matter, and carrying on, like, but that's the last he says. And he picks up his hat and his walking stick, and he walks out of the house. Just like that."

"He didn't say where he was going or what he meant to do?"

"No, sir."

"In which direction did he walk?"

"South."

"You didn't follow him?"

The man shifted. "Mrs. Harkness, she were screaming and carrying on, sir. We'd enough to do with her."

James nodded. "Very well. Does Mrs. Harkness have a relation—a sister, perhaps—nearby who could come to help her?"

The footman nodded. "Mrs. Phelps, sir. I'll go and fetch her this minute."

"Wait a moment. Stay with Mrs. Harkness until the doctor comes, you and her maid both. Once the doctor's here, then fetch Mrs. Phelps." The man nodded. He was accustomed to taking directions and, once instructed, showed something of a return to the footman's orderly manner. James turned to Mrs. Harkness, who lay motionless and silent on the sofa. Her eyes were closed, and she looked so still and calm James felt the need to touch her wrist. It was warm and her pulse, though rapid, was strong. "Madam. I'm going in search of your husband. I'll send word once I find him."

No response, not even a fluttering of the eyelids.

James's hat still hung neatly on a hook in the hall, and it seemed peculiar that it, of all things, was undisturbed and in the right place. Climbing back into the carriage, he touched his breast pocket and felt the reassuring presence of that foreign envelope. He didn't need to consider where Harkness might have gone in the seven hours he'd been absent. There was only one possible destination.

"Home, sir?" asked Barker, without much hope.

"No. St. Stephen's Tower."

* * *

Jenkins was still suffering as a result of Keenan's thrashing: that was obvious to Mary, although he tried to deny it. The best pace he could manage was a steady walk that soon slowed to a hobble. It cost him enormous effort. He was sweating profusely, his complexion gray, trying to suppress a wince with each step.

"Almost there," said Mary encouragingly. "Aren't we?" While Jenkins hadn't asked how much she knew or why she was curious, it was still safest to play the role of sidekick for as long as she could.

He nodded grimly. "Just round the corner."

"Shall I go ahead and see? It's number nine, right?" This second visit to the Wicks was pure optimism on Mary's part. She doubted Reid was there, but for once she would be happy to be wrong.

He nodded. "Go on."

As she scanned the row of houses, a couple of curtains twitched: nosy neighbors, once again. But Wick's house had no curtains—and who washed curtains on a Sunday?—which gave the house an abandoned feel. The black crepe bow was gone, its absence a vivid suggestion of how quickly a life could be forgotten.

"You moving in?"

Mary turned. A solemn, red-haired girl of about nine regarded her from the door of the house opposite. "Where?"

"There. Number nine."

"It's—empty?"

"They went this morning."

"Wasn't that quite sudden?"

"I seen them packing up, all night."

"Where did they go?"

She shrugged.

"Did the woman—Mrs. Wick, that is—pack everything on her own? Or was there a man helping her?" There had to have been. Jane Wick was neither decisive nor quick-moving by nature. Any sudden removal must have been at someone else's behest. The real question was, had Keenan or Reid moved the Wick family?

"Quinn! Quinn! What you doing?"

Both Mary and the girl jumped at this interruption: Peter Jenkins, of course, bearing down on them like a limping wolf. With a slight squeak of alarm, the girl promptly vanished into her house, the door thumping decisively behind her.

Mary sighed. "Jenkins."

"This ain't a time to muck about! Don't you understand?"

"I understand, Jenkins. That girl just told me that the Wicks moved out early this morning."

"That's rot! He'd have told me!"

Mary shrugged. "See for yourself. And after that, go back to your lodgings and see if your rent's been paid in advance, and how much."

Jenkins stared at her. "Why? What's it to you?"

She sighed. "If it's paid up, it means Reid knew he was

going and he probably packed up the Wick family. If it's not paid up, it's likely Keenan got rid of them all, quick."

He stared at her, slow wonder blossoming in his face. "I—that—you—why, you ain't so stupid as you pretend!"

She half smiled. "And when you've done that, come down to the building site. Hitch a ride on a cab or something."

His eyes went even rounder. "Palace Yard?"

Mary nodded. "I've a feeling the real answer is there."

Twenty-eight

Around Westminster, the streets were dusky and deserted. There was little here on a Sunday to attract pleasure seekers, and few residents to come and go. And in the unusual, magnified stillness of the place, the broad-shouldered man skulking in the shadows was highly noticeable. Mary stopped and tucked herself against a convenient pillar-box, the better to observe his progress. Yet she already knew where he was going.

The man was familiar—doubly so. That square head on those burly shoulders belonged to Keenan, she was certain. And not only that, but she now had an identity for the man who'd broken into the building site on Monday last. The man who'd rifled Harkness's office, chased her out into the street, and nearly caught her. He and Keenan were one and the same. And with that realization, she also understood why the theft hadn't been reported. If Harkness was working in cahoots with Keenan, it was part of their arrangement. If Harkness was trying to solve the problem of the site thefts, it was probably some sort of trap he'd laid. Either way, there was no use in involving the police. Not yet.

Mary watched, waiting for Keenan to plant his climbing grip in the wooden fence. Tonight, however, he hesitated. Glanced about. Walked the length of the wooden fence with an air of suspicion. As he neared her hiding spot not far from the corner, Mary readied herself to run. Her only chance of eluding Keenan was to gain a head start; large though he was, he was also swift. But he wasn't looking toward the street. His frown was concentrated on the fence — or rather, on something beyond. He turned back again, walked to the site entrance and examined the padlock. Then, with a glance over his shoulder, he simply lifted the latch and opened the gate.

Mary stared. He'd not used a key, which meant that the site was already unlocked. But that itself seemed impossible. Only Harkness — and perhaps the first commissioner himself — would hold a key to the site. Unless . . .

The rumble of carriage wheels made her tense again. This time, however, the moment she recognized the driver, she relaxed. She couldn't say she was precisely glad to see Barker, but she was relieved not to see someone else. The same was not true for him: as she stepped out of the shadow of the pillar-box, his frown deepened until his eyes all but disappeared. The carriage rolled to a reluctant halt, and he jumped down, nodding to her curtly.

He unfolded the steps, opened the door, and offered his hand upward with the solicitous gesture of a nurse to a child. "Mind your step, sir."

"You say that as though I've never climbed down from a carriage before."

"I say it because you've clearly taken leave of your senses, sir."

"I don't know how long I'll be."

The speaker finally emerged, leaning wearily on Barker's arm. His dark gaze scanned the street, coming to a startled, almost guilty halt as he saw Mary, not ten yards away. Mary's eyes widened, and she felt a stab of alarm—anguish, even—at the sight of him. Yet from the set of his lips, she knew the worst thing she could do was express concern. Coming toward the curb, she said in passably casual tones, "We do seem to keep meeting up."

He gave a brief huff of amusement and climbed down. "You followed Harkness?"

"Keenan."

"Seen him go in?"

"Just now. But not Harkness. Are you certain he's here?"

"I'd stake my appointment as safety inspector on it." He grinned ruefully.

Mary understood that he was offering a truce. "Come on, then—the gate's open, as though they're waiting for us."

"Pity; I was looking forward to scaling the fence."

"Very funny," she said severely. "If you can walk at a normal pace, you'll have done enough."

"Oh, not you, too. I've already been warned, you know, about the importance of complete bed rest."

"Glad to hear it." As she followed James toward the gate, she glanced back at Barker. He looked grim. On impulse, she said quietly, "I'll take good care of him."

"Suppose you can try," came the glum reply.

Through the palings of the gate, Mary and James saw Keenan emerge from the site office. His usual scowl was intensified, and he appeared to be muttering something—curses and maledictions, probably. Eventually, with an audible snarl, he stormed back into the site office. He remained there for perhaps half a minute, and when he reemerged, he was no more content. With a final growl of exasperation, he stalked toward the tower entrance, leaving the office door ajar—an unusual piece of carelessness for a thief. As he vanished into the base of the tower, Mary glanced at James. He nodded, and together they entered the site.

Mary paused for a moment to examine the padlock. It was intact rather than smashed, and when she pointed to it, James nodded again. "Harkness has the only key." His voice was taut.

Their boots rang loudly on the cobblestones in the quiet courtyard. Although the building was so nearly complete, the site had an air of desolation that made it seem more like an abandoned ruin than a triumphant architectural landmark. Or perhaps that was her imagination once again.

James pushed the office door wide open—or as far as it would go. It was blocked by something on the other side, and Mary's first thought was of Harkness. James's too, judging from the speed with which he darted inside. "Papers," he said gloomily, turning to Mary. "It's always papers." The light was dim in the little office now, with the sun plummeting low in the sky.

She looked carefully around the room, trying to match the chaos with her most recent memory of its contents. Things had certainly been shifted, but . . . "Has it been ransacked?"

James shrugged. "Who'd know? It's looked like this all week."

"Although . . ." Her gaze lingered on the desk. Its top left drawer was open by an inch, and she couldn't remember having seen it like that before. Carefully, she pulled the drawer out: it was completely empty but for an envelope—the same sort of envelope, she noted automatically, that had fallen from Reid's pocket. Harkness's personal stationery. On it was scrawled a simple message: *This week's payment is here.* Beside it was a sketch—a few lines, really, clumsily scrawled—of St. Stephen's Tower. A harsh black X marked the belfry.

"What have you found?"

"Come and look."

He stood just behind her shoulder, his breath lightly stirring her hair. "Damn, damn, damn," he said quietly.

"Melodramatic, isn't he?"

"I was thinking of the stairs."

The envelope was empty, but Mary pocketed it nevertheless. "Would you—might it be better if you—?"

"Stayed down here?" He was already walking steadily, grimly, across the yard. "Not a chance."

"Just how ill are you?"

"Well enough. Are you a girl or a boy at the moment?"

"I think I'd better be Mark."

"Good. If you ask again about my health, I'll smack you, Mark Quinn."

With a resigned sigh, she opened the small door to the tower stairs. "After you, Mr. Easton, sir."

Twenty-nine

It was a slow, torturous climb — much worse than the last one. Although James was quite ready to lean on her, they stopped to rest every twenty steps, then every dozen, then every few. He was breathless and shaky, with a pallor that couldn't be blamed entirely on the yellowing distortions of gaslight. At the one-third point, he collapsed onto the cool stone floor and remained there, in a huddle, for several minutes.

"James."

"Just a minute." He fumbled in his breast pocket and brought out a narrow parchment envelope. Tipping his head back, he poured the contents — a powder of some sort — into his mouth, swallowed, and made a face. "Gah. All right. What?"

She stared at the paper in his hands. "What — what the devil was that?"

"Willow-bark powder, of course. What did you think?" Amusement flickered across his weary features.

"Some dangerous poison brought back from my Oriental travels?" He grinned at her sheepish expression. "Powdered opium? The demon that's sapping my youth and beauty?"

"Listen," she said rather more severely than necessary, "we're losing time. I'm going up ahead to see what's happening."

He shook his head. "We're going together."

"That will take another hour, if not two. We can't wait that long. Keenan's already at the belfry, and I don't want to meet him on his way down."

He climbed to his feet, a trifle unsteady but already looking more energetic than when he arrived on site. "It won't take that long. I feel much better."

She examined his face suspiciously. "You don't look quite as ghastly, that's true."

"Still rubbish at flattery."

"Willow bark wouldn't have that kind of effect. Especially not such an immediate one. All it does is ease pain and fever."

He shrugged. "All right, so it wasn't pure willow bark. But let's not waste time bickering. Come on."

She couldn't argue. They resumed their climb on the narrower flights of stairs, winding their way higher into the hazy air, the sunset, the rapidly falling night, none of which they could see. James seemed to gain strength as they went. His hand on her shoulder became lighter, his breathing easier, his step quicker.

"What exactly was in that powder, James?"

"That's 'Mr. Easton' to you, Mark Quinn."

"Oh, stop dodging the question."

He sighed. "Mainly powdered willow bark, as I said. And something a friend of mine picked up in Germany. A mild stimulant derived from a tropical leaf. Nothing to be concerned about."

"Doesn't seem very mild to me. How much did you take?"

"What a nagging old granny you sound. Enough to get the job done."

"And after that, I suppose I'll have to scrape you from the cobblestones."

"Oh, I have Barker for that."

They climbed in silence until the final stretch, when James placed a hand on her arm. "We ought to have a plan."

"We don't even know what to expect. We'd need to know that before making a plan."

"Well, here's my theory: Harkness and Keenan are up there, conducting their business. I'd like to know whether Harkness is truly involved with the thefts, and to what extent. Let's get close and listen for as long we can before having to act."

"Of course. But what do you intend to do at that point?"

"Hold him until the police arrive."

"Hold Keenan? Good luck."

"The two of us together—three, perhaps . . ."

Mary looked at him. His eyes were very bright, even by gaslight. Glittering with suppressed fever, perhaps—but more likely the effects of that stimulant. He was vibrating with impatience and excitement, a rather un-James-like condition. She suddenly wondered if he'd be the steady, intelligent ally she had assumed—and then set aside that doubt. There simply wasn't time for it. Whatever happened, whatever he did, she would simply have to improvise and hope for the best.

As they crept up the final few steps, Mary was very glad she'd been up once before. The sun would now be low on the horizon, and she was uncertain of how well lit the belfry might be. Without a rough idea of its dimensions and layout, she'd have no idea what she was seeing and almost no chance of remaining unseen. It hardly counted as an advantage, but it comforted her nevertheless.

"Mary?" James was so close behind her that his whisper tickled her ear.

"Yes?"

"My physician warned me sternly against excitement of any sort."

She almost giggled. "Shut *up*, James."

"Can you see anything?"

"No, and I can't hear, either!"

But suddenly, she could. Male voices, clear and close at hand.

"You paying or not? I ain't got all night."

"Neither have I, Keenan." Harkness sounded oddly calm. "Neither have I."

The voices were so near that Mary instinctively shrank back into the warmth of James's body. He placed a hand on her shoulder. If it was meant to comfort, it did rather the reverse: his fingers trembled, very subtly and very quickly, and she wondered again about those powders he'd taken. She'd never noticed his hands shake before—had marveled, rather, at their steadiness under pressure. Tonight they vibrated.

"Well then?"

"Oh, you'll get what you deserve, Keenan. I'll make sure of that."

"You ain't threatening me, Harkness. I ain't afraid of you."

"Ah—and here is what's interesting: I'm no longer afraid of you."

There was a pause.

"You didn't think of that, did you? What happens when silly old Harkness is no longer frightened of you?"

Another pause.

"No smart rejoinder from you, Keenan? You're not generally short of one."

"Stop your blathering: you paying up or not?"

"I'm not." Harkness took a deep breath, and Mary heard the smile in his voice. "Did you hear me? I'm not going to pay you any longer, you blackmailing devil."

James sucked in his breath sharply. Mary tensed—it sounded loud in her ear—but Keenan and Harkness continued, fully absorbed in their exchange.

"I did a few sums earlier today," said Harkness conversationally. "D'you know how much you bled me for, Keenan? The total of what I've paid you and Wick both, these past ten months?" He didn't wait for a reply. "It seemed quite manageable at first, one pound a week. Then two. Even five. I could manage five, although I expect it was divided between you three, so to you it didn't seem so splendid after a while. It was ten pounds—ten pounds a week!—that broke me. Such a paltry sum, really: a couple of new dresses for my daughters, the cost of a party given by my wife. But all told it came to more than two hundred pounds.

"And here's what I'd like to know: I can see how I'd have spent it. I've a wife and family. Daughters are expensive and sons even more so. And I suppose Wick had a family, too—poor souls. But what did you do with your eighty pounds, Keenan? That's what I can't understand."

"Go to hell," snarled Keenan. "If you don't pay up, you know what'll happen to you."

"The question of hell is in the hands of the Almighty. But you might have gathered by now, Keenan, that I'm no longer afraid of what *you* might do to me. In fact, I'm almost looking forward to it."

There followed a long silence, during which Mary carefully leaned past the doorway at the top of the stairs.

James did likewise. The two men were, as she'd imagined, in a far corner of the belfry. Harkness had his hands braced against the half wall, as though he were admiring the effects of sunset over the London streets. His posture was deceptively casual, but the set of his shoulders, hunched and stiff, revealed his underlying tension. In contrast, Keenan, who stood facing him, leaned slightly forward, poised for a physical struggle. Yet there was a curious rigidity in his stance, as though he didn't know how to manage the situation before him. Harkness's desperate serenity robbed him of his most effective weapon: the threat of violence.

"Then why'd you call me here?" growled Keenan. He clenched and unclenched his fists as though he could feel Harkness's soft, loose neck between his fingers.

"Why, to tell you of my decision, of course."

"Up here? What's wrong with the office?"

Harkness smiled and looked out over the city. "It's a beautiful evening. I wanted to enjoy the view."

"I don't give a damn about the view."

"You might, if you consider what your future holds."

"What's that, then?"

"Breaking stones, at best."

For just a moment, Keenan blinked with surprise. Then he gave a sudden bark of laughter. "You outdone yourself there, Harky. Don't you know if I go to gaol, you're going, too? I'd sell myself to the devil himself to see you get more time than me."

Harkness, too, was smiling—a curious bend of his lips that had as little to do with humor as Keenan's laugh. "You're not as clever as I'd expected, Keenan. I confess to a touch of disappointment. You know," he went on, straightening now and leaning against the edge of the belfry, "you've a certain low, criminal cunning not uncommon to your class. But your problem, Keenan, is that you lack imagination. You can't possibly imagine what I'm thinking or feeling right now. And that will be your downfall."

"Rubbish," growled Keenan, swinging away sullenly. "All rubbish. How the hell you going to get me in trouble while covering over your own part? You took half the profits; you fixed the bloody books."

Harkness's gaze, intent on the glowing horizon, never wavered. That intense serenity transformed his entire face, returned to it color and even a little youth. And then Mary became aware of the greatest difference in his appearance: the twitch was gone. Harkness's left cheek was entirely still and smooth. "I've no interest in covering my own guilt. Far from it: I've left a letter detailing the entire scheme." He swung to meet Keenan's surprised face. "Yes, everything from the time I caught you thieving. I've set out why I agreed to turn a blind eye and even falsify the accounts in exchange for half the profits. Also how your friend Wick discovered our plan and began to blackmail me. It took me a while to work out that you were behind that neat trap, you know—setting him onto me like that. Such crookedness was entirely beyond my experience."

"No more, though," sneered Keenan.

"You're quite correct." Harkness's tone was austere, schoolmasterly. "I've done wrong, grievous wrong. And I shall atone for it."

"How?" Keenan's tone turned suspicious. "What's this letter, and where is it?"

"Ah: the low instinct for survival, coming once again to the surface. Suffice it to say, the letter's in a safe place. You'll not find it. But the authorities will; you may depend upon it, and they'll know precisely what happened."

"All right. Supposing this letter's real, and supposing some copper finds it, and supposing he believes all your rot. What's to say he'll find me? It's a big town, is London—supposing I stays in it." He stared at Harkness, who stood, unmoving, staring out over the darkening streets. "Eh? Supposing all that?"

Harkness blinked and smiled, as though emerging from a reverie. "D'you want to know what happened to Wick?"

Keenan's face became very still. "I know what happened. He fell."

"But how?" persisted Harkness. "And when, and why?"

"He just did, all right? Accidents happen—'specially here, it seems."

"I suppose they do. But you must wonder why he was up here."

"No. I don't." The voice, cold and stony, also held just the suggestion of a quiver.

Behind her, Mary could feel James holding his breath. If Harkness did intend goading Keenan into an explanation, this was a desperate and foolish method. It couldn't last. It was only remarkable that Keenan hadn't already exploded.

She crept forward another few inches, angling for a better view of Keenan's face. She would now be almost entirely visible to them in the doorway. There was no cover in the belfry, no small nook in which to tuck herself unnoticed. And over them all, the great bell loomed high in the tower's peak. Black inside, monstrous in scale, it hung there like a lofty, judging god, waiting for the puny humans below to do something definitive. To act rather than talk.

"I'll tell you."

"I said, I don't want to hear!" The sharp lash of Keenan's voice reverberated through the small space, ringing slightly in the bell's great cavern.

"It was his suggestion—Wick's, I mean—that we meet up here," said Harkness. He couldn't be oblivious of Keenan's rising panic. If anything, he seemed to welcome it. "He insisted, in fact. I didn't want to meet him at all, tried to put him off for as long as possible. He was only going to raise his demands, you know. Of course you know—you probably put him up to it. Didn't you, Keenan?"

The master bricklayer glowered, unmoving.

"No matter; we met, at Wick's demand, here in the belfry after dark. It was perhaps ten o'clock. I was late in arriving, and Wick was displeased. He upbraided me in most vulgar terms. And I—I had lost courage and permitted him to do so." Harkness's left eye twitched, just once. "Perhaps I regret that the most: losing sight of my position as a gentleman." He paused for a moment before a slight movement from Keenan returned him to the present. "No matter. Wick demanded an increase in his already outrageous bribe: twelve pounds a week, all for keeping silent about my careless bookkeeping.

"I said to you earlier that ten pounds a week broke me. I was a broken man already, although I didn't know it. But I knew I could not meet his increased demand and told the scoundrel so in no uncertain terms. He had the temerity to say he would go to my wife and tell her of the situation, that perhaps she would be willing to sell her jewels in order to preserve my good name. And he—he intimated that if her jewels were not sufficient to satisfy him . . . well, he spoke only as a low-born villain could . . ." Harkness paused again to swallow his outrage. When he spoke again, his voice was cool and detached. "No gentleman would suffer such an insult. I lost my temper, and we came to blows. We were standing so—Wick here, and I just where you are now."

Keenan made a startled gesture, then quickly controlled it. "I heard enough," he said in a low, guttural voice. But he made no attempt to depart. If anything, he inched closer to Harkness, spellbound by the tale.

"Wick was much stronger than I, of course: all that manual labor. And yet when he came at me, I managed to resist with a strength I hadn't known I possessed. We *grappled,*" said Harkness, almost in a tone of wonder. "I don't understand fighting—physical violence has always made me ill—but I wasn't afraid. If anything, I enjoyed it."

"You devil! You're enjoying this, too." Keenan launched himself at Harkness, seizing him by the throat. The older man stumbled back, falling heavily against the stone half wall. It must have hurt, for he was bent backward over the ledge, but he made no sound of pain or fear, even when Keenan began to throttle him, voice high now with fury. "You bloody devil! You pushed him, didn't you? You tricked him into coming here, and you pushed him off the ledge."

"Stop!" That clear, commanding voice was James's, echoing into the hollow of Big Ben as he sprang past Mary toward the two men. The belfry was small, James's legs were long, and in just a few strides he was upon them.

He wasn't quick enough. Keenan started up at the sound; beneath him, Harkness flailed. Their combined movement was enough to topple Harkness over the lip of the half wall. It was a curious way to fall, Mary noted mechanically. Harkness ought to have tipped back headfirst, if at all, and if so, he should have taken Keenan with him. Yet here they were, with Harkness outside the belfry and Keenan within, balanced precariously on his belly, on the ledge. There was a sharp, panicked cry—whether from Harkness or from Keenan, Mary couldn't be certain.

James dived forward and caught Keenan's thrashing legs, landing with a grunt and a thud. There was a collective, convulsive gasp. Then came only the wind whistling through the open chamber.

Keenan remained perfectly still, anchored by James's grip. The upper half of his body dangled outside the belfry, and he made no move to rise. Mary, half a step behind James, dashed toward the ledge and peered over. There, with his large, soft hands wrapped about Keenan's meaty forearms, was Harkness. His feet dangled against the roof tiles below, and he peered up with an oddly composed expression.

But at the sight of Mary's face poking over the edge, he frowned. "Quinn? What on earth are you doing here?"

Mary swallowed and remembered she was still in disguise. "Helping Mr. Easton, sir. Just hang on, and we'll get you up." She was about to add, "Don't panic," but it hardly seemed appropriate in Harkness's case; he was more serene than she'd ever seen him.

Keenan's face, however, wore an expression of dread and nausea. He dangled, inverted, his face growing steadily redder. "For God's sake, drag me back!" he cried hoarsely. It was a peculiarly passive position for such an active, aggressive man: if he kicked his legs, he risked dislodging James, his anchor. And Harkness was heavy.

Harkness looked mildly perplexed, as though he couldn't quite remember how he'd come to be dangling three hundred feet over the cobblestoned streets of Westminster. And then his expression cleared. "Is that you, Easton, keeping this scoundrel from falling to his death?"

James emitted a gasp, equal parts exertion and amusement. "Yes, Harkness. I haven't the weight to drag you both back up."

"Well, I shouldn't worry about that," replied Harkness in an astoundingly conversational tone. "I'm quite prepared to meet my Lord and Savior."

"So soon? Surely not."

Keenan's darkening face reflected Mary's astonishment. "This ain't no tea party!" he yelped. "You, boy! Help drag me back inside before my arms drop off!"

Mary grasped one of Keenan's legs and pulled, but her meager body weight was insufficient to make a real difference: Harkness and Keenan weighed at least twenty-five stone between them, and she and James weighed significantly less. To pull them up, against gravity, was impossible without some sort of aid. And there wasn't time to go for help.

She looked at James. "There's all sorts of rope up here. We could use that."

James nodded, sweat beginning to bead on his forehead. "Good. I'll show you the knots to use."

"There's a simpler solution, my boy," came Harkness's voice, much muffled by wind and stone. "I had hoped to take Keenan with me, but that clearly isn't to be, if you're holding him. But once he lets me go, you ought to be able to save him for the police."

There was an instant, general outcry.

"He's gone mad!"

"What the devil are you on about, Harkness?"

"What d'you mean, once he lets you go?"

"Just what I said," said Harkness, maddeningly cool. "I assume, Easton, that you and the lad heard enough of our conversation to work out what's happened."

James assented with a grunt.

"I'm out of choices, my dear boy. Death is my only desire now."

"You daft old fool!" snarled Keenan. "Go on, then, I'll let go of you, and you're welcome! I got witnesses as to say you wanted to die."

"No!" snapped James. "If you let him fall, Keenan, I'll push you over the edge myself. Harkness," he continued, trying to sound reasonable now, "we'll discuss this once you're safely in the belfry, not now. Quinn, get those ropes."

Mary scrambled toward the nearest coil of rope, a remainder from the installation of the great bell. She wrapped it about Keenan's ankles, knotted it soundly, and anchored the other end using rings embedded in the stone wall. And then the real labor began.

With their feet braced against the lip of the central air shaft, she and James began to pull. The rope was thick and strong, and there were no obstacles in their path. Keenan was nearly half inside to begin with, and Harkness a consistent, if dead, weight at the other end. Yet almost as they began to make progress, a furious tussle began on the precipice.

"Oi!" cried Keenan, "he's a-going, he's a-going."

"Hold him!" barked James. "As you value your life, hold on to him."

"He's let go of me!"

"Then hold tighter!"

They retracted the rope in hard-fought increments, one inch, even half an inch at a time. Sometimes they made no progress for the stretch of a minute, so great was the effort of raising those two large, struggling men. It was James, Mary thought, a rivulet of sweat running down her forehead. Despite his heroic efforts, he was beginning to flag. The hectic glitter in his eyes was gone, his color ashen beneath the rosy flush of exertion, his breath coming in short, sharp gasps.

He caught her assessing glance. "Pull harder!"

She nodded, although she was already pulling with all her might.

Somehow, somehow, Keenan's torso inched toward them, dragged painfully over the open ledge. He was very still and completely silent, waiting, holding, concentrating. At long last, his armpits hooked the edge of the half wall.

"Steady there!" gasped James, relief plain in his

exhausted face. "We're coming to help pull up Harkness."

It took them only seconds to reach the ledge. In that interval, with a single, defiant movement, Keenan threw his hands up. "There! Ain't that what you wanted?"

The scream that sliced the air was dreadful, shrill enough even to stir a ghostly echo from the bells. It seemed to pierce Mary's skull. Futile though it was to do so, she stumbled toward the ledge. Scanned the rows of neat shingles, the elaborate Gothic traceries, then craned below to the shadowy cobblestone yard. At that moment, the sun dropped fully below the horizon and a new, almost tangible darkness dropped over the city, cloaking from view the body she knew must be splayed below, broken and bloody.

An instant later, she cried out in surprise as a rough hand seized the back of her collar and she was whisked into the air to dangle, like Harkness, over the beautiful slanted roof of St. Stephen's Tower. The seam of her collar bit into her throat, constricting her airway; the tips of her boots grazed the stone of the belfry wall. It was Keenan, of course. What a fool she'd been to come anywhere near him, now that he was safe.

James rushed toward her, only to be stopped by a commanding gesture from Keenan. James stood perfectly still, his expression sick with horror. His lips worked, forming the first syllable of her name.

Alarmed though she was, Mary still had her wits. She

shook her head in a very slight movement. He mustn't reveal her gender now; doing so would only give Keenan more power, more delight in hurting her. She focused on James's face, tried to project her message using only her eyes.

"Thanks for the lift," Keenan said with a grin. "Sorry about Harkness."

"Bring the boy back inside," said James, his voice vibrating with tension and exhaustion. "Keenan, you don't know the trouble you're making for yourself."

"Don't I, though? Seems to me you're awful fond of this useless little whoreson. Seems as you'd do anything for him."

"He's a good lad." James's pulse hammered in his throat.

"Your special little lad, eh?" Keenan looked contemptuous. "You don't look the backdoor sort, but I suppose I don't know about all that Greek stuff."

She was so close. Every couple of seconds, the toe of one of her boots bumped against the half wall. She focused on that, at this moment her one scrap of hope. Better to think about that than of the choking sensation in her throat, the blood roaring in her ears, the sheer terror turning her limbs to water. If she could just gain half a second's purchase, a tiny bit of momentum . . . if only there was a handhold, a pillar, anything she could use to pull herself forward.

"What d'you want?"

Keenan grinned. "Now you're talking. What I want, Mr. Fancy Safety Engineer, is for you to forget this last couple hours ever happened. You ain't come here. You ain't seen Harky. And you most surely ain't seen me."

"Agreed," said James promptly. "Now bring him in."

"No," croaked Mary. James was entirely a man of his word. Without his testimony, they'd never convict Keenan, and they all knew it.

"Ain't nobody taught you not to contradict?" Keenan raised her yet higher and grinned as her breathing became labored. "Less you fight, longer you'll live."

"I've already agreed to your terms," said James. "Bring him in."

"Oh, that ain't all," said Keenan easily. "You're going to fix your report so whosoever asks, me and Wick got nothing to do with anything. We's just two harmless brickies minding our own business, and Wick's death's a proper tragedy."

"What else?"

As James and Keenan bargained, Mary's sensitive ears caught a new sound outside the tower. Above the remote babble of urban life, a new sound intruded: a long, shrill whistle, and then the heavy thud of boots on cobblestones. At least two pairs. Running.

James and Keenan seemed oblivious to this new development, near as it sounded. And, dangling in midair like a worm on a fishhook, Mary couldn't turn to see anything. But she closed her eyes and listened, and the noises began to sort themselves out in her mind, so clearly could she visualize them. A police whistle. A pair of bobbies giving chase. Even, perhaps, the clang of the site gate. The boots kept galloping, and now they changed in sound. They were no longer running flat-out but were instead taking smaller, faster paces. What could cause that? She reckoned she knew. And the thought of it made her open her eyes and smile broadly.

"What you grinning at?" snarled Keenan, jerking her close for better inspection.

It was all the chance she needed. "This," she said, and kicked him in the groin.

A roar of pain. A blow to the chin that damn near knocked her unconscious.

Blindly, Mary hung on, and after a few seconds realized she was clinging to the lip of the belfry. The hard pressure against her chin was the stone ledge. A steady trickle of blood seemed to confirm this, although she felt no pain.

"My God, Mary! Hold on!" James was there, his face white and frantic, wrapping his long hands about her forearms.

"Keenan! Where's Keenan!"

James didn't even glance back. "Sod Keenan; he's run off. Can you hold my wrists?"

She could. A minute later—surely less, although it felt like more—she tumbled over the ledge into his arms. He fell back onto the floor, squeezing her tightly, pressing her against his chest so hard it hurt. His heart was thumping at a furious pace, his chin digging into the top of her head.

"My God, Mary. Oh, my God. I thought—oh, Mary." He covered her hair and face with fierce kisses, and when she hugged him back, he groaned and laughed at the same time. "You careless, daring, vicious, damned little fool. You nearly died, purely for the satisfaction of kicking him in the—"

"I didn't," she protested, laughing now, too. "I miscalculated. I thought I was farther inside than I was."

"Oh, well, that's all right, then." He rolled her onto her back. "Idiot."

"Who's an idiot? You were about to agree to all of his outrageous conditions, just to—"

"To save your life," he agreed, kissing her again, so hard she could scarcely breathe. "Damned foolish of me."

"He'd never have kept his word. You'd have sworn all that, and he'd still have knocked me off the ledge, just for the fun of it."

"I suppose you're going to scold me now for letting him escape."

She examined his face carefully. His eyes were bloodshot, his pulse going far too quickly, and his skin hot and dry. Clearly, that dubious "stimulant" he had taken earlier was wearing off and in a moment he would be desperately ill—and grumpy to boot. But despite all this, she could think of no one else she wanted as much as this; no other place she'd rather be. "No," she said thoughtfully. "I'm not."

He feigned shock.

"I think he's been caught. Listen." They paused then, and through the wide air shaft they heard the echoes of heavy-booted steps, grunts of exertion, a roar of defiance. "The police are on their way up."

"Hmph."

"'Hmph'? That's all you can say?"

"Well, normally I'd be very pleased . . ."

"But not now?"

He kissed her again, deeply and sweetly. "How long have we? Five minutes?"

"Less, I think." Still, she clung to him and kissed him again.

"Bloody England—a bobby on every street corner."

"Mmm. And if we don't sort ourselves out, they'll arrest us, too."

"Only me, I think. I'm willing to risk it."

She laughed at that, struggling to slide out from beneath him. "And what of me and my spotless reputation?"

A new voice, sardonic despite its breathlessness, sounded in the room. "I'd say it's rather too late to worry about that, miss."

Mary closed her eyes and groaned. *Damn, damn, damn.*

James's head snapped up at the first syllable. Then a broad grin spread across his face and he collapsed back to the floor. "Thank God," he said, sounding suddenly exhausted. "Take us home, Barker."

Thirty

He didn't. Instead, after helping Barker to load James's shivering, barely conscious form into the carriage, Mary jumped down again. At Barker's questioning look, she shook her head. "I'll write." She didn't wait to hear his response or bid James a proper good-bye.

Neither did she return to the bloody scene at the foot of the tower. She'd seen bodies enough in her time, and she had no place there, besides. Already, even from a distance, she could see a good-size throng gathered about it: uniformed policemen, a police surgeon, detectives from the Yard, probably someone representing the Agency. Even Peter Jenkins. And, unless she was much mistaken, there was a scruffy, fair-haired chap nosing about in a discreet fashion: Octavius Jones. The liar—so much for resting on Sundays.

She didn't linger. Her task now was to return to the Agency and report fully. Physical exhaustion was now overlaid by so much nervous tension that less than half an hour later, she stood once more before Anne Treleaven and Felicity Frame in the austere attic. Anne managed to appear dignified even in a nightgown and robe, with her pale reddish hair swinging down her back in a tidy braid. The effect was startlingly girlish, and for the first time, Mary wondered whether Miss Treleaven wasn't a good deal younger than she'd always assumed. Felicity was dressed as if for a particularly elegant party, in peacock-blue silk and with ornately curled hair. In sharp contrast to her employers, Mary was dusty, bruised, and only now, beginning to shake with suppressed shock.

"Are you certain you're uninjured?" asked Anne. "Our physician is ready to see you at any time. Perhaps before you report . . ."

"No, thank you." Mary dropped into a chair and said, "Harkness claimed responsibility for Wick's death, Reid's disappeared, I don't know what's to happen to Jenkins, and Jones knows I'm female."

Felicity frowned.

Anne blinked. "You may be unhurt, but you'd better have a drink, my dear."

Her stomach churned at the idea, but Anne was insistent. And indeed, after a stiff measure of brandy, Mary felt warmth returning to her hands and feet, and a degree of organization to her thoughts. "I beg your pardon," she said, blushing at her own incoherence. "I'll begin again.

"According to my source—a laborer's assistant named Peter Jenkins—Keenan, Reid, and Wick were stealing materials from site stores and selling them. Harkness discovered their thefts but was somehow persuaded to overlook them; indeed, in exchange for a share of the income, Harkness began to falsify the site accounts to allow Keenan and Wick to continue their scheme. I've seen Harkness's bankbook, and he was seriously overdrawn; I expect he had other debts, too, which he had no means of repaying on his salary alone."

"Indeed," Anne said with a nod. "We've confirmed a number of loans, all on extortionate terms, with one of the more notorious moneylenders in London."

Mary nodded. "This arrangement might have worked. However, Wick — possibly prompted by Keenan — realized he could profit at both ends of this arrangement: he began to blackmail Harkness, threatening to expose his involvement with the scheme. It was a foolish idea: had Harkness called his bluff, Wick would only have put an end to his own illegal earnings. But for some reason, Harkness agreed to pay — possibly because the initial sum Wick demanded was manageable and because his own debts seemed increasingly urgent. But as Wick's demands got larger — by the end, Harkness was paying him ten pounds a week — Harkness became increasingly desperate. Keenan's black-market income was no longer enough to justifying paying off Wick, yet he couldn't extricate himself without getting caught.

"Wick demanded a meeting with Harkness, after dark, in the belfry. It's a sign of how deeply enmeshed Harkness felt that he agreed to meet Wick at all. But he did. That night, Wick proposed going to Mrs. Harkness and forcing her to find the money. He also threatened to force her to have sexual relations with him, as a form of payment."

"This is Harkness's own account?" asked Felicity.

"Yes. Wick may have wanted only to frighten Harkness, but he went too far: Harkness was incensed, they fought, and, as everyone knows, Wick went over the edge. It's still unclear whether he fell or was pushed.

"The week following Wick's death, Harkness paid Keenan one final blackmail installment. Their arrangement seems to have been for Keenan to take the money himself from Harkness's desk; at least, I saw Keenan enter the site after hours last Monday night. But that week, the first commissioner declared his intention to conduct a safety review of the building site. Harkness must have known at that point that he was caught. Any competent safety review would reveal the shortcuts he'd taken, the low building standards he'd accepted, in order to set aside more raw materials for Keenan to steal. James Easton's review also uncovered his highly dubious accounting practices."

"James Easton again," murmured Felicity. "What an interesting young man."

Mary had no idea how to respond to this, except by ignoring it. "With his professional integrity and personal reputation destroyed, Harkness believed his only choice was suicide. He decided if possible to take Keenan with him. So he lured Keenan to the belfry for an after-hours meeting.

"Keenan seems to have been close to Wick, and Harkness taunted him with the details of Wick's death. He successfully goaded Keenan into attacking him. And he might also have succeeded in dragging Keenan over the ledge with him, except that Mr. Easton caught them — caught Keenan, at any rate, and dragged him back to safety." Mary swallowed. She could still hear that scream echoing in her ears. "Keenan deliberately let go of Harkness."

After a pause, Anne asked, "How did you and Mr. Easton manage the arrest of Keenan? You can't have had time to send for help."

"That was a lucky accident," said Mary slowly. "I ran into Jenkins on Sunday afternoon, after Reid went missing. I asked Jenkins to check whether Reid had disappeared of his own accord. He had: Reid paid for Jenkins's lodgings, and on the evening he disappeared, settled with the landlord for the next two months. When Jenkins came to the site, as I'd told him to, a couple of policemen patrolling the area saw a boy run into the building site after hours, gave chase, and ended up catching Keenan on his way down the tower stairs."

"Quite ridiculously fortuitous," murmured Felicity.

Mary also smiled for the first time since entering the Agency. "Mr. Easton's coachman was also on the scene and realized that things had become violent. He was ahead of Jenkins and the policemen by a story or two, and I believe he was able to lend a hand." She released a long, slow breath. "I think those are the most important points . . ." She was suddenly unspeakably weary. Her eyelids were leaden. Her muscles ached and burned. A thick patch of dry blood on her chin stretched and stung each time she spoke. And an angry red crease along her throat, like a noose, was a stinging reminder of those terrifying minutes she'd hung suspended from Keenan's grip.

Anne nodded briskly. "There are a few loose ends, of course, but I expect we'll be able to tie those up tomorrow before we meet with the commissioner. By the by, his assessment of Harkness as 'reliable' couldn't have been further off the mark." She turned to Felicity. "D'you think the commissioner was testing us?"

Felicity blinked, surprised at the question. "I—I wouldn't have thought so."

"Mmm." Anne's jaw took on an obstinate angle. "We'll have to find out. There's just too much we don't know about him. About this case, overall."

Felicity's mouth was stubborn. "We'll discuss this further, of course." She turned back to Mary. "There's just one more thing."

Mary froze, halfway out of her chair. "Yes, Mrs. Frame."

"James Easton. What d'you intend to do about him?"

"I—I hadn't—that is, I don't yet know exactly what I'll say."

"But you intend to see him again."

"I can't just run away or disappear." The twin gazes of her employers seemed to bore through her. "I—I owe him a good-bye, at least." She felt a painful, unexpected bump of disappointment as the words left her mouth. Was there another solution to their situation? Not likely. Not if she valued her work, indeed her life, here at the Agency.

"You'll report to us the outcome of that interview."

"Of course."

Thirty-one

Wednesday, 13 July

Gordon Square, Bloomsbury

It was another sticky, soupy, stifling afternoon. The thunderstorm threatening the city all week had yet to materialize, and even by English standards, people talked about the weather a great deal at the moment. As her hansom cab turned into Gordon Square, Mary saw and felt the thick layer of straw coating the cobblestones, damping the sound of hooves along its length. The straw was put down for invalids, to help them rest, and she hoped it wasn't for James's benefit. After all, he hadn't been too ill to write her a note.

The patrician housekeeper opened the door and looked down the length of her nose at Mary. "Miss Quinn. Do come in."

She was shown up to the drawing room, where a stoutish, balding man greeted her with polite forbearance. "Miss Quinn. It's been quite some time since we met." The edge in his voice suggested, unmistakably, that it was a pity they were meeting now.

"Mr. Easton," she said politely. "How do you do."

The younger Mr. Easton reclined meekly on a sofa, draped to the chest in blankets. "Thank you for coming," he said. "I'd stand, but George would kill me."

Mary smiled and murmured something polite. Apparently, all the formalities were to be observed today. She hadn't been invited to remove her hat and gloves, so this meant a short call: fifteen minutes at most. It was for the best. A long, cozy visit would only prolong the pain of saying good-bye.

"Tea?" asked George.

"Thank you, no."

"Yes, she will," said James with sudden vigor. "And take off your hat, Mary—and George, do go away, there's a good chaperone."

George ruffled up, just like a rooster. "It's for Miss Quinn's own good, Jamie, and—"

"Oh, rubbish. Look at me on my sick bed: I'm hardly capable of ravishing her. And don't call me Jamie!"

After some spluttering, George retreated with the proviso that the drawing-room door remain open.

That accomplished, James offered Mary his most charming grin. "Come and sit beside me?"

She grinned. "You're a horrendous brat."

"George is a tyrant. The only way he'd agree to a visit was if I lay on this sofa while he supervised our conversation."

She laid her gloves on a side table. "What's so very urgent that it can't wait until you're well?"

"I wanted to see you."

She flushed with pleasure. Swallowed regret.

"And I want all the news. George won't tell me a thing, for fear of overexciting me."

"Well . . ." It had been such a long, intense few days since the tragedy at St. Stephen's Tower. "Big Ben rang for the first time on Monday. It sounds quite good, although the quarter-bells aren't going yet."

He gave her a look. "Real news, if you please. I'm not your maiden aunt."

She blushed hotly and said the first thing that came into her mind. "Keenan's been charged with murder. Although I expect you know that, as witness for the prosecution."

He nodded.

"They found Reid in Saffron Walden, newly married to Jane Wick. He and Keenan had agreed that if Reid left town with the Wick family and kept quiet, Keenan would leave them alone. I suppose that's not possible now—the Crown will certainly want him to give evidence."

James nodded. "He ought to be all right. The evidence against Keenan is strong."

"Reid's worried about his own part in the thefts, obviously, but he should receive some clemency for those. He was very upset about the blackmail. That caused the initial friction between the three brickies: Reid maintaining that it was wrong, and Keenan and Wick pressing him to keep silent."

"But profiting from stolen goods is all right?"

Mary wrinkled her nose. "There's a large moral difference. And from Reid's perspective, the thefts didn't directly harm anybody. They represented only a small percentage of the site budget, yet seemed a small fortune in comparison with his wages. He also tried to justify the theft of the money by doing right with it: he supported an injured errand boy and his sisters and subsidized the Wick family, too.

"We were right, you know, about the bruises he had on Monday: he and Wick had fought about Jane. She'd just told Reid she was pregnant again, and he was furious. Scolded Wick for 'wearing her out with babies,' and said any decent man would leave her alone for a bit."

James smiled. "You were right and I was wrong. I thought he was a drunken hothead, remember?"

She raised her eyebrows. "Admitting imperfections, now? You really are unwell."

"I'm the most generous of souls."

"Well, since you're feigning generosity, I want to ask you about Jenkins—the lad who led the police to the tower."

"What about him?"

"He's clever. Poor. The eldest of several, both parents dead. I don't suppose . . ."

James nodded. "Send him round to our offices. I'm

sure George will find something for him to do until I'm back, though it may only be sharpening pencils."

Mary grinned. "Count them first, mind. He's used to skimming off the top."

He snorted. "You do keep strange company."

There was a pause. Mary fidgeted with her gloves. How to bring up the real question she wanted to ask him . . . ? It seemed brutal, digging into matters that were so clearly sensitive ones. But she had to know—if only to understand how James might be feeling.

"What is it?"

There was no sense in hinting. Not with James. "What are the consequences for Easton Engineering, now that you know Harkness's letter was forged?"

"You mean, did he topple our reputation alongside his?" He made a face. "You'd think so, but oddly enough, no. I'm still not certain how." He paused. "Sometimes I think Harkness chose me because I'm young, and he hoped I'd be malleable. Or perhaps he thought me inexperienced and unlikely to know good practice from bad. Or—good God, perhaps he really did want me to meet the first commissioner, even in those circumstances. One last good deed, or something like that. I'll never truly know. But the result is that I have indeed met the first commissioner. Whether that will lead to anything, I couldn't begin to predict."

"And—you feel all right about that?"

"Of course not. I've played at politics now, dirtied

my hands, and it went disastrously. I regret nearly every minute I spent on that accursed site." His tone was so vehement that Mary recoiled. He caught her eye and half smiled. "Except, of course, those I spent with you." She made a sound of protest and he laughed. "It's true, it's true. It sounds trite and pat and appallingly clichéd, I know. But I mean it. Meeting you again is the one good thing to have come of the entire affair."

Fear and something else—a wild sort of joy—warred within her. This was dangerous territory. If she didn't speak soon, she never would. "I—there's something I need to tell you."

His gaze sharpened at the new guardedness in her tone. "What's that?"

Twice, she opened her mouth to begin.

Twice, she closed it again.

Finally, she said simply, "Who do you think I am?"

There was a pause. Then, slowly, "When I first met you, I thought you were a rich man's mistress. Then I learned you worked as a lady's companion. Now you tell me you're an aspiring journalist." His tone was wary. "Why d'you ask? Are there further developments?"

"Not exactly. More like . . . past omissions."

His expression was still, shuttered. "Go on."

"I—I'm a criminal. A former thief."

Whatever he'd been expecting, it wasn't this. His eyes flashed to hers, wide and startled. "What?"

"When I was twelve, I was tried and found guilty of housebreaking."

"That carries a death sentence."

"Yes. I escaped."

"But you're still wanted. If you were caught now, they'd hang you."

"Yes."

"You must be living under an assumed name."

"Yes."

He stared at her for a long minute, a complex blend of emotions struggling in his eyes.

Disbelief.

Affection, still.

And—yes—revulsion.

Here, at last, was the answer she needed in order to go on her way.

Finally, he said in a low, gruff tone, "Why are you telling me all this?"

"I wanted you to know the truth." The little jade pendant nestled against her collarbone was a constant reminder of her other truth. The one she could never tell anyone.

"But *why*?"

"Because . . ." And this was the hardest part—one of the most difficult things she'd said in years. "Because I didn't want you to care for me—for someone—about whom you knew so little." She paused. "You live by such clear, unambiguous principles. You condemned Harkness for stealing, when he should instead have reined in his family's greed. You despise yourself for condescending to play politics with Harkness and the commissioner. What I've just told you must change your feelings toward me."

He couldn't meet her gaze.

After several minutes, she said quietly, "Isn't that right?"

Again, no reply. Not even a look.

She took her gloves from the side table and stood, the swish of her skirts loud against the sofa leg. "I've enjoyed your friendship. Thank you for that." She longed to say more, to thank him for more than friendship. But she couldn't trust her voice.

When he finally spoke, she was already at the drawing-room door. "Why tell me now?"

She looked back at him, into dark, wounded eyes. "You'd rather I'd not told you at all?"

"Of course not." Suddenly angry. "But your life is in my hands now. Aren't you afraid I'll go to the police?"

"My life was in your hands on Sunday night. Nothing's changed since then, James. Not for me."

Thirty-two

She walked roughly westward. Walked carelessly and blindly, not minding which road she was taking and oblivious to the sights and smells about her. From time to time, when the shimmering wall of tears threatened to blind her entirely, she swiped at them with a glove. She needed a handkerchief. She never seemed to have a bloody handkerchief when she needed one.

Some minutes later, she realized somebody was keeping pace with her. A fair-haired man—tobacco-brown suit, rather rumpled—to her right, proffering a large square of clean linen. She stopped and gulped. "Octavius Jones."

He made an elaborate bow. "Miss Quinn. May I be of service? It does so trouble me to see a lady in distress."

"Does it? You must see rather a lot of them in your line of work."

"Your line, too—isn't it?" he asked, alert eyes belying his casual tone.

"Perhaps I'm not suited to it."

"Surely you're not booing your eyes out because you've lost your post as Mark Quinn."

"No," she admitted, resuming her walk. "I'm not."

"Care to tell me about it?"

"Certainly not. I notice you completely broke your word to me about publication." The story of Harkness's inglorious end had been the main feature—eight pages of "exclusive" coverage!—in Monday's *Eye*.

"I should hardly say so," he protested. "The circumstances were so different. You didn't tell me that Harkness was going to be killed that night."

"No." Mary slowed, thinking about James again. She'd not asked how he was managing after Harkness's grisly death. He must be troubled—and further grieved to know that Harkness's suspected failings were all true, after all.

"Cheer up," said Jones, chucking her under the chin with a cheeky smile. "Whoever he is, he's not worth it."

"Don't touch me," snapped Mary. "You haven't the faintest idea why I'm upset."

"Oh, it's almost always the same thing: affair of the heart, dreadful misunderstanding, things will never be the same again," he said glibly. "What you've got to do is look ahead. Think of what's to come!"

She blew her nose. Impossible to feel miserable in the face of such relentless obnoxiousness.

"That's it. You're a clever, energetic young woman. Lots to see and do. Well, this is where I turn off." He indicated the street. "So long for now, Miss Mark Quinn. I'll be seeing you again."

"I doubt it."

He swung back, offering his most charming, lopsided grin. "Oh, I don't. Not for a minute."

He vanished into the crowd. It was a trick that made her wonder whether he was merely a gutter-press journalist, as he claimed. Surely he was too sharp, too knowing? She would make a point of finding out, if they met again. Not that they would, despite his smug certainty. She detested bright-eyed know-it-alls who only talked and never listened, and Jones was no exception.

Energized by irritation, she resumed her usual brisk pace. As she came toward Regent's Park, a drop of rain struck her shoulder. Another splashed the brim of her hat. And then a proper light rain began, sending pedestrians scattering and street vendors to pack up their wares. She hadn't an umbrella with her. She didn't care. She began to walk again, returning to St. John's Wood by the quickest route. It wasn't the storm everyone was calling for, but that would come, too.

In its own time.